VADIM: CONQUER

A CLUB XXX NOVEL: BOOK SIX

LANA SKY

Conquer

Conquer By Lana Sky

Copyright © 2020 by Lana Sky
All rights reserved.

No part of this publication may be reproduced, distributed, or transmitted in any form or by any means, including photocopying, recording, or other electronic or mechanical methods, without the prior written permission of the author.

This is a work of fiction. Names, characters, businesses, places, events and incidents are either the products of the author's imagination or used in a fictitious manner. Any resemblance to actual persons, living or dead, or actual events is purely coincidental.

Cover Design and Interior Formatting by Charity Chimni
Proofreading by Charity Chimni

ACKNOWLEDGMENTS

Thanks so much to everyone who supported this draft along the way, including the many beta readers who provided encouragement along the way! Please keep in mind that this story includes dark, graphic, and explicit content matter that is not suitable for readers under the age of 18—or for readers who are uncomfortable with the following subject matter: explicit sex, mentions of sexual abuse, mentions of child abuse, graphic depictions of violence, and mentions of self-harm.

CHAPTER ONE

Insecurity thrives on doubt—but it doesn't help when reality reinforces every last one of those petty fears. Like when your new lover's ex-whatever-she-is-to-him comes back from the proverbial grave. It's easy to write off the concerns as paranoia at first, until the truth is staring you in the face, and there is no escaping it.

Knowing that Vadim had another woman in his life, no matter how he characterized her, scares me for reasons well beyond the obvious jealousy. Mainly because whenever I dare to picture such a woman…

One small consolation was that the mythical figure I'd conjured up seemed so unrealistic in my head, a part of me was convinced she couldn't possibly exist. She's always *beyond* beautiful—she had to be in order to become swept within the orbit of someone like him.

But here she is, in the flesh, and my self-deprecating fantasies didn't even do her justice. *Irina.* Tall and slender, her long, curling blond hair ends at her waist, and her beautiful features convey poise and confidence—high cheekbones, perfect pouty lips, and a figure to die for.

I self-consciously run my fingers over the skirt of my outfit, trying and failing to maintain my fake smile. My first thought is that she didn't come dressed to impress her daughter. A tight-fitting navy dress exposes a wealth of cleavage, clinging to her narrow hips, hugging every curve not shrouded by her tailored black jacket. I can't help but picture her with the man standing before me, their hands entwined…

And they look fucking perfect, despite the fact that Vadim is still wearing a pair of sweats, rumpled from riding.

My only consolation is an entirely selfish realization—she and Magda could be strangers for all the similarities they share. The latter is a damn near carbon copy of her father with his delicate bone structure, for one—even her expressions seem to mirror his. It could be safely assumed that Irina might not be related to her at all, save for their eyes.

Vadim had called it himself—*those eyes.* Ice-cold blue, their twin gazes tether them together more strongly than any one feature of his. And I hate myself for being so bothered by that fact.

Awkwardly, I linger at the back of the foyer while Vadim blocks the doorway, frozen solid. Some genuine sympathy creeps in, gnawing away at my nerves. For all of my selfish reservations, this woman has one title I can't deny—a mother. Who am I to blame her for coming to see her child, even if it's out of the gosh darn blue?

Channeling my own mother, I force a polite smile and try to meet her gaze. "Hello—"

"It's been a long time," Irina says softly without looking my way once. Her voice is lilting, tinged with a heavy accent I can't place—but I'm too distracted by where her gaze is focused to really give a damn. The way she eyes the man standing between us...

There is a word to describe it, I think. That longing, desperate expression.

If my brain weren't on red alert with dread, I'd be able to come up with the right description. Maybe *ownership*? That would certainly explain why my cheeks catch fire, and I sense my chin tilt defensively into the air. Stepping forward, I slip my hand into Vadim's—not jealously. Just... Reassuringly. A silent way to reinforce that I'm here on this battlefield with him.

Because, I sense, this very much is a battle.

Irina herself imparts the first warning shot as her gaze finally settles over me. Only my time with Magda helps me interpret the icy shift in those unsettlingly blue irises. *Annoyance.*

"I was hoping we could speak in private." Her gaze lowers to our clasped hands and Vadim's flex, gripping mine almost to the point of pain—but just as quickly, the tension loosens.

"Tiffany…" From this angle, I can't see his face. I don't need to in order to picture his expression. Haunting, dark eyes implicitly closed off. Before I know it, his wall goes up, solid stone against me—and that realization stings. Almost as much as the act of him slipping his hand from mine does. "Why don't you go for a walk?" he suggests without turning around.

Hurt sears through my chest a split second before my ears perk up, catching the subtle, deliberate inflection in his voice. *Walk.* In this context, that clearly means something else when paired with how his gaze flicks toward the kitchen —and the tiny, helpless figure still there, oblivious to our visitor's arrival.

"Okay." With difficulty, I turn away, sensing Irina enter the house—her presence is *that* overwhelming. Cloying rose-scented perfume itches my nostrils as her voice taunts me, a low hum.

"I've missed you, my Dima," she tells him in a way that makes my chest constrict. "God, how I've missed you…"

Only sheer pride prevents me from turning back to see their reunion unfold. Determined, I make it into the kitchen, and there I spot the true target of my so-called "walk." Instantly my priorities shift, and I bite back any lingering unease.

"You okay, honey?"

Magda watches me from the very back of the space, her arms crossed, her gaze wary. A tiny pang of panic makes me falter and brace my hand against the nearest counter. Did she see Irina? Hear her? Recognize her? If she has, I doubt even my mother's skills of social navigation will help me much in this instance…

"Is it the man?" she asks. In response to my raised eyebrow, she adds, "The big, scary man." Her tone strives to convey bravery. If only her eyes weren't bug-wide, her jaw clenched.

But at least her assumption is so far off base, I doubt she knows our visitor's true identity. Though, as for a big, scary man… *Maxim?* Forcing a smile, I shake my head. "No, honey. Just boring adult business. How about we go for a walk?"

"A walk?" she parrots suspiciously, her arms still crossed.

"Yes. I bet it's lovely out." I stroll boldly through the sliding glass door leading to the terrace and promptly feel my plan change on the fly once I realize that it's pitch-black dark outside.

"So…no walk," I confess. As my eyes scan the brightly lit terrace, they fall over one promising diversion, however. "What about a swim?"

"Now?"

I have to smirk at the alarm in Magda's tone. Like father like daughter. Reckless, impulsive decisions aren't her style.

"Yes," I say, strutting boldly to the edge of the pool. She lingers back, but I glance over my shoulder to find her watching me with avid interest, bathed in the glow of a few lamps placed strategically throughout the terrace. "You've never taken a night swim before?"

Her tiny lips press together, and I can practically see the gears in her brain whirling. Does she trust me enough to divulge whatever bit of information she's mulling over? Finally, she sighs. "I can't swim."

Her voice is so soft, so guarded. I suspect the lacking skill is a sore point for her, and I chalk it up as yet another failure of her last foster family.

"I can teach you," I suggest, fighting to keep the surprising amount of genuine desire from my voice. I actually want to —though with her birth mother seemingly back in the picture...

Who knows if I'll get the chance?

Be positive, Tiffy. Forcing yet another grin, I shrug. "I may be too rusty in riding to help you with your pony, but I, my girl, have swum to and fro many a yacht party in the middle of the night."

I look back again to find her lips twitching, fighting a smile. "What's a yacht party?"

It's my turn to be guarded. "I'll tell you when you're older."

Sighing, Magda wraps her arms around herself and rocks onto her heels. "I'm cold. Can we go back into the house now?"

Shit. Thinking quickly, I skip to the edge of the pool, say a prayer for this beautiful Chanel ensemble, and then I dive in. The water is a shock to the system, but nowhere near as cold as it could be—as I kick, I recall something Vadim said about it being heated. The second I break the surface, I'm faced with a tiny figure leaning eagerly over the edge of the pool.

With her wide-eyed, gleeful expression, I barely recognize the same surly little girl.

"You are going to get into *so* much trouble," she declares, sounding ecstatic at the prospect.

As I let my brain toy with what my potential punishments may be—at the hands of my handsome punisher, of course—I feel myself more than matching her excitement.

"God, I hope so."

"You're all wet," she adds more sternly. "And your clothes are all ruined. You'll probably catch a cold. I bet you'll get in *big* trouble too."

My lips twitch into a gleeful smile at the prospect of a disciplinarian Vadim. That is, if he isn't with Irina right now, bending her over the desk in his office, overcome with lust at her return. My gaze drifts to the house as I picture it...

There goes my smile. To hide my worried expression, I lean back, kicking my legs in an easy backstroke.

"Trouble? I laugh in the face of trouble! And what about you, little Miss? Don't tell me you're afraid?"

"I'm not!" She frowns and inches ever closer to the edge of the pool. As she eyes the water, her expression wavers in such a childlike display of hesitation that my heart swells at the adorableness of it all.

"Chicken?" I ask her playfully.

"I can't swim," she insists, sounding irritated at having to announce her weakness to the world a second time. So prideful, just like her father.

"I'll catch you," I suggest, swimming toward her. "I promise. Keep your feet together. Jump straight down—just whatever you do, don't panic. I've got you."

Her eyes narrow, her lips pursed in a damn near carbon copy of one of her father's wary expressions. "Promise?"

I stick out my pinky, deadly serious. "I promise."

Her eyes blaze as if she wants more than anything to deny that. Prove me wrong. So young, but so mistrustful already. I'm sure she'll refuse and go storming back into the house when she steps back, smoothing her hands over her beautiful new outfit.

"I'll always have your back," I tell her. "You can trust me."

She shoots me a fearful glance—glimpsed without her trademark mini-wall—and before I even have the chance to mull over the implications, she jumps into the pool. I lunge forward, slipping my arms around her the second I sense her start to flail. She claws at my arms, her tiny nails biting in, but I can tell that she's trying hard not to panic, even as she sputters at the air, her expression shocked.

"See?" Gently, I kick my legs, sending us further out into the water. "There's nothing to it."

She eyes me skeptically, her teeth chattering. But when I shift to let her kick on her own, she does, clinging to my arms as I steer her into the shallower end.

"Good job! It's not so bad, is it?" I praise as she paddles with all her might to stay afloat.

Her tiny lips twitch. Fighting a smile? A frown? In the end, an impishly self-satisfied grin shapes her mouth for just a second. I let her practice for a few more laps before bringing her to the end of the pool. The second she can touch down with her own feet, she lets me go, but her mouth is stretched wide. Definitely a smile this time.

"You'll teach me more?" she asks, barely managing to disguise her eagerness. "So, I can swim by myself?"

I nod and then playfully flick my wrist splashing her. "You've got it—"

"What on earth is going on here?"

We whip around to find Vadim standing at the opposite end of the pool, his arms crossed, the picture of playful discipline. I feel my toes curl, and my heart drop in the same conflicting motion. One might never guess that, seconds ago, he had to deal with a literal demon from his past. Staying in the pool feels preferable to confronting whatever reality might await inside the house.

His disarming smirk gives me no clue, only unnerving me further. "Whose idea was this?"

"She did it!" Magda scuttles from the water, waddling to his side as her sodden clothing clings to her tiny frame. Crossing her arms, she copies his posture, eyeing me disapprovingly. "I told her not to."

"And you were right," Vadim agrees, his tone ringing with authority. "Ena will kill me if you two track water throughout the house." His smile lessens the impact of that statement, however. Gone is the darkness I feel I should see in his gaze, and my unease nibbles deeper. Is Irina still here, lying in wait to meet her daughter?

Have they reconciled about her custody, already?

Together?

I try my damn hardest to make eye contact with Vadim as I swim to his corner, but his attention is fixated firmly on his daughter.

"What am I going to do with you?" He raises his hand to her, only to falter partway. Then something in his gaze hardens with resolve, and he tentatively ruffles one of her damp braids. Remarkably, she doesn't cringe from him—a fact that makes his dark eyes soften with such gentleness I bite back a groan. "You're soaked," he tells her, some real concern slipping into his teasing murmur. "Let's hope you don't catch a cold, *oui*?"

"Yeah," Magda says, wrinkling her button nose.

A teensy bit of guilt dampens my enthusiasm as I climb from the pool and rise to my feet. "Maybe you should grab us some towels? That way we won't make too much of a mess—"

"But I'm little," Magda says, shifting toward Vadim conspiratorially. She tugs on his pant leg like a queen commanding a servant. "You can pick me up, and I won't drip like *she* will."

The little minx. She's so intent on her apparent victory that she doesn't seem to notice she gave him permission to touch her. Permission he accepts with a strained look of awe so potent my heart aches.

"Right you are." He shrugs off his sweatshirt and drapes it over her before lifting her gingerly into his arms. She eyes me smugly from her new height, and I can't resist seizing a chunk of her hair as I come up beside them, giving it a tug.

"Tattletale."

She swats me off, and I finally meet Vadim's gaze from over her head. Only for him to turn away. "Let's head inside," he says.

I follow them into the house without complaint, and I'm relieved—yet unnerved—to find the lower level seemingly empty. Even Ena isn't lurking in view. Neither is a breathtaking blond with more of a claim to this budding family than I have.

But as we cross the foyer, Magda stiffens, clinging to Vadim to the point that he has to adjust her grip around his neck to keep her from accidentally choking him.

"What's wrong?" he asks, his expression drawn with concern.

She doesn't answer. Her eyes worriedly scan the corners of the foyer, her nostrils flaring. Out of fear of Maxim?

"No one's here, sweetheart," I say, stroking through her damp hair. As the words leave my mouth, however, I realize that I'm not even sure of that fact.

"That's right," Vadim insists, his tone hard. "No one."

He forges onward upstairs and pauses only to grab a towel for me from a hall closet before carrying Magda straight into her room. As he ushers her into the bathtub, it's as if his entire demeanor changes without him seeming to realize it. His voice deepens, soothing but stern as he urges her to wait while he runs the water until it's warm enough.

While I slip into her closet and procure a nightgown, he scours her bedroom for anything out of place and then turns back her blankets. By the time she emerges from the bath, bundled in a robe, he descends on her with an army of towels and patiently dries every last curl.

I'm completely enthralled. Like a shameless voyeur, I find myself leaning against the doorway to the closet, as he grabs her brush and diligently tackles her hair, braiding it with a skill that leaves me both awed and seething with jealousy. To think that only a few days ago, he'd been worried about failing her. As it turns out, he's damn good at this dad thing.

When Magda huddles beneath her blankets, freshly dressed and pampered, he starts to pull away.

"Wait!" She tugs at his hand until he stills. Then she scans her room with laser focus. Spotting her doll, Biphany, on the nightstand, she grabs it, tucking it under her arm. Vadim seems to read his cue and stoops to lift something else from the floor—two halves of a decapitated teddy bear.

Magda sighs with relief and eagerly grasps for the torn pieces.

"We should fix him, *non*?" Vadim suggests as he sits on the side of her bed.

Magda nods solemnly even as she crushes the deflated bear to her chest, damaged or not.

"He needs advanced surgery," she decides, eyeing It's head with a weary sigh. "Multiple stitches. A stuffing transfusion… You'll do it?" She looks so wary as she phrases the question, almost as if she's afraid he'll refuse.

And Vadim, well aware of the gravity of the task, nods with the demeanor of a world-renowned surgeon. "Of course. It will be a grueling surgery," he explains, stroking a bit of the bear's ivory fur. "But I'm sure that if he is a good lad, he'll come through. Maybe with a present to mark his bravery."

"Good." Magda closes her eyes, snuggling beneath her blankets. Within seconds, she's already drifting off.

Quietly, Vadim and I escape her room, shutting off the light and closing the door behind us. Once we reach the bedroom, however, Mommy and Daddy lose the "E for everyone" rating.

My thoughts instantly shift to Irina, and a question about her is already on the tip of my tongue when I sense Vadim come up behind me.

"*Merde.*" He grabs me, wrenching up my sodden dress and cups me directly between my legs. The desperation with which he does so tempers the answering lust sparking to life inside my belly. He's more possessive than sensual, yanking me around so swiftly I have to clutch his shoulders just to stay upright. His mouth finds my throat, lips parting, teeth latching with a searing nip that makes me gasp.

Lust ignites my blood like liquid fire—so potent that I almost forget the world-shattering event at the forefront. Almost.

"Irina," I rasp as he strokes me, applying devious pressure to my clit, enhancing the placement of my piercing. *Holy crap.* I nearly lose my train of thought, and then I realize as his eyes hungrily watch me bite down a moan—that's what he wants.

To distract me.

"Tell me what happened." With difficultly, I break away from him, backing up to put distance between us. My body hums, craving him, but I force myself to deny the desire and meet his gaze with what I hope passes for a stern expression. "Tell me. What did she want? Is she still holding up the adoption?"

He turns away, putting his back to me. A heavy sigh betrays the exhaustion he hid so well in front of Magda—and the alarming instability that has become his hallmark. How he rakes his hands through his hair. Trembles with emotion. Gets that hard, low note in his voice I've come to associate with some impulsive gesture—like tying me up. Twice.

"I will tell you everything," he swears, his shoulders hunched, body radiating tension. "If, you tell me something first…"

My breath catches as I advance a step toward him. "Anything."

"Tell me that you'll marry me." He whirls around, fixing me with the full intensity of his gaze, and I stagger backward. His eyes are so damn dark, so fucking earnest and determined all at once. My throat dampens, my body pulsating even as alarm bells go off at the back of my mind.

Only as he starts to advance do I fully register what he said. "Vadim—"

"Tomorrow," he interjects as he continues to approach, backing me into a corner. Within a heartbeat, I'm trapped, forced to crane my neck just to take him in. "I already have the paperwork drawn up. Together, we will file for joint custody over Magdalene—"

"Slow down!" I place my hand on his chest, my voice breaking.

"You will adopt her," he continues as if I'd never spoken. "My lawyer has already set plans in motion to expedite the request. All I need is your signature. I have a judge on my payroll, ready to validate them—"

"Wait!" I feel like I'm spinning, forced to brace myself against the wall just to gain some semblance of stability. "Tell me what happened. What did Irina—"

"Fuck Irina!" His voice booms, startling me with the ferocity. The vitriol. The...fear. Too late, he seems to realize his mistake. His eyes dart to the door, his head cocked to listen for any hint of Magda stirring.

While he's distracted, I take my chance and escape to the opposite end of the bed.

"Tell me what happened," I plead, making my voice as soothing as I can. "Talk to me—"

"She is irrelevant," he says coldly. "You tell *me*. Say yes."

"Vadim…" I lean against the wall, my face in my hands. "This is a lot to take in. Maybe if you explain what happened—"

"It doesn't matter what happened. You claimed you wanted a relationship with me. Or will you let a woman you've never even met be your excuse to run?"

I blink. "I'm sorry?"

He barks out a harsh laugh, pacing the length of the windows. "Sorry," he echoes, eyeing his hands as they curl and uncurl into fists. "You spend my money. Mother my daughter though you tease the idea of leaving when it suits you. Fuck me senseless. And yet, you won't marry me. You refuse to."

I gasp, stunned. "That's a bit of a low blow," I croak. A surprisingly painful one too. I place my hand over the center of my chest, startled by a real actual ache throbbing there. "Demanding a woman marry you after barely a month is a bit unprecedented. Especially when you won't tell me why—"

"You know I would do anything for you." He makes it sound like a crime on my part. Something awful and corrupting that I did to him. *This.* I made him break down his wall. I forced him to let me in. Let me see those dark, twisted parts of himself no one else ever has.

But from where I'm standing, he's not the one clutching at his literal heart, feeling it swell too big to fit in his chest.

"Tell me what you want, and you will have it," he demands. His voice, though softer, still resonates like thunder, radiating more conviction than I think I've heard from him until now. In so many ways, he reminds me of his brother. Where they lack in physical similarities, this is what they must share—a ruthless intensity when it comes to what they want.

No matter who stands in their way.

Something in me breaks in the face of this emotion, and I sway, forced to slump onto the end of the bed, too drained to stay standing.

"My money?" he prods, stepping forward. "You have it. My home? You have it. My—"

"I don't want anything from you," I confess in a whisper. As his expression falls, I race to add, "I mean, not physically. I don't want a transactional relationship with you. I want… Time. I just need *time*."

More time to heal from Jim. Time to think. Time to feel like being with him is my decision and not a product of hastiness or desperation—it shocks me to realize how much I truly want that—a natural progression with him. Nothing forced or faked.

I want this to be real.

"Just give me time." I gather the nerve to meet his expression and suck in a hopeful breath. His eyes are still narrowed, his jaw clenched—but that awful, bitter suspicion is gone, replaced by a hunger I'm too tired to deny. I raise my hands to the straps of my dress, guiding them down my shoulders as he tracks every bared bit of flesh with an expression that makes my toes curl. "Can you do that for me? Just give me time."

He doesn't answer. With one monstrous lunge on his part, I'm in his arms, swept toward the center of the bed. He strips my sodden clothing, groping the flesh underneath. I react to him wantonly, letting him drown my logical brain in friction and touching and heat.

But even as our lips meet, I sense that unspoken figure looming between us, growing harder to ignore with every surging beat of my pulse. *Irina.*

Irina. Irina. Irina!

Though I seem to be the only one in this bed haunted by her.

Vadim groans, sinking his fingers into my hair as he manipulates me beneath him—legs splayed, hips pinned against his. Gone is his usual restraint—he enters me with a commanding thrust, going so deep we both cry out. *Holy hell.* There isn't even time for my body to adjust to him before he rocks his hips, taking me whether I'm ready or not. Hungrily.

Recklessly.

His piercing batters my inner walls, his size straining my limits. It's a sensation almost verging on uncomfortable— and he moves in a way that makes me suspect, with a hint of alarm, that's just what he wants. To force me to focus on him, taking him fully. Lulled by his rhythm, my thoughts dissipate. Then reform, still fixated on that beautiful, mysterious blond.

But it's as if he knows the second my attention shifts from him. Growling, he reaches between us, his thumb grazing my clit, teasing me with the weight of my piercing.

I feel my head tip back, my eyes fluttering shut as the pleasure builds with every stroke.

More. More. More.

A burst of wetness eases his next stroke. The next... But that's where all similarities to carefree, normal sex end. The second he shifts, gripping my chin, his eyes boring into mine with more ferocity than his cock, I know...

This is something more.

Claiming.

Owning.

Dominating.

He slows his pace, making me arch into him, my eyes rolling, breaths feathering. I almost can't bear to meet his gaze like this, head-on. He looks at me so hauntingly. It's...insane.

Like I'm a lifeline he's clinging to, strengthening his grip with every thrust. Every startled moan he wrenches from my chest. Helpless, my knees curl around his waist, dragging him in despite the urgings of my brain to stop this. Resist. Fight.

But I can't.

He has me. All I can do is hold on, groaning as the pleasure builds and builds, and he times his movements with calculated, piercing thrusts. My orgasm is punishing—a wave that hits like a freight train, slamming into me before I realize it.

To savor his victory, his lips capture my startled cry, his body bucking against me as he strives toward his own release. All the while, he strokes me, cradles me to him. Cherishes me.

It's an intimacy I've never known. Not with any other man. Not even within myself during my deepest moments of self-reflection.

It's torture in its truest, rawest, most debasing form.

A pain I can't deny or escape.

A pleasure that will undo me.

CHAPTER TWO

He lets me rest, panting for air as he shifts to sit on the end of the bed, his back to me. Despite everything, I reach for him, sensing the bricks of his wall reforming too quickly to batter down.

What the hell happened in the space of time I was in the pool? Something vital. Something that's shaken him so thoroughly even sex can't clear his head.

Much like he did when Irina first inserted her presence into his life again, he's spiraling.

"Don't shut me out," I whisper, my voice rasping and broken. "This isn't a rejection. I promise. I promise—"

"Every time you look at me, I can see you plotting your escape." His voice. It's ice-cold, such a contrast to how he spoke to me just mere seconds ago. I go rigid, the air trapped in my chest, my hand frozen inches from him.

"You take what you can from me, but it is never enough, is it?" He stands, striding for the bathroom. His stiffened posture warns me not to follow. Regardless, his voice reaches back like the snap of a whip. "I prefer for you to spend my money."

"V-Vadim!" I watch him go, blinking frantically. It isn't until a searing warmth runs down my cheeks that I realize I'm crying, hurt by that implication way more than I want to be. It sounds so dirty. So vicious—using him. Maybe I have. Maybe I am.

But sometimes, manipulation is a two-way street.

I hear the water run, used as a barrier to disguise the sounds of what he's doing. Splashing water onto his face? Showering? The former, I suspect when he returns, dry save for his damp hair, mussed as if torn through by raking, ruthless fingers.

"What did she say to you?" I demand, alarmed by this shift in him. He isn't like this—driven by emotion. Wild.

Callous.

His eyes meet mine, so cold I gasp, shrinking in my seat. "What will it take?" he demands, stopping short just beyond the bed, utterly naked. When I sputter wordlessly, he crosses his arms, his chin cocked in that cruel, calculating way he does when only one thing is on his mind. Business. "Name your price. More money? Clothing? Shoes?"

"Don't do this." I shut my eyes just to get a reprieve from his icy exterior. "Don't hurt me. I am not rejecting you—"

"What do you call it then?" he counters. "When a man offers you the world, and you not only spit on his hand. You demand his thoughts. His secrets. You always ask for more."

I flinch. "I call it one thing—"

"What?"

"I'm scared!" My voice breaks, echoing so violently I'm sure Magda can hear it. We both wait, straining through the silence, but no other sound stirs. Just his frantic, furious—gosh, he's so angry—breaths, and my shallow whimpers as I fight back the tears I feel brewing.

"I'm scared, okay? I marry you in the heat of the moment when your thoughts are on your daughter—as they should be. But what happens in six months when the danger wears off?"

I draw my knees beneath my chin, hunched against the mattress as tears spill down my cheeks, wetting the sheets beneath me. "I'll tell you what. You realize that you're shackled to a..." My voice breaks. I'm channeling my ex-husband in this moment. What were the words he said to me on the eve of our divorce? "A lazy, selfish, self-centered, spoiled bitch who can't even run a home, let alone fend for herself. That's fine in a one-night stand," I add, laughing bitterly. "I know my limits. But do you? Do you want more children? I told you about my miscarriage, but I never told you why. It's not easy for me to get pregnant. Most doctors I consulted recommended IVF. Painful, expensive, grueling treatments that may or may not work. Are you willing to sign up for that? Are you willing to sign up for supporting someone who can't even hold a fucking job outside of one handed to her because her husband is prominent in a church? You claim I'm after your money? Money can only get you so far."

It can get you a life, beautiful on the outside, but jagged and agonizing within. A world wherein people only see your worth in a resume or who put a ring on your finger. A world I went on a wild, sexual goose chase just to escape.

"I'm not holding back out of fear for myself. I'm fearful for you! I don't… I don't want to disappoint you. I don't want you to wake up one day, bored, and go looking for another model. I don't want to be broken again. I *want* a relationship with you."

The mattress shifts. Warmth engulfs me, drawing me into a body that conforms to mine, strong and welcoming. He holds me so tightly I couldn't pull away, even if I wanted to. His voice bathes me in reassurance, so gentle that I relax instantly, my fear drained. He says something in French, too grated to decipher.

In this moment, I don't need to. I don't need anything from him but this. Silence. Nearness. Understanding.

I hide my face against his chest, seeking out any comfort in his embrace I can find. The real world can wait—because this conversation isn't over. Not by a long shot.

But for now, he relents.

And I have a fraction of more time.

I WAKE up before he does and escape into a robe, throwing on a nightgown underneath. Entering the hallway, I stop by Magda's room and peek in to find her still sleeping.

Thank God.

Craving silence, I steal into the kitchen and make myself a cup of tea.

I've barely taken a sip before my opponent appears across from me, dressed in a shirt and slacks that look as though he just tugged them on without any forethought. As he claims the seat at the end of the table, I sense the war horns being blown.

Another round is about to take place—because our battle isn't over.

"Look at me," he demands.

Because my gaze is on the window apparently, watching dawn claw across the horizon. When I risk sneaking a glance in his direction, I gasp, struck dumb by his expression. Gone is the icy rage from last night. He's too calm now.

Disarming in his persistence. He's brought weapons to this fight, I realize—a stack of documents that he places on the table and shoves toward me.

I glance at them, my heart racing. Sure enough, my worst fears are confirmed as I read the topmost line of the first page. *Petition to adopt…*

"Vadim—"

"I heard your concerns," he says, in a tone like thunder, though alarmingly quiet so as not to disturb anyone beyond this room. "Now, you hear mine. My daughter… You think I would offer her guardianship to you on a whim? That I would entrust her to anyone else? I've stood in the background of her life for too damn long, never would I jeopardize her safety or her trust. Never."

I set my tea aside, overwhelmed, and clutch my head in my hands, desperate to keep my thoughts focused. "Vadim, this is—"

"And I don't extend an offer of marriage lightly," he adds, easily cutting over me. "Do you know how many women have tried to seduce me? Fool me? Deceive me? I have seen through them all. Outsmarted them all." He's proud of that, I realize. Prideful, and defensive. "I knew from the second you approached me at that bar that you were different. Why? I wasn't your first choice," he says as if seeing right into my thoughts. My very soul. "I wasn't even your second or third. You approached me with no preconceived notions or deception, though I wanted to deny it. I did deny it. You approached me as a game," he says, his brow furrowing, eyes blazing. "To see if I could give you the fun you sought. Or not. You didn't care. If I failed, you would easily seek your fortune with someone else. It was so damn *easy* for you to find someone else."

His tone turns feral, and I picture him recalling all those men I'd taunted him with. Nearly run off to bed with. He's right, I'd treated it as a game—but only because he kept pushing me away. He hurt me, each time he did so.

"I had to fight to keep you entertained," he adds, gritting his teeth at the thought. Him, fight? As though he never has. Never sought a relationship with someone else before me—or maybe he *did*, I realize with growing horror…

Only for that person to reject him. Spurn him so badly he preferred to live his life closed-off, expecting only the worst from those who dared approach him. And the second he does let down his guard, that past rejection makes him spiral into paranoia.

Who was the culprit? Irina? Maxim? In this moment, I don't even think it matters who. They aren't the object of his focus now. His ire. His rage.

"I've plied you," he adds through gritted teeth. "Tempted you. Bought you. Fucked you. Tasted you. And yet it feels as if it's never enough. Like I'm always a heartbeat from losing you. You are still playing your game—"

"No!" I cringe at the woman he's describing and push back from the table. "I never manipulated you," I point out, shaking my head. "I never hurt you or tried to play mind games at your expense."

"Correct." He nods, his eyes are so dark I swear I can see myself reflected in them—a small, fragile woman on the verge of something both horrific and lifechanging. A realization. A mental breakdown. Who the hell knows?

"You just tease," he growls, palming the table with a quiet thud that sends my heart racing. "You give me a taste of everything I fucking never knew, and you threaten, every minute, to take it all away."

"Vadim…" I can't look at him anymore. I break, forfeiting the round to stare down at my hands. They're shaking. "What do you want from me?"

"I want everything." He sounds so hollow. So cold. A man denied warmth for so damn long he doesn't even remember what it feels like. Just that he craves it above all else. Jealously, he craves it. "Your body." But his tone implies something else. Something that makes me stiffen, desperate to head him off.

"Don't—"

"Your touch."

"Stop it—"

"Your taste. Your love—"

"Vadim!" I lurch to my feet, scrambling for the terrace door. My eyes are burning, vision blurring. Putting distance between us now is my only hope for escape. "I'm going for a walk."

"So you run," he snarls. "As is the case with everyone else, I am never enough to keep you."

I stagger, so wounded I nearly collapse right then and there. There's so much pain in his voice. Such awful, unending pain…

And a terrifying threat.

"Is this about whatever happened with Irina?" I say, deploying my own secret weapon. "Just tell me what she said—"

"You want time?" he questions. The telltale scrape of a chair over the flooring warns of him standing, his steps heavy. "You have it. But I suggest you not take too long. I am well used to the pain that comes from rejection by others—but Magdalene? My daughter will never know that pain again. *Never.* You can toy with me all you'd like, but I won't let you trap her in your web. Never will you be the one to take her happiness away."

His steps advance from the kitchen, moving toward the foyer.

"Leave or stay," he adds. "But know that I am done playing your game."

He retreats to some distant corner of the house, and I slump against the nearest wall, gasping for air. My chest feels so damn tight. Like it's caught in a vice, being crushed between desire and fear. Ultimatums are nothing new—Jim tossed out his fair share.

But none ever left me feeling like this…

Shaken to my fucking core. Beaten down to a fragile shell seconds from cracking. No one else in my entire life has ever left me so uncertain. Of myself. Of the world around me. Of my heart and every fiber making up the body I've spent twenty-eight years dwelling within.

I don't even process moving, but eventually, I find myself outside, sitting on the edge of the pool in the frigid morning air, shivering, my legs calf-deep in the water. I don't know how long I've sat like this. Just that my only tether to the real world comes in the form of a tiny, disapproving voice speaking to me from the direction of the house.

"Are you going to go swimming in your clothes again?"

I turn to find Magda watching me from the doorway of the kitchen. She's neatly dressed in a light blue skirt and magenta sweater. Someone took the time to brush her hair and braid it with meticulous care, securing two pigtails with pure white ribbons.

I don't know why I flinch at first. Vadim's her father, he should be the one to help her. And yet, I can't help but interpret the act as a threat, its warning simple. When it comes down to it, I'm not needed.

"No," I tell her, forcing a tired smile. "I'm just thinking." I kick my legs for emphasis, sending up a spray of water.

Warily, she slips from around the door and approaches me, her hands on her hips. "Can I play with Ainsley today?" she asks.

I sigh, turning my gaze to the churning waters of the bay beyond our quiet spot. "I don't know, honey. You'll have to ask your father—Mr. Vadim."

A glance from the corner of my eye reveals her pouting, but seemingly undeterred. "I'm hungry."

"Okay." I unfurl my sore limbs and follow her into the kitchen. There, I spot the time above the stove and realize that I've lost at least three hours, just staring into space. I'm freezing as a result, shivering violently as I adjust to the heat of the house.

After making Magda a bowl of cereal, I creep upstairs into the master bedroom, relieved to find it empty. I shower quickly and throw on a relatively casual outfit consisting of a light linen dress and a sweater. When I return downstairs, Magda's still seated at the table, but a larger figure dominates the space beside her.

He's adjusted his outfit, smoothing out the rumpled appearance to regain his polished composure. The only oddity to contrast his icy, businessman persona is the fact that he's manipulating a white teddy bear with utmost care.

It got a makeover, it seems. His fur is a brighter, cleaner white as if he took a trip through the washing machine. He's also been freshly stuffed, his head sewn back on and adorned with a tiny red scarf to hide the stitching around his neck.

"What do we think?" Vadim asks, holding the toy up for Magda's inspection.

She observes the bear critically and then nods in approval, reaching for it. Vadim watches as she tucks the bear under her arm, betraying a sentiment that makes my throat constrict.

It's like my torment alerts him to my presence before any other clue. His head jerks up, those dark eyes roving in my direction. Coldly, they graze over me before returning to his daughter as he smooths his fingers over one of her braids.

"Would you like to ride Dasha today?" he asks, referring to her pony.

She perks up. "Can we?" She's already lurching to her feet and bounding from the kitchen by the time he tells her yes. I step aside, my lips parting into a smile. But the expression lasts until the second I see Vadim's face.

Gone is the warmth he displayed around his daughter. That coldness sets in, hardening the line of his jaw and making his gaze so chilling, I'm frozen even in my sweater. The worst part is that his wall is down all the way, and there's nothing to temper the hostility. The raw pain he displays, making one fact overwhelmingly clear.

It's all my fault.

And yet, I can't seem to move. I'm frozen, caught like a deer in the headlights of this fragile truce until Magda comes racing back into the kitchen, her skirt swapped for jodhpurs, her riding helmet in place.

Like magic, Vadim's face transforms again, radiating warmth as he stands and follows her out. Before she steps over the threshold, however, she looks back, her gaze finding me.

"Are you going to come to watch?" she asks in that wary, hesitant tone. As if, like Vadim, she's guarding herself from me, still unsure.

I nod as enthusiastically as I can. "Of course!"

"Then come on." She squares her shoulders and marches off, her father in tow. And I promptly stagger to the nearest counter, gripping the edge so tightly my knuckles whiten.

Get it together, Tiffany, my inner bitch warns. But even she sounds shaken, a shadow of the guidance that has driven me since leaving Jim. That's the scary part. Everything I rebuilt of myself—everything I managed to salvage of the shadow I became—I can feel splintering around me, in danger of crumbling all over again. Will the resulting Tiffany be stronger or worse off in the aftermath? I don't know.

I don't know anything about myself anymore. My thinking has been corrupted, shaped by a man who seems to crave me one minute, only to push me away the next. Then crave again, somehow making me feel as though it's my fault for letting him shove. And if he keeps on shoving, I'm going to fall eventually.

Right, a part of me hisses. *So, grit your teeth, dig your heels in and stand firm. What do you want?*

Him. But on my terms, with enough time to ensure that this is really what he wants as well. I rushed into marriage with Jim and look how that turned out? I deserve the chance to convince myself in every way that life with Vadim is worth the inherent risks.

Because Jim hurt me so badly, it took a reckless vow of sexual exploration to get me back on my feet. Vadim? I can feel the echoes of that old pain where he is concerned—tenfold. He won't just break me if I lose him the same way.

This man could utterly destroy me.

And yet it's almost too easy to plaster a fake smile onto my face and skip out to the stable as if nothing is wrong. In one of the fenced-in pastures, I spot Magda, sitting astride her pony as Vadim directs her from the center of the paddock, holding a pink lead rope.

Watching them interact is always engrossing, but now with the sun shining and both of them fighting back grins? I'm helpless to resist. Creeping forward, I slip my fingers through the wooden slats of the fence and watch, my heart aching, my thoughts in disarray.

They move together so well, a beautiful synchrony. With gentle words and reminders, he corrects her posture and offers encouragement. With every word from him, she sits straighter, her eyes brightening, her lips twitching until a genuine grin unfurls despite herself. The potential relationship building between them could be something fearsome to behold—a partnership no one could ever come in between. But one with room for anyone else?

That remains to be seen. And I'm not the only one mulling that very question, I suspect. In the snatches of time that Magda's back is to him, Vadim's expression slips, revealing a tumult of contradicting emotions. Every now and again, he'll look at me, his gaze still accusatory. Wounded. But the second he senses his daughter's attention on him, he suppresses the darkness, greeting her only with the light.

It's like being tortured, over and over again, leaving me grasping the paddock for sole support as I'm teased with the full extent of his happiness and then stabbed with his anger.

Again. Again. Again.

I barely notice the sound of approaching footsteps, until a childish bit of laughter reaches my ears. From Magda, I realize in shock. She's practically bouncing in her saddle, waving frantically at a pair of figures advancing across the fields behind me.

Our intruders somehow made it past Ena, given the unofficial seal of approval to cut into the property from its west end. One of the figures sprints ahead, her dirty-blond hair flying out like a missile behind her. Within seconds, she's at the paddock gates, cooing. "Wow! He's so pretty," she says with all of the solemn awe a child can possess.

Magda beams, so proud from her perch. "*She* is pretty," she corrects. "Want to pet her?"

Ainsley looks to Vadim for permission, who tightens his grip on the lead rope and helps Magda down. Then he approaches the gate, allowing Ainsley inside, and stands watch as the girls fuss over the pony. It's adorably cute in the brief moments those dark, storming eyes avoid meeting mine.

But then they do, and the resulting chill is enough to drive me back from the paddock altogether. Wrapping my arms around my torso, I turn and spot the lone figure lingering on the path, her gaze wary and watchful over the trio behind me.

Sighing, I advance toward her, forcing a neutral smile. "Hey!"

"Hey," Francesca replies, though she barely takes her eyes off her sister to greet me. Both enemy subjects are dressed warmly—Ainsley in a pink sweater and jeans, Francesca in a black woolen dress and jacket. Her dark hair frames her face, hanging down her shoulders.

"I'm glad you came over," I say, genuinely pleased for Magda.

Francesca's lips part into a small grin. "It's good for Ains to play with someone her own age. Someone other than her brother Eric, at least. And I could use a break from the fighting."

"I hear you on that," I murmur, glancing over my shoulder. Even while outnumbered, Vadim maintains his trademark charm. Always the master manipulator, he has the girls spellbound, teaching them various parts of the horse mingled with jokes and exaggerated expressions that have them giggling.

"Cover your mouth, Ains!" Francesca calls as the girl sneezes mid-cackle. Then she turns to me, and something in my expression must trigger her alarm. "Sorry. I think she may be coming down with a cold… Are you okay? This isn't a bad time—"

"No, of course not!" I make my grin wider, playing up my own social charms. "How about we let the girls play and have our own playdate? I have the best wine—" I eye her warily with what I hope passes for a friendly chuckle. "You are twenty-one, right?"

"I don't really drink…" Her gaze strays again to her sister. Is she worried about Vadim?

With an awkward bit of guilt, I remember the whole tiny detail about him having kidnapped Ainsley once upon a time.

"Right," I say nervously. "Well, we could just hang around, and—"

"No." Francesca shakes her head, forcing a heavy sigh. "No, you're right. A glass of wine sounds great."

"Good!" I'm so relieved, I sway. "I could use a bit of adult time, to be honest."

At least time with an adult who isn't intent on consuming me, body, and soul.

CHAPTER THREE

"I got married young," I blurt out once Francesca and I are settled into lounge chairs, positioned halfway between the house and the stable. From this position, we have a clear view of our charges, but are far enough back to let the girls play in peace.

In my hand is a glass of wine, while hers rests untouched, balanced on the arm of her chair. Lacking her restraint, I drink deeply as my eyes trace the contours of Vadim's silhouette, visible from here.

"I was too young," I add, lowering my voice for my audience of one. "So young, I had no idea who I was or what I even wanted out of life. I let the thrill of belonging to someone completely shape me. In the end, it almost destroyed me. But, you don't want to hear about that," I add with a forced, hollow laugh. "Listen to me, babble on about nothing. How are things on your end?"

"Good," she says. But her brown eyes trace mine, too damn alert. Aware. There's something in her expression that makes me squirm until, helpless, I find myself desperate to spill more.

"You're not afraid?" I ask. "Of marrying Maxim?"

She averts her gaze from me and lifts her glass, taking a sip. "I was," she confesses after swallowing. "I was terrified as hell."

"But?" I prod, already halfway through my glass. Thankfully, I brought the bottle, leaving it perched against my calf.

She frowns. "He gets me better than anyone. And I may be young, but I've been through a lot. He gets me."

I'm instantly drawn to the unapologetic nature in her tone. No bullshit, I suspect. No love-blind sugar coating. Just raw honesty.

He gets me.

"Does Maxim know you're here? I have to say that I'm surprised you came over."

A hint of unease slips into her weary grin. "He's out of town," she says. I remember the conversation I'd overhead a few days ago between Vadim and Milton—Maxim was in Russia apparently, dealing with some kind of business disruption. "I told him Ainsley, and I were going out today —but I didn't say to where. Ainsley's been begging me for the past two days, and Lucius promised to cover for me. We have about an hour before we need to head back, though."

Lucius, I suspect, is the kind, older man who allowed Magda and I onto their property the other day. And his sudden leniency most likely has everything to do with the former's charms. I look over to find her relishing in the attention from both her father and her new friend—a different girl from the surly, brooding figure who came here just over a week ago.

"Is there a reason you're thinking about marriage?" Francesca asks, her tone gently probing.

With another sip of wine and a sigh, I relent. "Yes. There is a reason. A twenty-four-carat reason." I'm eyeing the fake engagement ring on my finger, but who knows what Vadim would spring for as the real deal. Something obscenely expensive, I suspect, and the thought of it terrifies me. Denying him terrifies me. As afraid as I am of the potential downfalls, I'm quickly realizing that I don't want to lose him. Not like this.

Because as volatile as his mood has been these past twenty-four hours, something tells me that one culprit is behind the shift. *Irina.* She said something to set him on edge, making him jump to a hasty marriage as his only solution.

"But I'm not ready," I admit out loud. "I'm not."

"And if Dima is anything like Maxim, you feel like you don't have a choice," Francesca says softly.

There's lingering pain in her voice, alluding to a wound that I suspect is every bit as deep as the one festering in my heart at the moment. Sadly, I tilt my glass as my gaze finds the sole cause of my torment. "I'll drink to that—"

"But," Francesca adds without lifting her glass to her mouth, "You can't have a relationship built on just one person's rules. There has to be a give and take…" She trails off, her gaze fixated somewhere in the distance. After a few seconds, she shakes her head and sighs. "I don't think you should let anyone pressure you if you aren't ready. You'll only lose yourself in the end."

"It's not that," I say, feeling some need to defend Vadim from the picture my dancing around the subject is creating. "It's just…"

I'm not sure just what point I'm trying to make. To avoid the subject entirely, I down the rest of my glass as the girls scamper around the paddock.

But the niggling, defensive feeling won't leave. Finally, with a sigh, I'm forced to confront it. "I lost myself once," I admit. "I swore to myself I'd never let it happen again."

Francesca eyes me simply, her gaze conveying more maturity than her age should allow her to. "Then don't," she says, as if it's that easy.

But in the realm of Vadim Gorgoshev, I'm not sure that anything truly is.

THE SECOND, Francesca and Ainsley leave, Vadim helps Magda cool down and stable Dasha while I watch from the safety of my lounge chair. Together, we finally return to the house, and I sense an even firmer boundary settling between us.

An ocean of emotional distance separates me from Vadim as we file into the kitchen, and he heads to the fridge, presumably to make dinner. He doesn't look my way once, his shoulders rigid, his warm tone solely reserved for his daughter.

"Spaghetti?" he suggests to her while rummaging through various cupboards.

"Okay." She nods in agreement, clutching her riding helmet to her chest.

"I'll get it ready. You go get washed up, *oui?*"

"Okay!" She dutifully sets off, and I don't even realize I'm following after her until his voice reaches me, a cautious rasp.

"Tiffany…"

"I should help her get ready," I say, practically running for the stairs. Magda looks surprised when I enter her room, but like the princess she is, she promptly points to her closet.

"I want to wear my pink pajamas," she declares, and like a good servant, I rush to obey.

As she showers, I lay out the clothing on her bed. The moment she reappears, I make a show of fussing over her, helping her towel dry her hair and braid it.

"You took a very steamy shower, you lobster," I tease, running my hand over her scalp. "You're still boiling."

"Can you teach me to swim tomorrow?" she asks, her eyelids heavy.

"Sure," I say, oddly touched by the request. At least someone wants me around. "As long as it's not too cold out. Maybe we can go out on the boat, too?"

She holds out her tiny hand, raising her pinky. "Promise?"

Chuckling, I curl my own pinky around hers. "Promise. Now let's go eat."

Clutching the newly restored It to her chest, she bounds downstairs for dinner.

But I don't follow right away. Instead, I retreat into the bedroom and strip my own clothing. Then I enter the shower and linger until the water runs cold, and my shivering serves as a cover for my own silent sobs.

Get a grip, Tiffy, I try to tell myself. *You're a bad bitch, remember? Stop second-guessing yourself!*

But that's all I seem capable of doing while in the realm of Vadim Gorgoshev. Second-guessing. Fearing. Doubting. Questioning.

Something that can feel this damn good, and yet hurt this damn much… It can't be real, can it? Let alone healthy?

I haven't decided by the time I finally leave the shower and slip into a robe. The second I take a step over the threshold to the bedroom, however, I stop short, my gaze fixated on the creature watching me from the edge of the bed.

He's stripped his shirt, wearing just his slacks, his hair mussed like it is only when he's been tearing through it ruthlessly. Dark, his eyes track my every movement, hunting me with a predator's intensity as I tentatively take a step. Then another.

Still holding my gaze, he rises to his feet. His eyes blaze anger, but as they trace the low neckline of my robe, the lids lower, his lips parting. My heart hammers in response, and I don't shy away from his gaze, even with the tension simmering between us.

Lust is the one language we speak that transcends all others, and I'm so desperate for a connection…

It's like I lose control over my body. Myself.

With Jim, sex was always used as leverage. Or as a reward, if I'd jumped through various hoops and pleased him enough to deign indulging me in the moment.

With Vadim, sex is wild. Untamable. Communication. It is the only way I seem to be able to understand him. In groping, hungry touches the second I come close enough. In a fierce, mind-melding kiss that renders me defenseless against him.

Hungrily, he grasps my hips, twisting around to shove me onto the bed. His gaze intent, he mounts the mattress after me. Hooking his fingers beneath my hips, he flips me onto my back, easing my legs apart before I can protest. This angle robs me of any leverage, forcing me to buck into him. Chase him. Crave him.

I shiver as he enters me, thrusting deep, taking what he can and battering down any resistance I may think to put up. His chest cages me in, his hands crushing me flat, controlling the pace. Angle. Everything. Mindless, I rock against him, letting him stretch me to my limits. Take me beyond them. Leave me quaking on the edge of sanity and then watch me fall.

This isn't over, I sense, even as we both gasp out in relief. Just a reprieve. A truce.

The real war is only beginning, and when he finally withdraws from me, spent, he collapses with his back to me, his shoulders rigid.

I go limp, panting against the sheets, my thoughts scattered, body still burning alight. If I had the strength to move, I would. Run far, far away—put distance between us any way I can.

Physically at least, because emotionally, we might as well be on different planets.

CHAPTER FOUR

I wake up, blinking at a partially darkened ceiling, though I'm not sure why. Closing my eyes, I'm already drifting back off when I hear it—a voice low with concern.

"Magda?" Vadim murmurs. I turn to find him rolling upright, dragging part of the sheet over his body. Magda stands on his end of the bed, her eyes half-closed, lips pursed. Seemingly in a daze, she tugs on his hand until he faces her.

"What is it, *ma chérie?*" Vadim questions, stroking her hair. But something makes him frown and press his palm to her forehead. "Shit! You're burning up." He lurches to his feet, snatching his pants from the floor. Once dressed, he lifts Magda into his arms, racing into the hall. "Ena!" I hear him shout. "Bring the car around! Now!"

"Vadim?" Shrugging off my exhaustion, I scramble to my feet and hunt for my discarded nightgown. By the time I make it downstairs, Vadim is already carrying Magda through the front entrance. Beyond them, a stern-faced Ena is waiting beside the compact gray car, opening the door to the backseat.

"Get her a change of clothes," Vadim commands, cutting his gaze to me. The raw, frantic desperation in his eyes takes my breath away, and I run off, anxious to help. Panting, I tear into Magda's room and find her gray suitcase under her bed. I snatch a change of clothing from her closet, along with pajamas and her toothbrush. Last but not least, I grab It and Biphany, still tucked beneath her blankets.

"I've got it!" I call as I peel down the stairs. But the front door is closed. When I wrench it open in confusion, I find the driveway empty.

And it's nearly a solid minute of staring before the truth sinks in.

They're gone.

And I've been left behind.

I SPEND all of five minutes searching the house for a phone before I realize that I don't even know Vadim's cell phone number should I find one. Or Ena's. Hell, I don't even know where the car keys are kept. A trip to the garage reveals nothing but mocking, empty vehicles I have no way of driving.

"Damn it!" I'm crying, I realize, as my hoarse sobs echo back to me. I'm not even hurt, not really. My overriding thought is that Magda needs her teddy bear. She needs her pajamas and a ribbon for her hair. She needs me to tuck her in—and God forbid she's sick enough to need intensive care…

I should be there.

I *need* to be there.

That driving thought has me running from the house on a whim, cutting through the woods that shroud the west side of the property. At the back of my mind, I try to imagine the picture I make—I'm barefoot, wearing only a thin nightgown, clutching a tiny suitcase to my chest. Only God knows how I appear to the older man approaching the edge of Maxim's property to meet me.

Lucius. He's wearing a suit, murmuring into an earpiece. "Stand down," he says to someone on the other end of the device before turning his attention to me. "Are you alright—"

"Please help me! I need to get to the hospital. Please. I need to be there. I don't know how. I don't…"

Lucius' expression shifts into one of stoic concern. As I shiver in anticipation of his reaction, he shrugs off his suit jacket and drapes it over me. Within minutes I'm being ushered into the back of a black car as he takes the wheel.

I barely even know what I'm saying. Just that Magda needs her bear. Her pajamas. Me.

"Do you know what hospital?" he asks gently.

I think I try to say something, but all I wind up doing is sobbing. Openly. Loudly. I don't even know why I'm upset. Maybe by the implicit understanding that this is it—my worst fear coming true. When hell breaks loose, I'm left behind, forced to scramble on my own. He didn't even think to wait for me, so used to forging ahead.

What kind of marriage would this be?

By the time we finally make it to the hospital, I'm resolved. Gritting my teeth, I swipe the tears from my face and school my expression into one of calm. I start to scramble from the backseat on my own, thanking Lucius profusely.

"Wait just a moment." He exits the car, but rather than open the door for me, he enters the hospital directly, leaving me to squirm and contemplate running in anyway. I deflate with relief, however, when he returns and presents me with not only a change of clothes—a sweater and pants with the price tags still on—but a sturdy pair of decent shoes and a visitor's badge with my name on it.

"She's in room 2207," he says after I quickly change in the backseat. How he knows as much is far too unsettling to question at the moment.

I'm more grateful than alarmed.

"Thank you," I tell him, grasping his hand. "Thank you so much!"

Inside, a woman at the front desk directs me to a set of elevators that bring me to the second floor. The moment I see the sign over the archway leading to the section of rooms Magda's belongs to, my heart sinks—Pediatric Intensive Care Unit.

When I gather the nerve to step over the threshold, I'm faced with yet another woman at the desk.

"Hello," I tell her, struggling to regain my charming persona. "I'm here to see the patient in 2207. My name is Tiffany Connors."

The woman nods and turns to her computer screen. Whatever she sees makes her frown and rise from her desk. "I'll be right back, Miss."

She disappears down a hallway only to return seconds later with Vadim in tow. He looks awful, a man apart from who he was only a few hours ago. The darkness once again has claimed his expression, but glimpsed without the filter of his wall...

It's terrifying.

"Thank you," he says to the clerk. Then he advances toward me and inclines his head to a small sitting room just off the unit entrance. "We need to talk."

I follow him, still clutching Magda's things to my chest. Before he can even say a word, I feel the need to place her suitcase on a nearby coffee table, open it and fish out It. "She needs this," I tell him, shoving the bear into his hands. "And I brought her brush and some ribbon."

He accepts the offering, but his expression doesn't ease one damn iota. If anything, the line of his jaw hardens against me. "You shouldn't have come."

I blink. "What… What do you mean? She needs her clothes and her bear, and—"

"I mean this is the time when she needs stability," Vadim says, his tone harsh. "A parent. Someone she can trust not to leave when she needs them the most. Someone who won't be cavalier with her health—"

"What…" I'm still processing his word usage. *Cavalier*—reckless. "What are you talking about?"

His eyes flash. In a violent motion, he tosses the bear across the room so hard it rebounds off a nearby couch, and I'm left stunned in the face of such a display.

"I mean, you refuse to adopt her," he growls, straining to keep his voice low. "You refuse to marry me. And now you want to tease her at a time when her health and safety is of the utmost importance? Was this your aim all along when you got her soaking wet in forty-degree weather? Slip out while she's rushed to the hospital? And what, you got cold feet and came back in guilt?"

I turn away from him, hunting for a chair, and I hurriedly perch myself on the edge of it. My brain is spinning, thoughts so tangled, it's almost painful to form coherence from his statements, pairing his anger with his words. But when I finally do, the resulting implication is soul-crushing.

"Are you saying I got her sick on purpose?" I whip my head around to face him. He doesn't even have the nerve to flinch. Look guilty. Anything but face me with such a cold, hostile expression.

I can feel something inside me crack—right in my chest. No therapy, sex, or wine could ever soothe this pain. And I know there's no way he could be doing this on purpose.

"You're upset," I say, staggering to my feet. "I can understand that. Let's just go see her—"

"No." He steps back, denying me the ability to reach for him. "You should leave."

A startled laugh escapes me before I can bite it back. "I'm not leaving her alone. No. I'm not." I picture the stoic figure who held a grudge against her father for leaving her in foster care, paired with the innocent girl who begged me to teach her to swim. "I'm not," I insist, shaking my head.

"She needs *me*," Vadim says, flicking his collar. "Someone she can trust."

"How…how dare you?" I can't breathe. My chest feels so damn tight. Looking at the man before me, I can't reconcile him with the figure who held me at night or bathed me with care. I'm numb, barely aware of the wetness sliding down my cheeks until my vision blurs, and I'm blinded by tears. "How dare you?"

"How dare I?" I sense him move—his shape distorted as more tears fall, impossible to stem. "You've already denied her once," he points out. "I think it's better if you leave now. Let her heal from your mistake, and your absence before your eventual departure hurts her more."

He grabs her suitcase and crosses the room, snatching It from the floor. Then he heads toward the unit, leaving me to scramble after him.

"Vadim, don't do this. Just let me see her—"

He stops short, so suddenly I nearly run into him. "I think it's best for everyone if you just go. Now. Ena will take you back to the house. Help yourself to what you wish. Just be gone by the time I return."

He marches forward, breezing past the front desk. When I try to follow, the woman seated there stands, her voice apologetic. "I'm sorry, Miss, but due to the nature of our unit, I can't let you by without permission from a parent or guardian."

I keep blinking at her as if that single action will make her disappear. Make this pain go away. I'll wake up in bed beside the Vadim I thought I knew, and this will all turn out to be some horrid nightmare.

I just keep blinking, as my legs move woodenly to navigate my way back into the elevator and down to the lobby. I keep blinking even as I find Ena waiting out front, his expression stern.

I just keep blinking.

But I never wake up from this nightmare.

CHAPTER FIVE

In a daze, I return to the house, but I don't go upstairs to pack, even though I should. I find myself sitting at the dining room table instead, too numb to do anything but stare at a pile of mocking, goddamn documents. He made it sound so damn simple. Sign a piece of paper, claim joint custody of a little girl—like it was something people did on a daily basis.

On a whim.

Though in his world, maybe they do. Maxim did it? I wonder if that's where his anger truly stems from. Maxim supposedly didn't hesitate to take on six children when asked. But when it comes to his one?

I balk.

Because that's what normal people do when presented with the gravity of caring for a child, a part of me insists. *Leave, Tiffy. Run.*

Run…

I find the strength to stand and make it upstairs, but I don't enter the closet first. I stagger into the bathroom, alarmed by the woman I find watching me from the mirror's surface. Her eyes are bloodshot, her hair a mess, her outfit totally unfashionable.

She's a stranger—though not entirely. I've glimpsed her before, hunched over the sink, or cowering after a fight with Jim. After he made her feel so damn worthless…

And my already low mood plummets. What was that promise I made to myself all those months ago? Never again.

Bracing my hands over the countertop, I fight to take a deep breath. The moment I manage to drag in enough air, I release it slowly, tilting my head up to the ceiling. The last time I found myself in this position, I gave myself only a second to come up with a game plan. Back then, it was simple—live, kick ass, make my list. Fuck the world —literally.

But now?

This newer decision forms slowly, coming together as I strip my clothing and enter the shower, turning the water as hot as I can stand. Surrendering to the torrent, I let the heat and steam wash away my pain and hurt, watching it all circle the drain like blood. Then I towel off, and enter the closet, taking just one outfit from the hangers.

It's a modest gray dress. Without thinking, I select the matching jacket, and complete the outfit with a black leather purse and heels. The resulting effect is a more confident woman than the disheveled waif in gift shop clothing. And yet it's still not enough. I have to run a brush through my hair and carefully apply enough makeup to disguise the red blotches from crying. Then I line my eyes with liner and spread a soft pink lipstick on my lips.

Only now do I feel like myself again.

When I finally return downstairs, I'm surprised to find Ena leaning against the front door. Spotting me, he cocks his head, his expression wary.

"You go back?" His tone surprises me almost as much as his neutral gaze. It isn't hostile, for once.

I nod, and he grunts in reply, lumbering to open the door. "I bring car around."

"I'll be there in a moment." With my head held high, I take a detour into the kitchen, grabbing the handful of documents from the dining room table. I flip through them, picking out the adoption papers pertaining to Magda, ignoring the rest. He had this all planned out meticulously, it seems—the bastard even left his pen.

Lifting it, I give myself one last chance to second-guess the decision…

Before I sign my name on every last page. As I watch the ink dry, I rip off my fake engagement ring and leave it right by the unsigned marriage documents.

And don't regret a damn thing.

A DIFFERENT WOMAN claims the ICU reception desk when I approach. She takes one look at me, and her frown deepens as though she's recalling some warning about a woman matching my description.

The second I slam a stack of documents down before her, however, her frown fades.

"I'm here to see the patient in room 2207," I say in my chirpiest voice with my most charming smile. "I'm her legal guardian."

The woman nods and rises to her feet, but this time she beckons me after her, down a wide hallway and past an open nurse's station. Another woman is already advancing to meet us, her gray suit practical, a sturdy briefcase tucked under her arm.

"Mrs. Gorgoshev!" She extends her hand to me, her smile warm, and I vaguely recognize her as Magda's social worker. Ms. Anderson.

"I wish I could stay longer," she says with a small laugh. "Current circumstances aside, I'll confess that I don't think I've seen Magda look happier in a long time. I have the doctor's information, and they'll keep me posted on her condition…" She breaks off, scanning my face, and I sense her smile widen as if she's desperate to reassure me the same way she must soothe those in her care. "Don't worry now.

She's a tough girl. And this visit is just a formality given her hospital admission. I have to get going, but I'll contact your husband about the next check-in. Have a wonderful day!"

She scampers off, leaving the nurse to continue forging the way through the small unit. There, in a room at the very back of the space, I find Magdalene, resting in bed, chatting animatedly to a figure who's seated beside her, holding her hand.

"…and then I wanna ride my pony, and—Tiffany!" Her tiny face breaks into a smile so wide it almost distracts from the alarming pallor of her skin. A sheen of sweat ghosts her forehead, gluing stray curls to the damp flesh. Gone are her neat braids, and the tousled style only enhances her similarities to the man nearby. While she may not be on a ventilator—thank God—a series of tubing extends from an IV. The mass of bandages looks monstrous encircling her fragile wrist. Not that the treatment has dampened her excitement any—she squirms, prevented from claiming the object I'm holding between two hands. "Is that for me?"

"It is," I tell her, placing a giant bear nearly as big as she is on the end of her bed. She beams, too exhausted I suspect, to feign disinterest.

The figure beside her quietly rises to his feet. I sense his eyes on me, unusually wide—with shock? It doesn't matter. In this moment, he doesn't exist, and I pour all of my attention into Magda as I pull up a free chair beside her.

"Where were you all day?" she demands, eyeing me with an eyebrow raised.

This time, I do make the mistake of glancing toward Vadim. His expression is guarded, impossible to read. I guess he spared Magdalene his little rant. He didn't even tell her I tried to visit.

But I don't have the heart to challenge that now—for Magda's sake. Instead, I smile and tug on one of her new bear's enormous arms. "I was trying to find the perfect friend to keep you company," I tease. "What shall you call him?"

"Hmmm." She bites her lip and shrugs. "I don't know yet."

"Well, you better think of something good." I slip out of my coat and fold it over the side of my chair.

"You're staying?" she asks, her expression brightening even more.

I nod. "Of course. In fact, I'm going to stay with you all night." As I speak, I fixate my gaze on the man standing near the doorway, letting every ounce of vitriol seep into my expression. It's so much I almost can't contain it without wanting to sob. Break.

But I don't.

"Whatever you need, I'm here. I'll always be here for *you*."

Vadim says nothing until he finally crosses the threshold, his back to us. "I'll get you some more water, *chérie*."

He leaves, and Magda promptly picks up whatever tale she was in the middle of conveying to him. Something about all of the things she wants to do once discharged from the hospital. Go on an airplane. See the beach. Ride her pony off the lead. Go bike riding. Eat ice cream.

I file away every request, determined to ensure she gets to do every last one.

"You came."

The grated voice draws me out of a light sleep, and I blink my eyes open to a spacious hospital room, lit only by a few dimmed lamps. Magda is sleeping, her chest rising and falling, her new bear practically swallowing her though she tried her damn hardest to wrestle it under one arm. It lies tucked beneath the blankets on her other side, with Biphany on her nightstand.

The sight of her erases any doubts that may have crept in as I slept. I have no regrets. Motherhood wasn't on my original list, but I can make an addendum. No relationships—*but* this one. For Magdalene.

As for her father?

I stiffen the second I sense him enter the room, his face in shadow, his posture rigid. "You signed the documents?" He doesn't sound doubtful—more prodding, as if this is his way of demanding proof.

Luckily for us both, I've come more than prepared to rub his nose in my decision.

Forcing out a cold laugh, I reach under my chair, snatching the adoption papers from my purse. I throw them at him, watching them scatter throughout the room like misshapen snowflakes.

"Yeah, I signed your fucking papers," I hiss.

Despite the vitriol, my voice is barely louder than a whisper, and I keep Magda in my line of sight, watching for any signs she might be awake. She looks so peaceful in this moment. So innocent. Even in my anger, I can't risk upsetting her. So, I direct every ounce of loathing I can into the harshest stage-whisper.

"But I did it for her," I croak, my throat tight. "Not you. As far as I'm concerned, I'm a single mother forced to share custody with an asshole who doesn't even have the privilege of being called my ex-husband. Congrats, Vadim. You're below Jim on the *people who have fucked me over* list. I hope you're pleased with yourself. Now take your fucking papers and get the hell out. In the morning, you can have time with her, considering you barred me all fucking day!"

He flinches so slightly it could be a trick of the light. Then that telltale muscle in his jaw twitches before his expression hardens with resolve. He crouches, carefully gathering up every last document. Then he tucks them under his arm and leaves.

And I'm more confused than ever, slumping in my seat, my eyes blinking fiercely. He should have been angry at my change of heart, right? Angry that I had the nerve to show up at all. Not…resigned?

Like baiting me into agreeing to take custody was his plan all along.

Because that would be far too cruel. Way too manipulative.

That would be unforgivable.

I WAKE up a second time to find Magda watching me from her bed, her blue eyes unreadable.

"How are you feeling?" I ask, placing my hand over one of hers.

"Better." She shrugs, ever the stoic. "But I'm hungry."

"Okay, honey." Yawning, I lurch to my feet and set off in search of a nurse. By the time her breakfast is served, and the nurse has finished her morning assessment—her vitals are improving, and pending another round of bloodwork, she could be discharged as early as tomorrow—Vadim arrives, and I promptly prepare to make my exit.

"You're leaving?" Magda watches me from over her breakfast tray, her eyes so wide that I assume she's been perfecting this innocent expression solely for moments like this. Gosh, she's so much like her father, but the comparison stings now more than it feels endearing.

An emotional terrorist with a devastating arsenal at her disposal.

"Yes, honey," I say, gathering up my coat as Vadim claims the chair on the opposite end of her bed. "I'll see you tonight."

I hesitate beside her only to change my mind at the last second. Boundaries be damned. Leaning down, I kiss her forehead. Her fever has broken, but she still feels clammy, her skin far too pale. "Don't have too much fun without me," I warn, tugging on one of her curls.

On my way out, I stop by the nurses' station and write down their number. Then I exit the hospital to find Ena waiting out front, as gruff as ever. But, as he steers the car back toward the house, he grunts in an uncharacteristic way. Then he speaks. "You no understand."

"I'm sorry?" I reply, aiming for politeness. I'm too tired to direct my anger at anyone but Vadim.

"You no understand," he insists, his jaw clenched as if speaking to me is an agonizing ordeal. And yet, he persists. "Mr. Vadim did not want to hurt you." He takes his time to phrase the words carefully. "He was scared. Scared of *her.*"

"Irina?" I ask, my nostrils flaring. How could something as momentous as Magda's mother returning out of the blue go ignored until now? It just serves as a testament to the emotional roller coaster Vadim and his life have set me on. At this point, I'm no longer aware of which way is up or down. I'm trapped, along for the ride. "Magda's mother?"

Ena nods, snorting in disgust. "She crazy. Mr. Vadim only want to protect the girl."

Protect. It's a strong word to use in the context of a mother seeking to reconnect with her child. One that I suspect Ena isn't using lightly.

"Do you know her?"

He nods, and in the rearview mirror, I see his upper lip pull back from his teeth, his eyes narrowed. "I know her. She is viper. From the old days. Mr. Vadim never saw it, but Ena did." He nods, smug. And yet there's a hint of regret shaping his features. "She cannot have girl. He did it for her."

It being ban me from seeing Magda when she needed me the most. It as in turning the tables and yet demanding my trust. It as in shattering any hope of us ever being in a healthy relationship.

"He told you?" Ena demands. "Of the old days?"

He phrases it all so carefully that I recognize the sensitivity of the subject he's referring to—Vadim's past.

"Yes," I say thickly. "He told me. He told me… That you saved his life."

Ena's lips twitch into a scowl. "No. That place? It was hell. And Vadim, he good at pretending. They all did."

"Pretending?"

He shrugs, frustrated by my lack of understanding. "He was the only one to ask for help," he adds with deliberate slowness. "The others. They pretend. He didn't."

I say nothing, disturbed by the picture he paints. A hellscape of abused victims too conditioned to their ordeals to show their pain. The one time Vadim did—allow himself to be vulnerable—he expected to die soon after.

But what does he expect from me?

Ena doesn't give me any insight on that front, falling silent —though I sense he wants to say more. Maybe I should let him? About Irina and Vadim and their murky past, clouding everyone's judgment.

Or I can seethe and wallow, and try to lick my wounds in peace.

God, I need to be angry with him. Hate him. I don't think I'll have anything left in me otherwise.

Once we reach the house, I grab some food from the kitchen and shower. Then I leave the master bedroom, slip on my coat, and head out onto the terrace. It's freezing out, but I ignore the chill and curl up on a wooden-framed lounger overlooking the water. Not for the first time, I indulge in the idea of leaving. Running away. Ignoring Vadim and his fucked-up life and going back to California.

It startles me to realize how much I miss it. My old family home in the heart of wine country. My parents, whom I've been avoiding pretty much since my divorce out of shame. A sudden longing for home rises up so swiftly I sob silently in the face of it, and I decide on the spot to stop letting guilt and manipulation run my life.

Vadim won. He got his way to an extent—but I plan on taking my power back tenfold. He wanted me to be a mother to his daughter, then fine. But that means nothing as far as *he* is concerned.

And it's best I prove that fact to us both.

Sooner rather than later.

CHAPTER SIX

I don't know how, but I must fall asleep because I startle to awareness as a shadow falls over me. It's cast by a suit jacket, I realize, one someone is in the process of draping over me. My eyes drift up, spotting a beautiful face, so haggard my heart aches in sympathy. No man should carry such scars so openly—such pain.

But then I blink, and reality comes surging back. I remember, and I nearly fall off the lounger in my rush to get away from him.

"Don't touch me!"

"I apologize." Vadim recoils, his expression shifting, his wall lifting. "I didn't mean to scare you." He sounds so damn defensive. As if I don't have the right to shrug off his jacket and lurch to my feet, marching as far from him as the terrace space will allow.

Only now—as my legs buckle beneath me—do I realize that I'm freezing. That my fingers are numb, my teeth chattering so fiercely my jaw aches.

"You can have the bed," Vadim says, his tone eerily level. Ice. "I'll sleep in my office—"

"I don't want to sleep anywhere you've been," I hiss.

He nods. "I'll have a guest bedroom made up for you, then."

"Fuck off!" I cross my arms, storming to the end of the pool. "I'm sure you're so twisted in the head that you think I'd rather freeze to death on purpose. Catch a cold like I supposedly infected Magda?"

From the corner of my eye, I see him flinch as if struck. "I'm sorry," he grates. "I didn't mean—"

"Don't talk to me about mean! I will never forgive you for this. Never." My eyes burn, and the desperate need to salvage my pride makes me reckless enough to risk adding, "So I hope you're prepared to do long-distance parenting."

My threat takes a second to register. The moment it does, his entire posture shifts, his height lengthening, eyes narrowing. "Long-distance?"

I shiver at the subtle way his voice drops a dangerous octave.

"How is Magda?" I demand, picking another battle to fight —the one regarding my leaving can wait. Preferably when my bags are already packed and a plane ticket booked. Even now, I still hear his voice, persistent. *You haven't asked yourself, will I let you go?*

I'm trapped in the memory—and now his past words feel more of a threat than anything else.

"She's fine," Vadim says, drawing my attention back to him. "The doctor believes it is a minor infection, but given her history, they decided to monitor her more carefully. She's improving, at least. If her vital signs are stable by the morning, and if she continues to take her antibiotic, she can be discharged within a few days."

"Good." I suck in a breath and face him fully, squaring my shoulders. Screw waiting. Reclaiming my independence is now or never. "Because when she's out of the hospital, I'm going back to California."

I can't explain the way his expression shifts. It's like watching a violent storm roll across the landscape. His eyes flash, posture sways, voice booming like thunder.

"So, you *still* leave—"

"Leaving you, yes," I say nastily. "But you wanted me to have joint custody of Magda? Well, you got your wish, because I'm taking her with me. One week. I'll bring her back after that, but that's how we'll do this from now on. I can't live with you anymore."

His eyes turn so damn cold I stiffen in the face of his anger. But suddenly, he deflates. Boneless, he staggers to a nearby chair and collapses onto the end of it. Both hands shake as he tears them through his hair, sending the dark curls flying in every direction. "You would take her from me?"

He sounds so damn hurt at the mere prospect. So wounded, that even in my rage I can't relish in causing him this kind of pain.

"No. I'm not taking her from you. But you wanted me to be a mother to her? This is what happens when there is no trust between two parents. They separate. I want to go home. You forced me into this. Besides, don't my parents deserve to meet the new grandchild they had no clue existed when I left? Magda deserves to spend time with me, in my home. Or was that all a lie, and all you wanted was yet another toy in your game?"

"No!" He forms a first, slamming it onto the cushioned surface beneath him. "Fine. You want to take her? Fine. You want to leave me? *Fine.* But then admit it. All you wanted from me was to take, wasn't it? My money. My lust. Now my child—"

"No!" I'm blinking rapidly, but nothing can stop the tears from falling. "I wanted to love you! I could have if you just trusted me! Gave me time, like I asked."

It terrifies me to realize how close I'd been to getting there. Falling in love with him. Only now can I admit it to myself.

All along, I'd been on the edge of abandon.

"*You* ruined us, not me." I push past him and storm into the house. I navigate the layout in a blur and find Ena waiting for me out front, already in the driver's seat of the gray car. When I slip into the backseat, Vadim appears in the doorway of the house, his expression stricken.

I watch him as the car finally pulls off, but I fight back any more tears and angrily swipe away those already fallen. By the time I reach the hospital, I've nearly regained my composure, and when I enter Magda's room, I'm my charming, carefree self once more.

And no one will ever knock her down again.

MAGDA ISN'T DISCHARGED until a full four days after her admission. Though the doctor approves her traveling via plane, he cautions against an excess of sugar or exercise, at least for a week.

The latter prescription she takes the most umbrage at.

"I feel fine," she insists as I bundle her into the backseat while Ena watches on, his arms crossed. In our wake, Vadim follows at a safe distance, packing her things into the trunk. It's the first time in days that we've managed to be together in her presence for longer than the few tense seconds it takes to trade-off.

God, I can't even look at him.

"I should be able to ride my pony," Magda insists as I slide onto the seat beside her. "Right?" She glances mournfully at Vadim as he enters the front passenger's side.

"I'm afraid not, *chérie*," he says, calmly but firm. "But once you're fully recovered, I'll take you riding every day, *ça va?*"

"Okay." That seems to mollify her, and she sits back in her seat, clutching It to her chest. Despite her ever-growing collection, that bear is the one toy she's rarely without, battered to hell and back with signs of her affection.

Does that bother me? Maybe. Even if I'm determined to cut Vadim out of my life, as long as she's a part of it, he'll always be there. A festering wound encased in synthetic fucking fur.

"What's wrong?" Magda asks, adjusting her grip on It.

Forcing a grin, I shake my head. "N-Nothing!"

When we reach the house, Vadim heads for the trunk while I take Magda inside. As we head up to her room, I finally gather up the nerve to speak.

"Honey…" I guide her to the bed and crouch down as she sits on the edge of the mattress. Taking both her hands in mine, I force her to meet my gaze. "I've decided that I need to go back home, to where I'm from. All this cold is giving me wrinkles."

She frowns and wriggles her hands away. For a split second, she can't disguise the panic that shapes her features, widening her eyes and making her lips part. "Why?" she demands, crossing her arms, strangling her bear in the process. "Why are you leaving?"

I playfully tug on one of her braids. "I miss the sun, honey. And I think we could both use a walk along the beach. That's why I want you to come with me."

"Really?" Her expression brightens before something quickly makes her temper her excitement. "Is Vadim coming?" She says his name so carefully—as though she's deliberately avoiding calling him anything else. And the wary note in her voice paired with another uneasy frown makes me realize that she *does* want him to come. Even if she won't admit it.

Damn.

"Not at first," I say, with an enthusiasm I don't feel. "He has some business, and we need a girl's trip anyway. But maybe later in the week. Besides, you'll be back before you know it, and you can ride Dasha by then. At least this way, you won't be tempted."

She frowns, the gears in her brain turning. Then she nods. "Okay! When are we going?"

"Tomorrow."

She shrugs, kicking her legs, but doesn't argue. Feeling brave enough to risk it, I head into her closet and rifle through the hangers. "What would you like to bring?"

"Hmm…" She bounds to her feet and marches past me. "My sweater," she declares, fingering a turquoise ensemble. "And this."

"Okay."

We have an armful of items assembled by the time Vadim appears in the doorway, her suitcase in hand. He sets it on the floor, his jaw rigid as he spots the clothing I promptly place on the bed. I start folding various items, aware of his gaze boring a hole through the back of my neck.

When Magda shuffles from the closet carrying a stack of nightgowns, she inclines her head in his direction. "When are you coming?" Another rare hint of unease creeps into her voice.

"I… I'm not sure yet, *chérie*," he admits. From the corner of my eye, I see him crouch down to her level, his expression pained but neutral for her sake. His eyes dart toward me, and I turn away, folding a dress into thirds. "I have a lot of business to attend to. But I want you to have this. I promise to call you every single day."

"A phone?" Magda exclaims. I turn to find her brandishing a blue model with a touch screen. Wide-eyed, she meets his gaze, and he ruffles her hair.

"I am always just one call away," he tells her, cutting his gaze to me. "Always."

"Can we go swimming in the ocean?" she asks, her eyes still on her phone. I don't know if she's directing the question at him or me.

"Maybe," Vadim says before I can form a reply. "But anything you do will be a lot easier if you have this, hmm?" He pulls yet another present from nowhere—a blue and white polka dot fanny pack. Magda snatches for it, her eyes bug-wide.

"You can keep your phone in it, as well as your insulin supplies," Vadim explains while helping her strap the bag around her waist. "It is very important that you keep them safe. Especially when you play. No one else should ever take your medicine but you. Understood?"

She nods solemnly.

"And don't worry about your pony." He breaks his stern, fatherly character long enough to ruffle her braids, his smile strained. "Mr. Ena will take care of all of the horses while you're gone."

"Okay!" She climbs onto the bed, looking nothing like the sickly girl rushed to the hospital four days ago.

"Help me finish packing," I say to her gently. "And then we can eat dinner. We have an early flight tomorrow."

"Flight? We're going on an airplane?" Judging from her tone, a plane ride seems almost as appealing as riding her pony.

"Yes," Vadim cuts in before I can reply. "Your very own private plane, all to yourself."

I stiffen, biting back a retort. So much for the two commercial flights I'd booked last night. I know without bothering to ask that the bastard took the "liberty" of canceling them. I want to be pissed. Furious, even—but in this case, logic counters my irritation. It's probably not good for Magda to be squeezed onto a plane with hundreds of other people, anyway. So, I force a grin.

"You'll love it, honey. Now, why don't you go get washed up for dinner? Vadim and I will be downstairs."

I push past him and enter the doorway before I can fully process his startled grunt. He's on my heels, his breaths tainting the air, steps unsteady.

"Finally," he rasps once we reach the first floor. "We can talk—"

"No talking," I hiss, striding into the kitchen. "Just boundaries. You don't come near my parent's home without permission. You don't come near me. If you want to see Magda, you make arrangements for somewhere else, and I will bring her to you. Understood?"

I whirl to face him and suck in a breath. *Damn.* His expression is too open, and I'd give anything for the shelter of his wall. In lieu of it, the full extent of his gaze renders me weak. He's never looked so open as his dark eyes blaze with hurt. My knees buckle, throat hitches. I can't face him like this—so I turn to the row of windows overlooking the bay instead.

"I mean it," I whisper, my gaze on the churning waters in the distance. "You don't follow me—us. You don't pop up unannounced. If I didn't already tell Magda you'd come, I'd request you stay away from California entirely—"

"So you think to ban me from your world?" he demands, his tone that stormy, grated cadence that makes me quiver. "Rather than talk to me? I am sorry that I—"

"Sorry doesn't cut it!" My voice breaks, and I hate myself. Still, it's too late now, blinking back tears, I soldier on. "You accused me of trying to kill your daughter through reckless intent. Then you barred me from her hospital room. You told me to leave. Well, this is me, *leaving*."

"If you would just listen to reason, I wouldn't be forced to such measures," he growls—yet in a tone far too low for Magda to hear from upstairs. Regardless, his heavy footsteps resonate like gunshots, advancing toward me.

I scramble to a distant corner, but he's right on my heels. Too fast. I'm defenseless as he seizes my wrist in an iron grip, his breath fire against my ear.

"All I wanted was for you to hear me out," he growls, his chest hard against my back, his hips pressing against my ass. "But it seems you only want to take from me—"

"I'm hungry."

We both whirl around to find Magda standing in the doorway, holding It crushed to her chest, her new fanny pack still slung around her waist. And it's as if we both flip some internal switch. I slap on a fake grin while Vadim swallows his fearsome scowl in favor of a neutral smile. He heads for the freezer while I turn on the oven and usher Magda to the dining room table.

"What are you in the mood for, honey?" I ask, ruffling her hair.

She taps her chin with a tiny finger and then shrugs. "Pizza?"

"Pizza it is." Vadim diligently sets about warming her a meal while I cajole her into a conversation that I pray distracts her from whatever she might have overheard.

When the food is finally ready, we eat in a terse, awkward silence broken only by Magda's oblivious, innocent chatter.

And I realize that my divorce from Jim, as painful as it was, was a cakewalk compared to this.

This is torture.

Unbearable agony.

Because in this case, I can't just walk away.

CHAPTER SEVEN

Ena drives us to the airport in the morning, and we arrive in Cali by noon. It's a surreal experience, returning to my home state via a private runway rather than a commercial queue. Unsurprisingly, Vadim arranged for a car to pick us up, but as I hasten Magda into the backseat, I realize that I never even told my parents I was coming.

In fact, I haven't spoken to them at all in roughly…

A month? Two months? It's amazing what shame will do to a person, driving them from even their most cherished relationships. I toy with the idea of calling them now, only to chicken out.

An hour's heads up is the least of my concerns when it comes to them, all things considered. As the driver takes off, I wrestle with the best way to spring my new life choices on my parents. Well, I'm alive for one. And, I'm not destitute, pregnant, or addicted to drugs—but in some ways, I'm no better off. Pseudo-married to a billionaire, the newly adoptive mother of his daughter, and I'm addicted to *him*. Vadim Gorgoshev.

Which reality might cause my parents less stress?

"You lived here?" Magda asks, drawing my attention to her. She has It balanced on her lap, still wide-eyed from the plane ride. If I weren't too busy seething, I'd wish Vadim could have seen her reactions—utter fascinated interest—to the inner workings of the takeoff and landing. I think in addition to her interest in boats, planes are a newfound discovery as far as her hobbies are concerned.

"Yes," I tell her, smoothing back her tousled braids. "I used to live here."

Until a brooding businessman and his magic cock lured me away into a world of manipulation and mind games. It all has the makings of some sordid fairytale.

Too enthralled by the landscape beyond the windows, Magda falls silent until the car pulls up before a set of wrought iron gates, adorned with the phrase *"Connors Residence"* in elegant script.

"You lived *here?*" She sounds far more skeptical now, and I bristle at the doubt.

"Yes, I lived here." But, as I join her in gaping out of the window, I can admit that the place is impressive when glimpsed from the outside.

My father's estate is a minor offshoot of his brother's—my uncle Conroy—vineyard, which supplies a world-renowned label internationally. By virtue of its location, the property is impressive, though it has nothing on the rustic charm of Vadim's place.

Still, I didn't grow up a pauper, to be sure. Our house, my mother's pride and joy, is a four-story white stone Victorian style villa draped in rose vines and oodles of prestige that come with being "old money." Or so my father used to say.

Everything looks nearly the same as when I left it. The rose bushes, and begonias lining the paved stone paths. The tennis courts beyond the house and the acres of wine country looming just beyond the front walkway. I've never appreciated it more. In fact, I think I'm more eager than Magda to escape the car and stretch my legs. First things first, I circle around to the trunk and assist the driver with her bags. The second I lift Magda's gray suitcase, a familiar booming voice calls out.

"Tiffy? Sweetheart? Is that you?"

"Daddy!" I run to the front porch as he descends the few steps to meet me. Within seconds, I'm in his arms, inhaling his trademark scent of cologne, whiskey, and cigar smoke. He's wearing his typical polo and light wash jeans, I find as I pull back, his graying blond hair windswept back from his face.

"Where the hell have you been?" he asks with mock seriousness, his blue eyes twinkling. "I think your mother was about to send in the national guard."

"Tiffany?" As if on cue, a slender woman with reddish curls appears in the entryway, her hair coiffed, her outfit one-hundred-percent authentic vintage Chanel. Her eyes widen dramatically as she spots me, her lips breaking into one of her signature charming grins.

At least until she spots Magda scuttling up the steps after me and said grin slips at the edges.

"This is Magdalene," I say, getting it out of the way now. Sighing, I glance from Daddy to my mother and shrug. "It's a long story."

"It's a good thing you came during my afternoon wine," my mother snipes from over her half-empty glass. We're in the sunroom overlooking the garden while Magda inspects the blooming flowerbeds under my father's watchful eye.

"This situation may be far harder to understand otherwise, darling." Tilting her head back, my mother promptly drains her glass and smacks her lips. Satiated, she reaches for a nearby bottle and pours herself a refill. "Now tell it again, from the beginning."

"I'm dating someone," I reiterate, choosing the safest of options to describe Vadim. "Magda is his daughter. He's… away on business. I decided to give us the week off and come spend time with you guys."

"Hmph." Fifty-four years of well honed-bullshit detecting are concentrated in the look my mother levels my way.

Desperate to escape her scrutiny, I stand and approach one of the screen windows, watching Magda dutifully follow my father from bed to bed. He entrusted her with a watering can it seems, his voice a soothing hum audible even from here. Gently, he tells her how much or how little to give each plant, sprinkling every bit of advice with charming jokes. The familiarity hits me like a kick in the gut, and I realize just how much I've missed this. Missed them.

At least, when they aren't playing detective into my personal life.

"Did you hear me, Tiffany Ann?" My mother snaps in her no-nonsense chirp deployed only in emergencies. "I insist we must meet him this… What was his name again?"

"Vadim," I rasp without turning to face her. "And I told you, he's on business—"

"Poppycock. He can't spare a few hours to come to visit you? Or meet the strangers forced to accommodate his child? What kind of man is this?"

I bite my lip. Disparaging Vadim as some kind of deadbeat, absentee father too busy for social connections could help in the long run when I later tell them that I'm co-parenting Magda and separated from him. But…

I can't lie about his character, not even as angry as I am.

"He's busy, but if I ask, I'm sure he'll make the time," I say, conceding the point to her.

She nods and savors her victory by topping up her glass of wine yet again. "Well, I'll run off and find Gwendolyn so that she can prepare a guest bedroom. I wish you would have informed us sooner. We could have prepared toys or something… Honestly, it's as if you enjoy taunting me. I know I've been asking for a grandchild, but I'd prefer a teensy bit of notice." She sniffs, takes another sip, and all is forgiven. With a wave of her hand, she clears the air. "I'll see you at dinner, dear. Though if you want to rest, I can excuse you this once." She hesitates and reaches out, fingering a lock of my hair. "You look exhausted, darling. Have you been moisturizing? Your skin is—"

"I'm just tired from the flight," I say with a forced smile. "Thanks for accommodating us on such short notice."

"Anything for you, dear." She saunters off to find Gwen, our maid who's been with the family for over a decade. In her absence, I stand and creep back to the screen partition separating this space from the outside. Magda and my father have taken a break from flowering, it seems. They sit back to back on a decorative stone stool, each tearing into a fresh orange picked from one of the trees scattered throughout the yard.

Squaring my shoulders, I step out and join them.

"Ah, Tiffy, just in time!" Daddy rises to his feet, wiping his hands on his jeans. "I need to go get some fertilizer from the shed. You can keep the little miss company, and both of you can prepare to get your hands dirty." He winks and takes off in the direction of the tennis courts where the garden shed is.

Sighing, I claim his spot on the stool and watch Magda gingerly peel her orange and take a tentative bite.

"Good, huh?" I ask as her nose wrinkles in pleasure. "I used to love mornings here. We'd always have fresh juice for breakfast."

Something in my tone must make her frown, the orange paused midway to her mouth. Setting the fruit on her lap, she crosses her legs, her eyes downcast. "Are you never coming back?" I barely recognize the small voice as belonging to the same bold girl I've gotten to know these past few days. "Back home?"

I stiffen, my lips parting as I fight to find the right words. In the end, all I can say is, "What makes you ask that?"

She shoots me a funny look, her eyebrow raised defiantly. "I'm not a baby," she declares, her tone its usual haughty cadence. "I heard you fighting."

"Ah…" I lean back, nudging her shoulder. "Eavesdropper. What did you hear?"

"I know you're angry with Vadim," she says, resuming her inspection of the orange. "I know he made you sign legal papers, even though you didn't want to."

Damn. I grit my teeth, my cheeks flaming. "So, you weren't sleeping then, either."

She makes a small noise in her throat and meets my gaze. "He made you say you'll take care of me," she says, a childish summary of what really transpired. Still, the hurt in her voice reveals that she understood as much all the same. "You didn't want to?"

"Oh, no. Honey…" I turn around and grab her shoulders, forcing her to face me. "It's not you. I will always be there for you, got it?"

She nods, swayed by the conviction in my voice—almost as much as I am.

"What's happening between Vadim and me… It's grown-up stuff, and you know better than anyone that grown-ups are stupid."

She cocks her head, seeming to mull it over. Then she nods and takes a bite from her orange. "Stupid," she agrees with her mouth full.

I chuckle and tug a lock of her hair, but her revelation as a grade-A spy leads to far more questions. The main one revolving around the fuzzy, white bear resting on the ground between her legs. I let her go and lift It by his battered body. Vadim did a careful, precise job re-stuffing him. A loving job, betraying so much care for its owner, my heart throbs in the face of it.

"You knew who Vadim was to you before you went to the Robinsons, didn't you?" I ask as my fingers trace the nearly invisible row of stitches hiding beneath It's new scarf.

Magda takes her time peeling a fresh section of orange and takes a bite. Then she nods. "Last time I was sick…" She trails off, her nose wrinkling, and I suspect those memories aren't ones she likes to relive. Much like her father, she compartmentalizes her emotions, preferring to maintain control over them in lieu of expressing too much. "When I woke up, one of the nurses asked me if I like the bear my Daddy left me—" she nods to It. "She had been on vacation, I think. She later came back and told me she'd made a mistake, and it had been donated, but I knew she was lying."

And she knew that her father had vanished after that point, leaving her alone in foster care. I can't resist stroking my hand along one of her pigtails. Surprisingly she doesn't cringe from the contact. "I'm so sorry, honey," I tell her.

I can't imagine the pain she must have felt being so young, trying to process such conflicting emotions. But if she remembers Vadim, I have to wonder if she remembers anyone else.

"Can I ask you another question?"

She nods, her expression guarded.

"Do you know anything about your mother? Your birth mother?" I'm trying my damned hardest to keep any hint of jealousy or emotion from my voice. But I must fail because she goes rigid, her tiny shoulders stiff. Frowning, I add, "Anything before you went to the—"

"No! I don't remember." She turns away, crossing her arms. The reaction is so out of character for her, I'm taken aback.

"Okay." I can take a hint—an off-limits topic. For now. "I'm sorry if I upset you. We don't have to talk about anything you don't want to."

To cement our truce, I stroke her back until her posture relaxes, and she starts to kick her legs again.

Sensing another opportunity, I decide to aim for a seemingly safer topic next. "I heard you singing a song," I add carefully, easing my fingers through her braid. This approach seems to land with less of a defensive reaction. "Where did you learn it?"

She shrugs and kicks her legs out before her one by one. "It was always in my head. After I woke up, I mean. It's nice."

And the man who spent ten straight days singing it to her still has no clue just how much it meant to her. How much *he* meant to her.

"I don't want to come in between you and your dad," I tell her, my voice thick. Only belatedly do I realize that it's the first time I referred to Vadim's identity out loud in explicit terms.

She stiffens, but says nothing, still peeling her orange.

"I don't want you to think I'm trying to pretend to be your mother, either," I add, though I'm not sure why I feel the need to say it. Maybe for my own peace of mind? "But I'll be here, no matter what you need from me. Always. You're stuck with me, kiddo—" I nudge her with my elbow. "Whether you like it or not."

She carefully works away the last bit of her orange peel. Then she takes the sizeable remainder of fruit and shoves it into her mouth. Her cheeks bulge, barely able to contain it, and I make a show of fussing over her, swiping at her face with the end of my shirt.

"Messy girl!"

We break into laughter, so loud and raucous that I don't notice my father returning until he sets a crate of ripe fertilizer right at our feet. I cringe, but Magda lurches upright, her gaze inquisitive.

"Is that animal feces?" she asks, with awe coloring her voice rather than the disgust I think would be standard for a girl of her age. "Like cow poop?"

"Genuine, goddamn cow shit," Daddy says with a chuckle. "Don't go repeating that. This stuff we put on the flowers though, not in the vegetable garden. But it makes the flowers bloom really nice, especially those damn crotchety lilies."

Magda listens to him wide-eyed, absorbing every detail. When she looks up and spots my expression, she giggles. "It's like plant food," she explains, revealing a hint of her intellect. "It contains nutrients and microbes that help them grow."

"Right you are, Missy," Daddy says. "Why don't you come with me and we'll sprinkle this around. Let's let Tiffy go get some rest—" he shoots me an apologetic glance. "You look wrecked, sweetheart."

"Thanks, Daddy…"

Considering that both parents have mentioned my appearance in a negative way, I decide to take the hint and enter the house, heading up for my old room. In so many ways, it's just as I left it. Juvenile—decorated in shades of bright pink—childish, and superficial. The girl who once slept beneath this frothy, bubblegum-colored canopy spent her final nights here dreaming of what life would be like as Mrs. James Walker. Boy, what a letdown that turned out to be.

Nearly ten years later and this Tiffy has learned her lesson. Dreaming is for fools. But even as I strip my clothing, change into a nightgown, and crawl beneath my old hot pink comforter, a man sneaks into my head regardless.

His presence is more consuming than Jim could ever hope to be.

He's insistent, promising me the world…

But all I seem capable of doing is spitting onto his hand.

CHAPTER EIGHT

I had forgotten how hard it can be to sleep alone. To forgo the teasing warmth of another figure, their body close to yours, their touch pervasive—as if they can't bear to let you go.

I wake up somehow more exhausted than I was when I laid down in the first place. My nap, it seems, has stretched way beyond dinner, I realize as I scramble to my feet and view the world beyond my windows. Not only did I sleep through the evening meal, but I also tossed and turned right through the night, and it now looks to be mid-morning.

In a daze, I stagger into my old bathroom and try to wake up with a hot shower. Afterward, I brush my teeth, blow out my hair, and skip one of my Chanel ensembles in favor of an old T-shirt and jeans fished from my closet.

By the time I scramble downstairs, Gwen is in the kitchen preparing what looks like lunch.

"Hello, Ms. Tiffany," she calls as I scramble past, following the faint sounds of girlish chatter into the sunroom.

Sure enough, Mother and Daddy are in the garden, fussing about their plants while a tiny figure races between them, carrying out various tasks with an eagerness that betrays yet another newfound interest to add to Vadim's list. A gardener in the making, Magda beams with unabashed joy as she chases my father with a water pail before fetching a pair of pruning shears for my mother.

And she isn't the only one uncharacteristically animated. My mother hasn't graced the garden with her presence in about fifteen years since one of the influential socialites in her country club declared gardening passé. Though I doubt the flowers are what drew her out into the fresh air and unfashionable sunlight.

Magda is wearing an outfit I know for a fact I didn't buy for her—an adorable, frilly white dress with frothy sleeves that makes her look more like a little princess than ever—even with her polka dot fanny pack strapped to her waist. Someone elaborately braided her hair as well, adorning it with flowers and an excess of yellow ribbon. In fact, she resembles a seven-year-old Tiffy—whose tortured visage could be found in one of many portraits hanging throughout the house—whose mother enjoyed dressing her up like a doll. Magda, however, doesn't seem to mind the fuss.

Her cheeks glow a healthy pink, her eyes shining as Daddy speaks to her, no doubt explaining gardening techniques and the process behind their actions. And while my mother appears to be pruning one of the rose bushes, I realize that more often than not, those freshly trimmed roses seem to wind up in Magda's hair.

When I finally leave the house and join them, my mother jumps so badly she nearly drops her shears like a criminal caught in the act.

"Tiffy," she says shrilly. "We thought you were still sleeping. We went ahead and had breakfast already, but I had Gwen save you a plate."

"We had pancakes!" Magda pitches in from across the lawn, where my father is instructing her on how to best tell if the oranges on the tree are ripe enough to pick.

"Pancakes?" Horror constricts my voice. "Magda has diabetes—"

"We know," Daddy says. "Little Missy was very informative and gave us a list of her dietary restrictions, and we had Gwen whip up the best goddamn healthy nut pancakes a girl could ask for."

"Language, Harold," my mother sniffs.

"I'm sorry. I didn't think I'd sleep that long…" I falter, unsure of why I even feel the sense of guilt that I do. "It looks like you guys made out okay without me."

"Yes," Daddy says in that reassuring way only he can. "We got little Missy to bed, and even made sure she got her phone call."

I raise an eyebrow. "Phone call?"

"With her father, darling," Mother interjects, her tone suspicious.

"Oh, right…"

"Don't tire yourself out too much," she adds. "I was planning on showing Magdalene all of your old pageant dresses. Oh, I'm sure she'll look just darling in that old blue one with the silk, and that imported bit of lace. You remember the one."

"I don't think her father will be putting her in any pageants," I point out.

But Mother rolls her eyes. "She can use them for dress-up, darling. I've already offered her the pick of the lot. And she promised to take very good care of them, haven't you, sweetheart?"

"Yes, Ma'am." Magda nods, the picture of pure charm. I realize in horror that she's every bit as much of a social chameleon as Vadim. It's an awe-inspiring and yet terrifying skill to witness in action. Especially considering that my mother once threatened to stab a mover who made the mistake of assuming a box of my old pageant dresses was meant for Goodwill. She clung to those damn things with such sentiment I was sure she'd insist on them all following her into the grave.

"If you're planning on sticking around, Tiffy, then why don't you give us a hand?" Daddy asks. "Magdalene here wants to try whipping up her own batch of fresh OJ. You used to be a damn good little picker. Let's see if you still got it in you."

I approach them warily and yet find myself biting back a smile. The cynical part of me warns that the fact that she isn't mine by blood means I shouldn't take such pride in watching her eyes light up with joy as she finds a ripe fruit on her first try. I shouldn't relish how seamlessly she's blending into my family, or that she seems to love my childhood home already.

I shouldn't be skipping ahead, envisioning Christmases or other holidays spent here with her. And I definitely shouldn't be picturing another figure alongside her, imagining how he'd look with his lips wet with fresh orange juice, his dark curls filled with roses.

But I do.

And I am.

And nothing I tell myself seems capable of stopping it.

BY THE TIME NIGHT FALLS, Magda is the one who tires out first. She barely manages to keep her eyes open during dinner. I feel the need to take her hand once her plate is cleared away just to make sure I can get her upstairs without her falling asleep along the way.

As we leave the dining room, my mother's voice chases me, one of her stern reminders. "Don't forget, Tiffy, darling! We need to meet this businessman of yours. Preferably before the end of the week. He wouldn't want to make a bad impression, now would he?"

I do my best to ignore her as I lead Magda into the guest bedroom and help her dress in a fresh nightgown and braid her hair. She's seemingly on the verge of drifting off when suddenly she bolts upright and scrambles for something on her nightstand—her fanny pack, from which she withdraws her blue cell phone. As I watch in confusion, she dials a number and holds the receiver to her ear.

The moment I assume someone picks up on the other end, her body relaxes, and she slumps against the pillows, It clutched in her free hand.

"Yes, I had fun," she says tiredly, her words slurring. But I can sense the effort she makes to keep talking, humoring the figure speaking to her in a gentle, insistent hum. But eventually, her replies come further apart until I feel the urge to gingerly pry the phone from her grasp before she nods off altogether.

"Goodnight, *ma chérie*," a gruff voice urges from the other end, so gentle and soothing I nearly break in the face of it.

"Wait," I croak before he can hang up.

I hear his breath catch, and the seconds tick by as I gather up the nerve to keep speaking. "I... My parents want to meet you," I blurt in a rush. "I think it's best, even if... They should meet you. For Magda's sake. Later we can come up with a lie to—" I break off, my eyes on a drowsy, barely coherent Magda. After what she overheard the last time, I've learned my lesson about speaking freely around her. "We can devise an *explanation* for how things really are," I say, changing tact. "But not now. They deserve to at least get to know you first."

Silence, so thick I can feel it constricting my throat falls. Just when I'm on the verge of suffocating, his voice returns, far more cautious than the warm, honeyed tone he used with Magda.

"I can be on the plane within the hour."

"Okay?" My tongue stiffens, making the word an awkward question.

"Goodnight," Vadim says.

"Bye." I hang up and drop the phone back on the nightstand as if burned. After kissing Magda on the cheek and ensuring her toys are within her reach, I creep from her room and enter mine. My mother—as knowing as she is—ensured that Magda had the suite just one door down.

THIS TIME, I don't sleep deeply enough to miss the telltale patter of her getting up hours later. Yawning, I wash up and get dressed and manage to catch her just as she pads out of her room, fully clothed, fanny pack in place, her curls tousled.

"I'm supposed to help with the weeding today," she tells me, her expression so serious that I can't resist ruffling her messy hair.

"What about some braids first, sleepyhead?" She follows me into my old room, and I set her up at my vanity, watching her scan our surroundings with barely concealed interest.

"This was your room?" she asks, sounding skeptical once more.

I nod, but even I can admit that the décor and color scheme is a little outdated. "Sit still."

I smooth a brush through her hair, and I'm finishing the second plait when I realize a fact that makes me stiffen. "Vadim is coming today," I confess, surprised by how her features light up for a split second before she reigns in any excitement behind one of her neutral masks. "But my parents don't really know the full…details."

She nods, and I'm sure that a child as perceptive as she is picked up on way more nuances about those "details" than anyone else has.

"Lying is wrong," I say to preface my next request. "But, probing questions are annoying, and my mother is the queen of them."

"So, we have to pretend?" Magda inquires, an eyebrow raised. *Damn.* She's copied her father's inflection—when he's in the middle of devising a devious twist or laying the foundation of some mind game or another. As if she's testing me, waiting to see if I'll say the right thing.

Or fail entirely.

"Not pretend," I say softly.

To stall for time, I rifle through the drawers of my vanity, finding an old stash of hair ribbon. I select two light blue strands and weave them through the ends of her braids, tying them into bows.

"Let's think of it more as…evading. Whatever we're comfortable defending, we defend. And what we're not, we compromise on. And not by lying," I add, turning her chair so that she faces me. "But just by cleverly avoiding the truth. For now."

My convoluted way of explaining that while Vadim and I may pretend to be a couple now, the reality couldn't be further from the truth.

She nods, appearing to mull it over. Then she squares her shoulders and hops from the chair.

"Can I go to the garden now? I wanted to help out early."

"Sure." I tug one of her braids and watch her skip off. Then I claim her vacated seat and try to give myself my own "lying is for the benefit of society" pep talk. I don't think I've made much progress by the time a commotion rising from downstairs warns of the impending approach of yet another visitor.

Much to my mother's chagrin.

"Tiffy," she scolds as I descend the stairs and—sure enough —discover an unfamiliar black car cruising up the driveway.

"Is it too much to ask for a bit of forewarning as to when we can expect your guests?"

I murmur some form of an apology as I slip through the front door, beating the pack just in time to head off the figure climbing from the vehicle's driver's seat. Vadim, it seems, took the tactical approach of driving himself rather than hiring a driver to do so. His outfit also strikes me as deliberately calculated—a casual mixture of a less formal dark brown suit with a looser white dress shirt underneath and no tie.

The result is a man who looks no less approachable than any other suitor hoping to make a good first impression, be them a billionaire or not.

God. It's unfair. I can sense every little extent he's gone through to ensure as much. He probably forced himself to eat something during the plane ride because he isn't shaking, his features refreshed after days of chronic lack of sleep. His hair has been neatly arranged, and I can imagine him having to physically stop himself from raking his fingers through it.

He eyes me warily as I circle the car and approach him, my arms crossed.

"You don't plan on staying long?" I ask when he doesn't move to grab a suitcase from the trunk. His nostrils twitch —he didn't miss the audible relief in my voice.

"I booked a hotel," he says. "I was able to schedule some business meetings while I'm here."

Though he avoids mentioning a timeframe as to when he'll depart. I sense myself frown, but I decide to leave that battle for another day.

"Tiffy?" I hear my mother calling from the front steps. "Are you going to introduce your gentleman caller or have him stand out in the hot sun all day?"

Here goes nothing… I inhale raggedly. Then I extend my hand for Vadim's. Any shock he might feel at the gesture is damn near instantly suppressed, replaced by one of his light, quick smiles. He grabs for me in return, and his heat runs through me like a lance, enhancing the aches and pains I'd been able to ignore until this moment.

The soreness of tossing and turning at night—too many nights—while in bed alone. The throbbing awareness of how long it's been since I've had him inside me—such a strange thing to notice, all things considered. A reprieve from passionless sex was one of the many benefits of my separation from Jim, but this…

Being taunted with Vadim's nearness is a torture I wouldn't wish upon anyone.

Though maybe I'm alone in that regard. He loosens his grip on my hand, releasing me and turns his attention to the backseat of the car. I'm surprised to find that—in lieu of a suitcase—he did bring a few items with him. A bouquet of gorgeous roses that must have cost a fortune, as well as three neatly wrapped boxes.

I'm flashed back to when I accompanied him to his brother's home, insisting upon bringing presents. I think I'd explained it away as social etiquette—but I have a feeling he took those words to heart, studying such a concept as thoroughly as his foray into kink.

"Help me with these?" he asks, his tone soft—but he isn't speaking to me. A small figure bounds to his side, her smile beaming.

"Okay!" she chirps, playing the role of a precocious innocent so thoroughly I almost forget that I'd asked her to. She holds her arms out while Vadim piles each present on top of the other. Then she leads the way into the house as my parents watch on.

I think it should bother me a little, the approval I find in my mother's eyes as she takes in Vadim's slender frame and handsome visage. My father, on the other hand, seems more interested in studying the quality of his tailored suit and rented car.

"Mother, Daddy, this is Vadim," I say once we're all crowded into the foyer.

"Welcome!" My mother exclaims, drifting forward to plant a French-style kiss on each of his cheeks. "I apologize for the lack of proper fanfare. If I would have known you were coming so soon—" She breaks character just long enough to shoot me a glare, "I would have prepared better. Regardless, I'll have Gwen whip up a marvelous lunch. Do you plan on staying long?"

"As long as I'm welcome to," Vadim says, his accent adding an extra flair to his usual charm. "Though, I do have business that may call me away later, unfortunately."

Smart man, laying the foundation for an easy escape route should the need arise.

"Welcome, Vadim," Daddy says, eyeing him skeptically. As Magda hovers near his side, I finally make out the telltale signs of dirt stains on the cuffs of their jeans, their hands equally filthy.

"Looks like someone's been having fun," Vadim remarks, inspecting his daughter from head to toe.

"I've been helping," she says in response to his questioning look. Her eyes brim with excitement, and I don't think I've ever seen her so animated. "We're waging war against those goddamn caterpillars—"

"And, she's been a good little gardening assistant," my father says quickly. He places his hand on her shoulder and shoots her a conspiratorial wink.

Meanwhile, my mother's cheeks flush blood-red, and I half-expect her to faint. "Please, come and sit—Tiffy, show him into the sunroom, will you? I'll have Gwen prepare some tea. I'm sure you're exhausted."

"That would be lovely, thank you," Vadim says, his smile so breathtaking that even my mother's nerves seem put at ease. For now, at least. "And please, accept these small tokens of my appreciation for taking such good care of Magdalene."

He offers my mother the roses, and she simpers. Internally, I know that, like me, she's tallied up the potential cost of such a gesture and is more than pleased with her estimate. Material value means little to her, but in terms of hospitality, every good hostess appreciates being rewarded for her efforts.

And she shoots me yet another glare before flouncing off, murmuring something about needing Grandmamma's old crystal vase.

Two of the presents, Vadim has divided between my parents, saving the final one for Magdalene.

"I thought I heard you mention something the other day about working in the garden," he says teasingly as she rips open her package to discover a blue apron, complete with her own miniature gardening tools. She flashes one of those rare grins and throws her arms around his waist in the semblance of something that could be called a hug before she takes off, dragging my father with her.

Alone with Vadim, the awkward tension sets in, too potent for even my mother's best hosting abilities to conquer.

"I... I'll show you to the sunroom," I tell him before guiding him through the house and out into the sun-dappled space. Beyond the screen walls, we can make out Magda standing patiently by as my father crouches on a gardening pad, cursing up a storm.

Rather than sit, Vadim strips his suit jacket and escapes into the fresh air to join them, much to Magda's apparent delight.

I hang back, observing from a safe distance as he crouches down, no doubt ruining his priceless suit, and watches intently as she shows him how to use her new tools, her laughter infectious, smile contagious.

Soon my own lips are twitching despite myself, my heart throbbing as I watch them interact, easily including my father into their beautiful dynamic. Almost like…

Almost like a real family. The thought unfurls, too dangerous to indulge in. But I'm weak in this fight, and the fantasies persist.

CHAPTER NINE

I think my only saving grace when it comes to the potential of my mother murdering me in a fit of rage and burying me out in the garden is that Vadim doesn't plan on spending the night—thus sparing her the trouble of having to scramble to prepare another guest bedroom. Instead, she whips poor Gwen into a frenzy in her attempt to produce a meal "worthy" of our guests.

The result is a grand affair of roasted chicken, vegetables, and a dessert catered specifically to both Magda and Vadim's dietary needs. Somehow, Mother manages to arrange all of this while seeming as though meticulously planned meals and priceless, antique cutlery are trivial things someone might pull out as an everyday occurrence. In other words, I'm rendered inadequate, watching a master at work.

She somehow manages to get Vadim to let his guard down in ways that I suspect even he isn't comfortable with—not intentionally. There's a softness to his posture I'm not used to glimpsing in the presence of others. He's still without his suit jacket, having had to change into a spare pair of my father's slacks after his became coated in muck from the garden.

"Do tell us how you met Tiffany," my mother instructs as she savors her third glass of wine for the evening. Ruthlessly, she inspects him in between swallows, hunting for any minor flaw to seize upon. "Our dear girl has her charms, but I'm curious as to what might attract someone of your... caliber." It's a testament to her skill of social navigation that she somehow manages to make the insult both sting and sound endearing all at once. I'm still not forgiven for the lack of notice, it seems.

"What might attract me?" Vadim laughs, and his eyes take on a soft, faraway gleam I'm sure is one-hundred percent intentional. It has to be. "Your daughter is..."

His gaze finds me, hesitant, and clouded with uncertainty. I can imagine him agonizing over the right words to say. How to say them. In the end, he clearly states, "When I met her, I noticed her instantly—the moment she entered the room, every other man did as well." That hard note betrays a jealousy only I know the true extent of. An envy that led him to foil any attempt I made to forge a connection with another man. "She nearly slipped past me without a second glance," he admits. "But, I was determined to earn her attention."

His tone... His expression.

My throat goes dry, and I grapple for my own wine glass, inhaling the liquid within.

"That's our Tiffy," Daddy pitches in with a bellowing laugh. "She can be a whirlwind. Let's just hope you haven't gotten a taste of her temper yet. She's an ace sulker—can hold a grudge for days. But just when you think she'll hate you forever, she bakes you the most terrible cake you ever did taste as a peace offering. And you know what they say about redheads…"

He winks.

My mother fans herself.

Magda grins mischievously. It doesn't escape my notice that she managed to wedge herself in between my father and Vadim. Both of them seem intent on "accidentally" slipping extra slices of sugar-free cake onto her plate. I don't think there's another little girl alive in danger of being so thoroughly spoiled.

"What *do* they say about redheads, Harold?" My mother lobbies him with a barely concealed bit of bait.

Bait that he wisely sidesteps with a contrite nod of his head. "That they are beautiful, intelligent creatures worthy of utter worship and devotion, sweetheart," he says.

Satisfied, she takes a congratulatory sip of wine.

"How long did you say you were planning on staying, Vadim?" she asks a second time. "We would love to have you. Tomorrow, Magdalene is going to model some of Tiffy's old pageant dresses. As long as I have your permission, she can have as many of them as she'd like.

They were all handmade by some of the best designers of the time. I'm sure she'll look just darling in them."

"I agree," Vadim says earnestly. His eyes, however, cut toward me, cautiously guarded. If he's looking for a clue as to how to reply, I look down at my hands rather than convey an answer either way. Left to scramble for his own response, he says, "But I'm afraid my business may call me away."

"What is it you do exactly?" Daddy asks, raising an eyebrow. "I'm in investments, myself."

"I work in pharmaceuticals," Vadim explains. "Mainly German-based companies. Have you heard of Eingel Industries?"

My father's eyes widen—he's impressed. "Heard of it? I have stock in it!" He laughs heartily, smacking his hand on the table. "Damn, it's been performing like a beauty these past few quarters. Son of a bitch—"

"Harold!" My mother sniffs in disgust.

"It's one of many entities under my control," Vadim confesses. "Lately, I will admit that I've been trying to take a lighter approach to the business aspect, however, so that I can spend as much time as possible with Magdalene."

Both of my parents nod in approval, and I sense that we're nearing a dangerous line that I doubt we ever crossed with Jim. They like him. They *really* like him.

God, they like him too much.

And when his voice takes on that deep, disarming rasp, I know I'm royally screwed.

"I want to thank you for your hospitality," he says. While his voice resonates throughout the room, loud enough for everyone to hear, I feel like it's directed solely toward me, running down my spine in an ominous thrill of vibration. "For my daughter, especially. I can't tell you what your kindness means to us both."

"Oh, it's nothing, darling." My mother dabs at her lips with a napkin, her cheeks pink, and my father coughs in that way he does when things become too emotional for his comfort.

"It's no problem," he declares, rising from his chair. "How about us three interlopers go sip lemonade and watch the stars while Tiffy and Vadim get reacquainted, huh?"

"Okay!" Magda lurches to her feet, following at his heels while my mother reluctantly rises as well.

"Night darling," she murmurs to me, planting a kiss on my cheek. In a voice too low for Vadim to hear, she whispers, "Very good catch, darling."

And I want to melt into a puddle of shame as they finally leave the dining room.

"I don't have to stay," Vadim says, rising to his feet. "I'll be in town at least until it's time for Magda to come home. Then I'll—"

"Wait." I suck in a breath and let it out slowly while parsing my options. Finally, I make up my mind and face him. Self-preservation trumps pride, and I eye his collar rather than meet his gaze. I'm not brave enough. "We need to talk."

Preferably—given how our last few conversations have gone—somewhere far out of my parents' earshot. And Magda's for that matter.

Vadim frowns and, for the first time, a teeny hint of unease gnaws through my wall of anger. Could his hesitation be because he'd already picked up some floozy who—as I was in our first days of meeting—is now lounging around his suite, waiting for her next delivery of designer clothing? I let myself indulge in the possibility as though it were real.

And jealousy claws through my chest so violently I have to smother a gasp. Could I even blame him if he did have another woman in the wings? *No,* I realize as I scan his face and catch the glimpses of exhaustion, he's so cleverly disguised until now. I couldn't, even if I wanted to.

And maybe he *has,* merely to drive that stake through my chest—punish me. "If you've already made plans—"

"No," he says quickly, though his frown only deepens. "No… It's that my hotel suite this time isn't what you're used to."

I raise an eyebrow, my dread building, jealousy seething. "Oh?"

He seems to deflate and rakes his fingers through his hair, disrupting yet another aspect of his polished façade. "It's just that, I wasn't planning on sharing it with anyone."

"I'm not staying," I add, even as my curiosity is piqued tenfold. "We just need to discuss some logistics."

"Alright." He stands, and we take a detour into the sunroom to reclaim his jacket. In the distance, Magda is barely visible, sitting on my father's lap, pointing up at the stars in the sky as both he and my mother babble on.

It's a heartwarming sight even I can't deny.

Vadim, however? His expression melts, conveying such tenderness…

I have to turn away and nearly run out to his car just to escape it. His hotel, I quickly realize, is on the outskirts of my old hometown, about ten minutes from my family's home—the narrowest adherence to my previous guidelines regarding his distance from me. And he wasn't lying about his room.

I'm taken aback as I follow him into the narrow, efficient setup. Gone is the sprawling, luxurious penthouse booked by a bachelor accustomed to picking up escorts at random when the urge struck. This small, yet comfortable, suite is the preference for a man solely intent on business over pleasure. Even the bed is a modest full instead of a massive king.

Instead, the star attraction is a sleek modern style office in the corner, complete with a mini, circular conference table.

I take up one end while Vadim collapses onto a chair across from me. His stricken expression makes something inside me flinch, and I hesitate, unsure of what to say. He looks so damn tired. Exhausted. Like a man waiting for his execution to finally commence. He's had enough of this torture.

But so have I.

"Tell me something that will make me forgive you," I demand, letting every ounce of raw anger and pain seep into my voice. "Though believe me when I say that I don't ever think I can."

The pure intensity of my emotions seems to take him back. His posture sprawls out without an ounce of poise to guide it, his fingers raking through his hair—in this moment, comfort takes precedence over putting on a show. He's fully unguarded, his wall in shambles, and my heart sinks. I'm not sure if I'm well equipped enough to face him like this.

Gritting my teeth, I'm willing to try, though. "You hurt me," I add before he can say a word in his own defense. "You really did. How dare you accuse me of wanting to harm Magda?" I'm blinking furiously, desperate to keep from crying. "How dare you?"

"I'm not sorry for what I did," he admits, his tone firm. Stubborn, even. The blatant honesty tempers the pain ripping through my chest—at least he's not lying or trying to manipulate. It's the truth. "I will always put Magdalene first. Always. But... It wasn't until I saw you upset that I realized I should have gone about it differently. I know you would never purposefully hurt her." It seems to kill him to admit as much—the calculating, manipulative Vadim fucked up. He went too far to reach his aims. "You were supposed to demand money," he continues, his voice lacking any inflection. He could seem robotic if it weren't for the vast wealth of emotion contorting his expression. His hair is a mess, his eyes fixated on something beyond me. "Money or something else of value to you—"

"You think I'm that much of a gold-digging bitch?" I lurch to my feet and spin around, definitely on the verge of tears now.

"But I've seen how you are with her," he mutters as if oblivious to my reaction. He's speaking without his filter this time—saying plainly whatever thoughts are in his head. A man with nothing left to lose and the world to gain. "You could extort me, but I know you wouldn't do the same to her. I could live with that. I had to live with that. You weren't supposed to…"

"What?" I whirl to face him, my arms crossed, posture livid.

"Want *me*," he confesses, his eyes meeting mine without an ounce of anger or defensiveness. "My money, material things, yes. I told myself I could lose your interest, if it meant keeping you for Magdalene. It would damn near kill me," he adds, his hand at his throat, stroking the remnants of his scar. "But I could endure it. I could forfeit your body. This game. But never, would I gamble something more."

"I don't know what kind of women you usually consort with," I croak through clenched teeth, "but most don't shack up with a man they barely know and fall in love with his daughter for money. Most women don't forgive mind game, after mind game for money! Most women don't beg for more from a man only to get his fucking money!"

"But most people are more than content to use *me*," he counters, snarling. Lunging.

We're toe to toe in an instant, and I'm woefully unprepared for the vitriol in his voice. His gaze. All of it directed at me. Beyond me. At the whole damn world, he's raging.

"My mother? A whore who sold me into slavery for the price of a year's worth of rent," he snarls. "My father was a monster who inducted me into his family of vipers, pitting me against his true heir every fucking waking moment. My whole life has been spent at the whims of others. Trying to assume what it is they want. How to achieve it. How to prostrate myself for their fucking benefit. No one has ever offered me their love—"

"You're wrong," I say, standing fearlessly in the midst of his tirade. Even as his eyes take on that cold, mistrustful gleam, his teeth bared. I don't look away. "Everyone loves you! Ena. Milton. Your old partner, Hiram. Even Maxim, I think, loves you in his own way."

Why else would his henchman drive me to the hospital at five in the morning? Lucius may be kind, but I doubt his concern would extend beyond the boundaries of what his employer would allow.

The fact that he greeted me at all was testament enough—Maxim permitted him to.

"You're just too blind to see it. Your instinct is to always assume the worst. Always lash out when you feel stretched too thin."

"My instinct?" he echoes in a dangerous, vicious hum. His hand raises to my throat, his thumb tracing a quivering artery. I shiver, a heartbeat away from backing down...

But I stay, enduring the ominous caress, even as he curls his fingers around my neck entirely.

"My instinct is telling me that you're lying," he tells me softly. "You only aim to get inside my head. Because, your love? I want it," he admits in a growl so resonating I sway. "But I am not stupid enough to think I could ever have it. Ever have you. Not without a price."

"Why?" I counter, forcing myself to meet his gaze. The more I challenge him, the more unsteady his dark irises become, glazed over and unfocused. Crazed. "Why can't I *just* love you? Why can't you *just* trust me? Like when the mother of your child comes calling, and all I want is to know how to help you—"

"Because..." He encircles my throat in his fist, applying pressure...pressure. More. As I gasp, his eyes flash, nostrils flaring. Like my fear is a welcome addition to this tension—something he's used to navigating. Manipulating. "Because who could love me?" He says it all so fervently... I think he means it.

Every last word.

As if in emphasis, he tightens his grip slowly, letting me feel the flesh of my throat conform around his fingers. Collapse. My breaths feather at first, followed by that terrifying constriction of my windpipe. The building terror that he's cutting off my air. Choking me—but in the gentlest, lingering of ways.

Because I'm not resisting him. A fact he only realizes just as my breathing wheezes, a hair's breadth from being cut off completely.

"*Merde!*" He lets me go, staggering away from me, horrified. Panting, he stares down at his hands, his voice a broken rasp, "I'm sorry—"

"Don't be," I say, my voice surprisingly strong even as my throat aches slightly with the remnants of his touch. "At least you aren't hiding how you really feel for fucking once. Is that what you want to do to me? Hurt me?"

"No!" His eyes flash at the mere idea of it. "Never—"

"But you have," I cut over him. "You are. Every fucking time you push me away. Play with my mind. How can I trust you if you won't even trust me?"

"I've let you into my life," he points out, regaining his stiff, imposing posture. At his sides, his fingers curl and uncurl again—a mere hint as to the extent of his frustration. "I've let you around my daughter. You don't call that trust?"

"I don't know anymore," I admit, my voice breaking. "But I trusted *you*. That is what love is. Sometimes, it means being a petty bitch and second-guessing everything, but in the end, I trusted you."

Despite how he fucks with my head. Plays with my soul. Makes me hate him. Want him. Crave him.

"So now what?" he wonders with a cold, harsh laugh. "You leave after tempting me with the one thing I will never have?"

"No!" I scoff in exasperation. I think I even stomp my foot, I'm so frustrated. "You always had it!" I practically shout at him. "Always! You were just too fucking paranoid to see it."

And I refused to. Why? Who falls in love with a stranger after barely a few weeks?

But how many strangers are like Vadim?

As tormented as him?

As beautiful as him?

As utterly frustrating as him?

"But what was I to you, huh?" I demand nastily. "Collateral? A tramp you could just throw away—"

"Never!" He's before me in an instant, his hands cupping my skull, drawing me into him. Near my ear, he croaks, his voice hoarse, "You were what happiness always was to me. A futile dream always out of reach. At least before…"

"Before what?" I'm trying so damn hard to maintain my composure. My anger. My hurt. But it's splintering, breaking apart with every second his breath bastes my throat. With his fingers caressing my skin. His gaze so deep and unending I'm drowning in it.

"Before you taunted me with it." His eyes slide shut as his mouth grazes my lower jaw brazenly, his lips parted, tasting me. Inhaling me. "That's what you've done, isn't it? Tease me. Dangle a world I never imagined for myself, but you never reveal the fucking price—"

"Because there isn't one!" My voice lacks any real anger. I'm lost in the urgency of his touch, my hips arching into him before I can help it. "You can't buy love."

"Only take it," he says with a fervor that leaves me reeling. Hungry, he grips me tighter, drawing me further against him. "Claim it—"

"No. You *earn* it," I snap, devastated by the fact that he truly seems to mean those words. A man so lost he sees affection as something worth stealing, never his to take without a struggle. "It is given freely. Like when you let a man put his hands around your throat because you know he won't hurt you."

He blinks, his eyes fluttering open, dark with confusion. As I watch, they glaze over, hardened with resolve.

"I *will* earn you," he tells me. But when he presses his mouth to mine, I doubt a verbal confession is on his mind.

Because conversation never gets us very far in the long run. Only one form of communication seems to supersede all others when it comes to the two of us.

And he initiates this discussion with his touch sliding down to my ass, snatching me into him. Gasping, I run my hands down his chest, letting my nails rake at the fabric of his shirt, gouging the flesh underneath. He sucks in a startled breath, his gaze radiating confusion—but the confusion quickly morphs into something else when I keep traveling lower, finding the fastenings of his pants.

With a deftness I didn't even know I was capable of, I unhook the front clasp and yank down the zipper. Waiting beyond the barrier is his cock, stiffening against me, pulsating so strongly I swear I can count his heartbeat like this.

His very being is in the palm of my hand.

And groaning, he submits to me, letting me cradle him… and then tighten my grip so firmly he lurches, a growl revving in his throat. His hands grip me in retaliation, snatching me to him, grinding me over the contours of his body.

And we both cry out.

Days without him and my body reacts as though I've committed a crime. The ultimate act of self-harm—denying myself of this. Him.

Sensation returns like a gut punch, drowning me in a heat so potent it's like I'm burning alive.

But in this instance, I'm not suffering alone.

He grunts at the feel of me as if punched with every grasping handful. Ruthless, his lips capture mine, his hands roving, nails scraping. Groping. Claiming. I'm putty in his hands, a slave to his whims as he drags me toward the bed. Only to change tact at the last minute and shove me against the window instead.

He spins me to face the glass as his body cages me in from behind. I feel his hands in my hair, working their way down to my shoulders. My throat. He encircles it, gripping it again, tightening those slender fingers. Tighter. Tighter. At the same time, I feel him grinding himself shamelessly against my lower back, teasing his erection to the point of straining against the confines of his boxers.

It has to be uncomfortable, I realize somewhere at the back of my mind. Painful. But it's like he waits until the second I'm writhing, my thighs grinding together just to find relief.

The second I do, he cradles my throat, guiding my head back until our gazes connect from this angle—me straining up, him staring down, his eyes unfocused, glazed with lust.

A silent understanding passes between us. One that makes me buck into his grip and brace my hands over the window glass. Without hesitation, he plunges his hand beneath the skirt of my dress, finding my thong, wrenching it down my legs.

I writhe shamelessly, arching into his touch. Gasping out when his grip on my throat cinches—tighter than before. My eyes water, my lungs straining, lips parting.

But at the same time, he brushes his thumb over my clit, pairing the physical discomfort with pleasure and…

Holy, gosh darn *kink*.

My brain melts, every nerve going haywire. There is something inherently sinful when he stops holding back. Reacts without calculation or forethought. Adjusting his grip on me with one hand, he wrenches me onto him, plunging inside me on the first thrust.

It's fire.

The force and pressure apply friction to my piercing from the inside, and I yelp at the sensation, feeling an orgasm build damn near instantaneously.

Rather than feed the flames, he rocks his hips, withdrawing just as swiftly. His grip on my throat returns, applying more pressure as his lips feather kisses down my collar. The conflicting actions make my body go limp, my eyes rolling as he slams back in.

In.

Again.

Again.

I let him pin me against the window glass, murmuring praises. Gasps. *Nothing* as he controls my intake of air, teasing me with just enough space to gasp before his fingers clench. Body rocks. Cock thrums against my inner walls.

Rippling convulsions assault me, contorting my body from the inside out.

Never in my life have I come so violently before. I almost fear the incredible rise because I know the fall could be deadly. Only his grip serves as my sole safety net as the pleasure ebbs and flows in shattering waves.

"You *do* want something from me," he grates into my ear as I mewl wordlessly, on the brink of another earth-shattering release. "My love, is that it? I can't give it," he confesses, bucking so hard I'm sandwiched between him and the window glass, my body bared for anyone passing by who happens to look up.

My addled, deranged mind skips ahead, envisioning a future with him. Exhibition with him, letting the world watch him take me like this. Claim me like this…

Pain sears through my earlobe, and with difficultly, I refocus my waning senses on him. His teeth nip me again, ensuring he has my full attention.

"My love? You've already taken it from me," he growls, his body thrumming as he jerks, spilling himself inside me, heightening the depths of his confession. "*Always.* From the first fucking time you teased me with your praise. You've taken this from me…"

HIS BED, as it turns out, is too damn small for us to even lay on comfortably. We wind up lying naked on a sheet spread before the window, watching the world advance beyond this realm, bathed in darkness.

In the dizzying comedown, he only moves to salvage something from his pants, pressing it to his ear in the dark. "Goodnight, *ma chérie*," I hear him murmur, revealing the sole person worthy of drawing his attention in this moment. Even now, he strives to keep his promise to her, always. "I will see you tomorrow. Please tell Tiffany's parents she decided not to return too late and risk waking anyone. Goodnight."

He hangs up and settles down beside me, forcing a physical connection I have no chance of resisting—his arms encircle me, a prison of heat.

Silence falls again. Finally…

"I guess this means no more trolling the bars for fake wives. No more bringing strange women to your penthouse suites," I tell him, stroking his bare chest, loving how the moonlight paints him in silvery tones. "It seems as though you may be a family man now."

"What a fate," he says mournfully. One of his hands runs through my hair while the other possessively cups my hip. "And you can no longer flaunt your skills at attracting a variety of different men, it seems. Never will anyone else have you."

"Never ever," I agree with playful despondence. "But…"

I shift, craning my neck to see his face more clearly. The man is the picture of contentment, his eyes gleaming in the dark, his lips devoid of their natural resting frown. If I squint, his expression could almost be deemed a smile, soft and curling like the fall of his hair.

"There is one obstacle we need to overcome," I tell him sternly.

He raises an eyebrow. "Oh."

"Yes." Sighing, I collapse against him, nestling into his touch. "We need to get you a million more books on kink. All the research you could ever need."

Holy crap. My throat still aches, but damn was it worth it. Already, my body is humming at whatever tricks the man could have in store. I'm tempted to risk pissing him off again if only to experience the depths of his depravity all over again. Jim made normal sex into an ordeal.

With Vadim, makeup sex is a world unto itself, let alone the vanilla stuff. A woman could get seriously drugged on his cock. Though, I could think of far worse fates.

Like being stupid enough to lose him for good.

"I'm an idiot for bringing this up now, I know I am," I confess, apologizing in advance with a kiss pressed against his nipple. "But I need to know…"

The one question I've been avoiding up until this moment, dancing around my feelings for him—as well as the shadows looming in his past.

"Who is Irina? Who was she to you? What did she say?"

"Irina…" He sighs, and rolls onto his side, capturing me in his arms, drawing me against him, my back against his chest. His mouth settles against the back of my skull, his hands on my breasts. The heaviness in his voice tempers any lust the position inspires. In some ways, I feel like what It is to Magda—a security blanket, being crushed for comfort. "We were not lovers," he says into my hair. "I need you to understand that, because when I describe our relationship… It was never sexual. But given the nature of our environment at the time, sex with another was not a necessity."

I wince, my heart aching for him, as it does every time I try to picture the horrific trappings of his childhood.

"Emotional connection, however?" he continues gruffly. "That was a commodity we both sought with an almost addicted fervor. But not in the way you are thinking. More like… The need to feel superior. Challenged. Our games revolved around the manipulation of others. Our captors. Our clients. We were damn good at utilizing those we could control to the fullest extent—and relishing in that power. It was all we had."

I slip my arms from his protective cocoon and tentatively stroke the length of his arm, sensing his need for something reassuring. Something to tether him from that darkness. He grunts, gripping me even tighter while lowering his mouth to my throat.

"We were kept like dolls," he explains, his tone empty. Lifeless. "Locked into rooms for clients to pick from the way one might select a garment from a rack. Those who couldn't learn to turn off their pain—perform and endure— didn't last. But I endured, and Irina? She *thrived*. We were both young when we came to him. I might have been thirteen? Fourteen? She wasn't much older, a beauty from Eastern Europe trafficked by her own family to pay off gambling debts. We were...*favorites,* of our owner," he says, his voice hitching over the word. *Favorites.* He's used it before I realize, and I suspect that term means more than the superficial definition. It was a shackle.

"The sick bastard used us more than the others. Demanded more from us. He dangled our appeal before his most prized clients, and we did what we could to beat each other at the game. If she could learn political secrets from one powerful dignitary, then I would learn firsthand intelligence from another. If she gained a necklace as a token, then I would cajole a more expensive trinket from my own abuser. We traded knowledge and money and companionship, each of us fighting to cement their role as the better player. The strongest. The coldest. We were just children," he admits, his voice deepening. "Surviving the only way we knew how. And that way involved backstabbing and intrigue. If Irina were assigned to a client she didn't like, I would be manipulated to perform in her place. If there were a punishment awaiting her for food she'd stolen, or rules she'd broken, I somehow would be the one to wind up lashed. I let her use me as her scapegoat," he adds, his voice thickening as if only now can he admit that to himself. "I let her take from me. Toy with me… Abandon me when she saw her own escape."

And in the process, he learned to mistrust those around him, seeing any and all forms of communication as strictly transactional.

"I never begrudged her then," he admits, flexing his fingers over my breasts, making me shiver in a tormented mixture of pleasure from his touch and disgust at his words. "But our owner, the Collector… He enjoyed his favorites too much, and so sick a man he was… He aimed to breed us— but not on our own terms, mind you. I don't even know how advanced the technology was back then, but one by one, we were dragged off to the medical suite. Strapped down. Prodded. Poked. Our liberties and DNA taken as though we were animals in a kennel, matched with the intent for our offspring to be bought and sold. My turn came not long before I escaped," he adds coldly. "I was sure I'd torched the place to ashes, burning all traces of those experiments."

"So…you think Irina took your 'samples' for Magda?" I don't know how to say it without sounding foolish. A naïve innocent crudely narrating the darkest details of his past as though they're a spectacle to gape over.

But if anything, some of the tension from him eases, his lips nuzzling my heated flesh. And for the first time, I reconcile the fact that he's holding me at all—not staring into place, numbly recounting this like the few other times we've broached this topic.

"Irina was always cunning," he says. "Cunning and calculating. Those times she used me to her own ends? She always had a token on the other end to make up for it, or so she saw them as. For instance, after I'd be whipped for her crimes, she'd sneak a priceless jewel into my chambers. Or a sweet. Though those gifts were always predicated by a desire on her part to use me again. They always carried a price."

And thus, a brooding, ice-cold transactional man was born from the darkness of such a cruel life.

"If she did manage to get a hold of our 'samples.' Have Magdalene… To her, the girl would only ever be a token. A means to an end—and by dangling her before me, eventually, there will be a price to be paid in return."

But in the case of his daughter, I don't think he'll hesitate to pay it, whatever it may be.

"What did she want when she came by the house?" I ask warily.

"Nothing," he rasps, but his voice is gruff with unease. Unsteady. "*Nothing.* She told me she 'missed me,' then she left. No mention of Magdalene. Not even a fucking confirmation or a threat. And *that* is what…frightens me. She always wants something. Everything is a means to an end."

"But Magda isn't a token," I whisper, matching his apparent protectiveness.

"Nor a toy," he agrees. "And I am not the same broken little boy she left behind."

I shiver at the ferocity in his tone, my heart aching for him. Thinking quickly, I resist his grip enough to twist around to face him and loop my arms around his neck. Desperate to distract him, I kiss a path up from his collar bone to his mouth, grinding my hips with every teasing peck.

He lunges into the kiss, pinning me beneath him, easily parting my legs.

And this time, I let him take from me.

Whatever he needs.

All that he can salvage.

Everything.

CHAPTER TEN

We return to my parents' house in the morning to find Magda once again in the garden, but this time sampling frozen treats—sugar-free I see at a glance—on a picnic blanket spread out beneath one of the orange trees. Mother and Daddy sit on either side of her, each cajoling her into trying a new delicacy, their laughter carefree.

My heart swells in my chest. I don't think I've ever seen them so relaxed—let alone my mother willingly sit so close to the actual earth. Her eyes sparkle as she runs her fingers through Magda's loose curls as Daddy shapes orange peels with his tongue to make her giggle.

"Your kid is a master manipulator," I tell Vadim in awe as we watch her work from the obscurity of the sunroom. "I think someone will wind up with a very good haul at Christmas."

His jaw clenches at that, his gaze constricted with an emotion I can't read just yet. Something every bit as tender and delicate as the freshly blooming flowers spreading their petals throughout the garden. If I stumble too close to it now, I might wind up crushing it.

So instead, I coax him out where we join the makeshift picnic much to Magda's delight. Soon enough, rather than just two peons to fawn over her, her court grows to four, and every bit the little princess, she plays her role to the fullest extent.

"Can we go to the beach?" she asks, once we've eaten lunch and my parents have gone off in search of more things to placate her with—my father with the promise of showing her his power tools once he's cleaned the shed, and my mother in the process of fetching every dress I'd ever worn from storage.

"The beach…" Vadim locks eyes with me, conceding the decision to my discretion, I suspect. Something tells me he's well aware of the sensitive ground venturing into town treads upon for me.

But my past wounds aren't Magda's problem.

"I can show you my old haunts," I tell her, tugging at a curl. "I loved hanging out on Faraday beach."

Just like that, we bundle into the car and enter the town I haven't stepped foot in since my divorce was finalized over six months ago. It's one of those small, overly beautiful, secretly judgmental, and cloistered coastal towns with none of the allure of say, Orange County, but twice the charm.

I'm pleased to find most of my old favorite cafes and boutiques are still in business, gearing up for the peak tourist season.

"You lived here," Magda says, this time with utter confidence, her eyes on a gaggle of giggling blond teens decked out in matching designer fashions.

"Hey!" I elbow her in the shoulder as we leave the car parked beyond the boardwalk. "I would never walk in an identical cluster. I was the trendsetter, not the follower."

Her sly grin tells me she doubts that assessment.

Still, we trailblaze our own path through the beach bum clones, lazily patrolling the boardwalk before skimming past the water as Magda skips through the waves, her sandals in hand, her smile infectious.

"Something tells me you're considering investing in a beach house," I taunt Vadim once I spy the way he's watching her. Avidly, like a man who thought he'd never see the sun experiencing a full-on supernova up close and personal.

"Already in the process of closing on one," he admits, running his finger along the collar of his casual button-down. "Seeing your family's home sold me on vacationing in wine country."

I have to wonder if this purchase came before or after our makeup session last night. Judging from his smirk, he won't tell.

I lean against him rather than prod, slipping my hand in his as his other arm goes around me. I crave this nearness now more than ever—because as much as I hate to admit it, there is a reason I preferred to stay on the East coast, shacking up with a sexy, handsome billionaire rather than come back home.

Being here still stings.

We've passed the seaside diner Jim took me to early on in our relationship. And the spot on the beach where he proposed—but with a stand-in ring because his father's credit line at the jewelry store hadn't gone through at the time. Now, we're nearing the overlook where he liked to stroll, showing me off like arm candy before he tired of me.

I'm doing my best to ignore the poisonous nostalgia, but my mood must plummet to the point that even Vadim senses it.

"Let's take a break," he suggests, stopping short before a row of white picnic tables positioned with a view of where the boardwalk intersects the beach. "How about some ice cream?"

"Okay!" Magda takes his hand without a second thought, and they head off toward a frozen treat stand a few paces away. I find myself scanning the stream of traffic combing through the boardwalk as I wait, letting my brain run rampant with vicious scenarios.

I wonder if Jim is enjoying life with his new baby and harlot. If he takes her here, to these places, and she's dumb enough to assume they belong to her alone. If they both expect that I'm somewhere in hiding, living off his alimony payments and seething with jealousy.

I think that's the part that alarms me the most. I'm *not* seething. I'm pissed—so very pissed with myself and the fact that I suffered for so long. Lied to myself for so long.

And all for what?

To discover that the world beyond my marriage could be ten times more beautiful, and sexier and fulfilling. And I never had to change the person I was—not really. Dumb, lazy Tiffy could thrive when given the chance, with or without a relationship to assign her value.

Fuck Jim, may he rot in marital bliss.

But, because the world is cruel, I think I wind up conjuring him from thin air.

I almost mistake him for another balding, beer-gut sporting beachgoer at first. But no. No one else could sport that smug posture, like a peacock strutting, wanting the whole world to see the gussied-up, naïve little hen he'd cajoled into marrying him. His hen looks even younger than Francesca when glimpsed out in the open and not scurrying from me in the church corridors or cowering in Jim's shadow.

She's slender, with ginger waves curling down her back, a baby balanced on her hip. He has his arm around her, showing off the sexy young piece of ass a washed-up man his age managed to score.

But shock isn't what has me lurching to my feet, toying with the idea of running back to the car. Just pain. Because I recognize that look on her face—the thin-lipped smile, and simpering expression. God, how could I face myself in the mirror every day and not see it before?

But they see me. Jim cocks his head, frowning once he spots an unwelcome addition to his fawning crowd. He squints as if unsure if it really is me—dressed in a sexy, A-line beige sundress, my hair hanging loose in the style he never liked, my makeup bold and obvious.

His lips twitch in that ugly way, a hallmark of his irritation. Most often glimpsed when I said the wrong thing or seemingly embarrassed him, and he felt the need to "set me straight" with some cruel tirade. Rather than approach me, he tugs his new bride closer, almost protectively.

Because in his tiny brain, I'm still in love with him. Still pining for him. I bet he thinks I followed him here on purpose, waited for him.

Fuck him.

I don't even realize I'm taking a step forward until a pair of tiny arms goes around my waist. "Mommy!" a little girl chirps, clamoring for my attention. "We got you ice cream! Do you like it?"

A masculine arm encircles my shoulders, as the child—who I'm startled to recognize as Magda—flanks my opposite side.

"Here you go, baby," Vadim murmurs, pressing a cone piled high with strawberry ice cream into my hand, his lips soft on my cheek. And yet his voice is loud enough for anyone within ten yards to easily here. "It's about time we got back, don't you think?"

Like orderlies guiding a wayward patient, he and Magda block me in, forcing me down the length of the boardwalk. Purposefully I suspect. And yet, I can't resist glancing back, just enough to see Jim's face.

"Keep walking," Vadim tells me, his tone gently insistent. "Let's savor this moment."

Savor…

He couldn't know who Jim is, could he? I look over to find him and Magda trading conspiratorial winks, and then it clicks. Hell, yes, he knows.

And he intervened to give me a revenge too sweet to have devised on my own.

"You two and your mind games," I murmur, equally awed and impressed.

Poor Jim. He'll probably spend all night wondering if it really was me he saw—the woman he supposedly defeated —or a stranger with a beautiful life he could only dream of.

I'VE NEVER DREADED LEAVING my parents' home more. Even Magda seems to sulk at the prospect after a week spent gardening and playing dress up in my old wardrobe. Vadim, ever the resigned stoic, is the one level-headed enough to muster us to the airport after three days spent in utter bliss.

"I mean it, Tiffy," my mother scolds as she and Daddy follow us out to the car. "We expect you back for the summer holidays. And Magdalene, darling, I'll take you to all of the clubs once they open. Oh, all of the girls will find you so darling, and we can get you into tennis lessons, and maybe if your father *does* decide to try out a pageant or two—"

"Stay in the muck, kid," Daddy says with a knowing wink. "You'll learn more rooting through the dirt than you ever could in some fancy dress."

"Oh, Harold," my mother whines in exasperation.

They fuss as Vadim claims the driver's seat, and we make our escape. In the end, the journey home isn't anywhere near as daunting as I'd initially thought. Travel with one stoic—and a mini-stoic in tow—is an experience in of itself. Especially when Magda struggles to hide her excitement during her second plane trip, and Vadim loses himself in the pure joy of watching her eagerly prattle about plane engines and aerodynamics.

When she finally tires out, I find myself seated beside him, my head on his shoulder, his fingers lazily parting my hair.

"How did you know?" I ask, eyeing the clouds rolling beneath us beyond the windows. "About my ex?"

He shrugs, his expression neutral. "I noticed you were uncomfortable, and I made a logical leap to the obvious conclusion."

Fair enough. But as I submit to his gentle stroking, he adds, "And, I may or may not have researched the man the second I learned you were divorced."

"Oh," I croak, stunned by the implications of that confession. Seemingly harmless. But seemingly *not*, considering Vadim's wealth of resources. Not to mention his knack for manipulation.

"I don't think your arrival caused his ill mood, however," he explains, going a step further in his assessment of my ex's mental state than even I did. "It seems that persistent rumors of his infidelity may have reached the leadership of your old parish. Poor James may have been relieved of his duties for the time being, given the rumor of impropriety."

I gasp and bolt upright, placing my hand on his chest. "You didn't! You devil!" I'm grinning ear to ear, though, even as I feign utter shock. "I, good Sir, am a lady far beyond the machinations of revenge."

"Of course," he concedes, drawing me back to him, his lips brushing my forehead. "As am I. As am I…"

Hours later, when we finally pull up to the house, I'm alarmed to find that I'm not anywhere near as homesick as I'd assumed I would be. My family home in California is a beautiful oasis, but when glimpsed in the dappling evening sunset that reflects like embers over the water, I have to admit that Vadim's home has a certain charm to it.

Even Magda seems affected, skipping up the front walkway, It dangling from her hand. She moves assuredly, with the knowledge that this is hers. Her *home*.

But somewhere between the last section of the path and the front door, she stops short. The color drains from her face, and Vadim is before her instantly.

"What's wrong?" He crouches down, fervently feeling along her forehead. Then he frowns. "Look at me, *chérie*."

Magda doesn't even seem to realize he's there. Her nostrils flare, her chest heaving as if she's struggling for air. Desperate to breathe.

"Magdalene," Vadim says in a stern tone. She blinks, startled, and refocuses on his face.

"I smelled something," she says, her voice devoid of its usual charm. The resulting effect is a hollow, broken tone that makes me approach her, sinking down beside Vadim. "Do you smell it?"

I sniff and shrug. "Roses?"

Her eyes widen, and she nods, clutching It so tightly her knuckles are white.

"Oh." Vadim chuckles, ruffling her hair. "Ena has a secret green thumb," he explains, rising to his feet. "Give him time, and this house will resemble the garden at Tiffany's family home."

That seems to mollify her. As if flipping that pesky internal switch, she's back to her animated self, rearing to enter the house.

"Can we see my pony?" she asks as Vadim gathers our bags and finally unlocks the front door.

"Of course," he says indulgently. "Let's put our things away quickly, *non*? I'm sure we can make it out to our friends before dark."

They both hasten inside while I take my time savoring the view. Could I learn to call this place home as well? The second I see Magda bound up the stairs, filling the hall with childish clatter, I start to believe I could.

"I'll make dinner," I call as Vadim returns downstairs, dressed in a casual pair of slacks and a loose-fitting dress shirt while Magda scampers after him in her riding gear. They race out onto the terrace, Magda's giggles lingering long after they fade from view.

Left alone, I decide to hone my domestic skills and consider whipping up a meal from scratch. What might I cook safely without risking everyone's health? Frowning, I open the fridge and peruse the ingredients that Ena's stocked it with. Finding nothing promising—other than a potential salad— I start toward the pantry, hoping for more convenient options. Like cereal.

Intent on my task, I slip past the fridge, skirting the counter…

And promptly stop short.

A woman is seated at the dining room table, her legs crossed, her slim fingers—each tipped with a sharpened ruby fingernail—tracing patters over the glass surface, her expression the picture of contemplation.

My blood runs cold as she looks up, meeting my gaze.

"I'm surprised, to be honest," she says, her voice an odd mixture of cutting notes and lilting cadence. Shifting to face me fully, she crosses her arms, observing me with a judgmental flick of her gaze. Her navy dress helps her blend into the monochromatic background, and I wonder, horrified, just how long she's been sitting here.

Did Magda run right by her?

Or Vadim…

"Dima was always so secretive about his ideal type of woman," Irina continues, her pink lips quirked in a smirk that doesn't reach her gaze. Regardless, I stagger back, putting the counter between us, my fingers inching toward one of the drawers containing utensils. The sharp kind.

"How did you even get in here—"

"I'd assumed, it was because his standards were higher than he'd care to admit," she says, continuing as if I'd never spoken. "He was always so…obsessive with perfection." She frowns wistfully, her head cocked, gaze reflective. Then she shakes her head, sending her blond waves tumbling down her shoulders. "I will admit that it is disappointing to realize that I was wrong. The boy he was could never resist a sweet. Cheap, tawdry, fleeting joy."

I stiffen, recognizing an insult when I hear it. Squaring my shoulders, I swallow hard, schooling my expression into a mask of cool politeness. At the same time, my eyes dart to the glass door, hunting for Vadim. Ena. *Anyone.*

But with no witness in sight, my only course of action is to stay on guard. "You should go——"

"You asked me how I got in," Irina says, rising to her feet. With enviable grace, she smooths her hands down her front, drawing attention to her ample curves and tiny waist. Deliberately, I suspect—and just as she intends, I brush my hand along my simple dress skirt, mentally comparing the contrasting picture we must make.

As if aware of the thought, she smiles. "I'm sure you're smart enough to figure it out."

I flinch. "I'm guessing it wasn't with the permission of security."

Though she looks so slender in comparison to Ena's bulk, could she have incapacitated the bodyguard somehow? My stomach twists into knots at the thought—as surly as he can be, Vadim wouldn't want him hurt.

Neither do I.

"Security," Irina parrots, purring the word. "As in Boris Ena. Trust Vadim to draw the iciest, most ruthless bastard of the lot to his side. Luckily for me, I remember his...blind spots."

She winks, her eyelids lowered. At the back of my mind, I recognize the expression as a cruel imitation of one of Magda's. Her surly, brooding look when she's mulling over how to get her way during a round of monopoly. The second I see it, I know she's already won.

And I back up another hasty step. "Did you hurt him?"

She shrugs as her eyes scan the room while her body languidly approaches the counter. Frowning, she swipes her finger over the polished surface, scowling at imaginary dust. "I don't have to hurt him," she says, her voice alarmingly soft. "Just outsmart him. And you insinuated permission, I'm assuming. Well, there you have it—" She spreads her arms wide as if to exclaim, *"ta da!"* In the process, a whiff of her perfume teases my nose, the deceptively sweet scent of roses. "Vadim knows better than anyone my skills of evasion," she boasts. "Take his hiding behind such lax 'security' as proof that he knew I'd return. He all but asked me to."

I back up another step as she slips onto a stool. With my hand extended behind me, I finally manage to grasp the handle of a drawer. Yanking it open, I feel through the assorted cutlery, finding nothing useful. Forks…spoons— no knives.

"You're saying Vadim invited you here?" I ask, desperate to feign nonchalance.

Her expression flattens, her gaze clouding over. "You're mouthier than I'd assume he could tolerate." Only a subtle, harsh note of inflection reveals her anger.

And yet it's as bracing as touching a hot stove—every nerve prickles with awareness, warning that I'm in danger of being burned.

"Are you here for Magda, then?" I ask, mainly to keep her talking as I inch back another step, feeling the edge of the drawer brush my lower back.

But if I'd wanted to distract her, I've succeeded. She scoffs. "Magdalene? Magdalene is…flawed." She flicks her fingers as if swatting the mere idea of the girl away. "I can give Dima other children. Perfect children. But can you?"

I'm too stunned by her words—and their disturbing implications—that I barely notice her slip around the counter, her gaze fixated on me. And then my brain finally processes her insult and the sheer, cruel accuracy with which it was aimed.

"Tiffany Connors," she says as crisply as if reciting from a book. "Your gynecologist has quite the extensive record on you. Endometriosis. Poly Cystic Ovarian Syndrome. The occasional hormone imbalances. Even if you weren't on birth control, Dima could fuck you raw for a month, and you still wouldn't conceive, would you?"

Fire sears my cheeks. I blink, too startled to move, even as she slinks closer, her smile knowing.

"And I'm sure he has been fucking you." She reaches out, swiping the tip of her nail along my cheek.

I recoil so violently I wind up slamming the drawer over my wrist. Only gritting my teeth can keep me from crying out. "D-Don't touch me—"

"*Touch* you. Have you ever asked yourself why Vadim can? Why he does?" Her smile is feral, her eyes glittering in the shadow cast by the light falling onto her face from this angle. "It doesn't come naturally to him, but you know that. He's pretending, winding you up, his little toy. He'll watch you spin and spin until you serve your purpose. He's always been that way. Cruel. I suppose it explains why he's gotten as far as he has. Amassed the empire he has. I doubt you even know the true extent of it…" Her tone shifts as she glances down, her teeth clenched.

"What do you mean?" I ask, tentatively licking my lips.

She cackles. "You don't, do you? My resourceful boy's all grown up, but I'll admit that he's turned out far more ruthless than I could imagine. Though considering who his mentor was, how could he not?"

Mentor? Hiram, the man who rescued him?

"What are you saying?"

"Oh, darling…" Her eyes gleam with mock pity. "Have you ever stopped to ask yourself how a man his age could amass such a fortune so quickly? Especially given his lack of…let's call it a traditional upbringing. Has he told you of his family? Their legacy? Don't tell me you are so naïve to believe he could rise above it all unscathed?"

Denying her is my first instinct. I even start to, my lips parting. But something stops me, and another question forms on my tongue instead. "Why do you care? If he is toying with me? If you don't want Magdalene, then why are you here?"

"Why?" She chuckles, and leans back against the island, her hair spilling down her shoulders, her body positioned provocatively. "Because after more than ten damn years, my Dima has finally grown bored of waiting for me," she declares. "He is *provoking* me. Drawing me out the way he knew how to all along." She traces her bottom lip with the wet tip of her tongue, her gaze distant. "By daring to pretend I don't exist. By replacing me with puppets."

She rights herself, pushing past me for the foyer. "But I will remind him soon enough. This was always a game, my darling. You're just a pawn in it..."

Her steps fade, and I crane my neck to watch her vanish around the corner. *Damn.* I'm shaking, my knees buckling, my wrist throbbing as I wrench it from the painful clutches of the drawer.

Then I'm already halfway to the terrace door, my fingers grasping at the handle. My first fully coherent thought is to run to the stable. Warn Vadim.

And I don't even see the blow coming.

A force slams into me from behind, and I go down hard, landing on my side in the shadow of the dining table. Dazed, I turn, scrambling for purchase over the flooring. I only catch a glimpse of silver, flashing through the air before…

Pain!

It's so sharp and all-consuming I can't breathe. The air leaves my lungs, my body drained of everything but fiery agony centered around my left shoulder. Again. Again.

A distant thudding registers with the remaining logical part of my brain—pairing the sickening sound with that of a butcher, plunging a blade into a hunk of meat. Stabbing through it.

I can't move.

I can't even scream.

But my only coherent thought is of Vadim.

And Magda.

God, I can sense them, tramping across the terrace, their laughter raucous as my attacker retreats. I hear Magda first, her tiny voice high-pitched with excitement. "Can we have pizza again?"

"Of course," Vadim says, sounding closer. "Go get washed up—"

"Don't!" It takes everything I have to claw at the floor and drag myself behind the counter and out of view. "Vadim, don't let her in!"

Silence falls with the swiftness of a candle being blown out. Or maybe I'm just losing consciousness? Either way, I feel like I'm hearing everything as if from underwater, muffled, and distant.

"*Chérie*," Vadim says, his voice garbled. "I left my…at… stable…go fetch for me?"

A heartbeat later, heavy footsteps rush to my side, and I sense warm fingers prodding my forehead. "Look at me," Vadim urges in a tone so hoarse it makes my heart ache. "Look at me!"

But I can't.

My vision is already blurring, darkening around the edges…

Until I can't see anything at all.

CHAPTER ELEVEN

I feel so warm. So peaceful. I almost dread opening my eyes because it feels damn good to just float in this colorless ether. At least until I hear the voice.

His voice.

"Look at me, beautiful," he commands in a tone that cuts through the peaceful haze like a knife. "Open your eyes. Please, open your eyes."

When I do, the world returns in blurred snippets of color and contrasting shadow. Even in this dreamy state, I'm convinced the face coming into focus will from here on out be the most beautiful sight I've ever witnessed.

Dark eyes framed by dizzyingly long eyelashes fixate on me, narrowed with worry. That same concern tightens the line of a gorgeous mouth, the lips so pink. The face of an angel, his expression contorts with relief as I blink to take more of him in.

"Thank God." He seems closer, his gaze tortured. "Can you speak? Say something."

A tattered giggle edges his words. From me? My body feels loosely connected, as if threaded together with the thinnest string. Somehow, I manage to make my lips move, my voice high-pitched and breathy.

"You are so pretty," I tell him seriously. "The prettiest person *ever*. Like ever. In forever…"

He frowns, glancing beyond me. "What did you give her?"

"Due to the position of the wounds, the doctor ordered a mildly strong sedative to prevent further trauma during the suturing process," a woman explains in crisp, hilarious tones. "The effects will wear off in a few hours." Her voice drifts away, and another tattered giggle bubbles from my chest.

"Drugged?" I ask Vadim, amused by his worried frown. He's sexy in his normal resting state, but when emotionally aroused—even with concern—the man looks divine. "I probably would have married you if you asked nicely," I blurt, too warm and comfy to care about how the confession may land. "You didn't have to drug me."

"Drug you? I should have *protected* you." He smooths his fingers through my hair as more of our surroundings come into focus. We're in a room—plain, with light blue walls— but I don't recognize the style as belonging to his house. Or his bedroom, for that matter…

And I have tentacles, I realize with a dazed, childish bit of horror. Tubes snake out of both my arms, feeding into various blinking, beeping machines.

"Uh, oh," I say, still giggling harder now than ever. "Did I have an accident?"

"Get some sleep," Vadim urges, apparently deciding that the hazy, dreamy darkness is the best place for me to be. "Sleep. I'll be here. Always, I'll be here."

But will he? A voice in my head is telling me no, using one painful fact as the winning argument.

"I could give you a baby," I tell him out loud, watching his face change as the boast registers. Rather than hopeful, he looks stricken. Like I've struck him. Mortally wounded. Because he knows I might be lying? But deep down, I don't think I am.

Even if I may or may not be totally high.

"I could," I insist, my voice breathier than ever. "I mean it. I *want* to—"

"Stop talking, beauty," he commands, stroking his fingers through my hair. "All I need now is for you to rest. That is all I want from you. Your health. Nothing else."

I nod obediently, letting my eyes close as exhaustion washes over me like a wave—but one last thought tickles my conscious mind before I can drift off completely.

"Are you shady, Vadim?" I ask him sleepily. For some reason, a bitchy voice is in my head, implying as much. Taunting as much. "Do you do bad things—"

"Sleep." His voice resonates with way more authority this time.

But even as I comply, I sense his presence surround me persistently, more potent than any drug.

MY SECOND ATTEMPT at waking up isn't as fun as the first. I groan even before I blink my eyes open to a dimly lit room and a tired, handsome face.

"Better?" Vadim asks, his fingers stroking my cheek.

I nod and wince. "I'm not high anymore," I confess, my voice rasping. "But the tradeoff is that I feel like I got hit by a truck."

And in a way, I have—a psychotic, blond, beautiful truck my memories tell me. I shiver at reliving them, choosing to focus on Vadim instead. He's frowning, his jaw clenched, that muscle twitching.

"Four stab wounds. Fifty-two stitches in total," he confesses, his tone blunt. "Spanning from your left shoulder down to your hip. They are deep, but all avoided any vital organs, thank God. Still, you will need to take care to ensure you heal without any complications. An infection could be difficult to recover from, and the surgeon warned that, given that the injuries to your shoulder sliced through muscle, you will be in pain."

I wince. "That sounds about right."

"Should I get the nurse?"

Grunting with the effort, I shake my head. "No. I'll live…" Though a part of me shudders at the realization that Irina didn't intend as much by accident. She *deliberately* avoided killing me. Why?

One look at the man across from me, and I can guess the answer—this was merely a warning, to him alone.

"Where is Magda?" I ask, alarmed when I don't see her.

The hint of a smile sneaks into the corner of his mouth, so beautiful and unexpected that my physical pain is all but forgotten. "Charming your nurses into giving her more crayons, I suspect. She already has them wrapped around her finger." His gaze softens a fraction, and I sense a part of him takes pride in his socially adept offspring. Like father like daughter.

Or could such skill stem from her mother?

I suck in a breath as my brain finally dares to connect the dots of the pain searing through my left side to the vague images circling my scattered memories. Fifty-two stitches. That beats my previous record—stemming from a drunken yacht accident—by double digits.

"Irina," I croak, and Vadim stiffens, his gaze unreadable. But this time, he isn't hiding behind his wall. "*She* attacked me—"

"I don't know how she got in," he swears, leaning forward to grip my hand, unconsciously pressing my fingers against his chest, near his heart. He's seated beside me, his rumpled dress shirt betraying at least a few hours of vigil by my bedside—and something inside me heats and melts. At least in the brief second wherein I forget his psycho ex-partner in crime.

A horrible, sobering thought makes me slip my hand from his and utilize what little energy I have to brush his cheek, seeking out the contours of his haggard expression. "She doesn't want Magda," I tell him softly, a relief within itself. And, in so many ways, a tragedy for a child who, some might say, was abandoned by both parents at some point. "She wants *you*."

His eyes blaze, his throat constricting around a hard swallow. And… I think, deep down, he already knew that.

He was afraid of that very reality.

"I don't know how she got past Ena," he says hoarsely. "He didn't even see her. He was beside himself…" He sighs and runs the fingers of his free hand through his already mussed hair. "I hired ten more guards to cycle out at random intervals. I'm selling the house. Our new location is somewhere unlisted, impossible to trace. She won't come near you again."

I sink against my pillows, overwhelmed by the raw note of possession in his voice. The conviction with which he swears something so assuredly. Its power.

"Did Magda see…"

"No. I heard your warning." He takes my hand again, bringing it to his mouth, running his lips over my knuckles. "I entered the house first and distracted her before she saw anything. As far as she knows, you opened a cupboard of glass dishes with a faulty shelf, fell over and cut yourself— but she is intelligent," he admits, sadness crossing his features. "Too intelligent. Your parents, however, received the same story. I believe they accepted it, for what it's worth."

"Thank you…" The thought of him reaching out to my parents, given his lack of familial ties, means more to me than I would have expected.

But my relief is countered by concern for Magda. My heart aches for her—and pounds ferociously in the same breath. I don't think I've ever felt a desire to protect another so strongly before. Every time I think of her in danger…my blood boils.

"Irina doesn't want her," I reiterate, my voice cold. "She said she was…flawed—"

"She won't ever touch her." Vadim stands, turning his back to me, both hands in his hair, his posture rigid. Slowly, he starts to pace the length of the room, and my pulse flutters the more I watch him. Gone is the pain—replacing it is steely, terrifying anger. "Never. I will kill her before I let that happen—"

"You knew." Gingerly, I shift around, groaning as fire shoots through my side. It's intense—I can feel each, individual puncture wound. Four, he said? Their placement makes it hard to find a comfortable position without being reminded of my injuries every time I take a breath. Intentionally, I suspect. And if Vadim really grew up with Irina as he claimed, then he most likely is well aware of her capabilities. "*That's* why you really tried to push me away. Not only for Magda."

In his own, twisted, broken logic—he wanted me to run. But in me, the master manipulator met his match.

His hands fall as he turns to face me, his eyes scanning my battered frame. "How do you feel?" he asks, a deliberate change in subject.

I wince and twist my hips into a slightly more comfortable position. "Not dead, at least." I force a laugh that he doesn't return. "What happened? When you found me."

He crosses over to a single window betraying a view of the darkening sky. "Magda raced me back to the house, but I started inside before she did. I saw the blood first," he confesses. "I sent her back to the stable to fetch something. Called Ena. I held you down to apply pressure to your wounds while he raced us to the hospital."

"And Magda? Don't tell me you left her there alone."

He cocks his head, his frown deepening. Layers enhance the tormented expression, creating a grimace shaped by both pain and…confusion. "Not quite—"

"Tiffany!" Magda waltzes into the room as if on cue, armed with a massive box of crayons and a stack of printer paper. I'm not sure how much time I've lost being stuck in this bed already—a day, maybe longer? Someone, however, took up my hair brushing duties in my absence, as well as dressed her in a lilac dress—though it clashes with her trusty fanny pack—complete with matching hair ribbons. The only detail glaringly out of place is a massive amount of glittery, unicorn stickers climbing up the length of her left arm.

"Pretty," I say, as she marches to my side, squeezing past Vadim. Reaching out, I stroke the gaudiest sticker—a pink unicorn bunny with big blue eyes. "Where did you get such swag, honey?" Call it a hunch, but they don't quite seem like Vadim's style.

She shoots her father a wary glance, but I can tell she's bursting at the seams with this new secret. "Ainsley gave them to me," she says, flashing that rare, ripe grin as she shows off her decked-out arm. "We had a sleepover."

"A sleepover?" I feel my eyebrows shoot up as I glance at Vadim while seriously considering the fact that I may actually still be high.

He doesn't meet my gaze, his frown surly, though as he looks down on Magda—and her obvious joy—his lips soften again. "A sleepover," he concedes.

That's it. I *am* hallucinating. As quickly as I dare, I sit upright, making him face me. He looks on edge, as if I've caught him with his pants down. Or, even worse in his mind, I caught him at a moment when he'd been desperate enough to go to the one person he seems to hate more than anyone.

Solely for Magda's sake.

"*Francesca* watched over her," he finally admits. "And her siblings."

But not the main, dominant member of that household— his brother Maxim. Not too long ago, he was out of the country. Could he still be gone?

Yet, the idea of Vadim crossing the invisible boundary between the property is a sight so unexpected—and at its core, so damn selfless, with such tender motivations—my heart almost can't contain it.

"Can I go back tonight?" Magda asks. She's curled up on his vacated chair, her gaze fixated on a drawing she's in the process of scribbling with a red crayon. At a glance, she's the picture of childish nonchalance—but her eyes betray her. Every few seconds, she glances hopefully at Vadim, her bottom lip dangerously close to a pout.

"Not tonight, *ma chérie*," Vadim says, moving toward her to ruffle her hair. She deflates, but relents to his touch, her nose wrinkling. "We're going to our new home tonight, remember? So that we can get it ready for Tiffany's return."

She nods, turning her attention to me. "No glass this time," she says solemnly. But damn…

Much like Vadim, I sense she's well versed in doublespeak— and my heart swells again. Literally.

A series of beeping machines goes off, and Vadim scrambles for a nurse. After checking my vital signs, she deems me no closer to dying than at any other moment throughout the day. Still, he's frowning, unconvinced.

"You need rest," he declares, brushing his lips over my forehead. "I'll come back tonight after Magda's in bed. Ena will watch over her this time. You'll have three guards on you at all times. You're safe." He sounds so confident in that fact, but as he pulls away, I suspect his reassurances were more for himself than me. He looks so exhausted as the waning daylight casts shadows over his haggard features. Worn. And yet, as he hasn't failed to do since her arrival, he swallows down any discomfort as he faces Magda.

"Let's go, *chérie*," he calls to her. "I'm sure Tiffany appreciates your many creations."

As battered as he is, the man cracks a tired smile at the sight of her drawings scattered all over my side table. I spot one and reach for it, wincing with the effort.

"This is lovely," I croon, glancing over a misshapen blob formed of black crayon that may or may not be an animal of some kind.

"It's It," Magda says seriously. She slips from the chair and gathers her belongings. Squished into the cushions of the seat behind her is a small white bear that she clings to even while juggling her pilfered art supplies. "He can protect you. From falling onto glass."

I laugh, but when I look up from the page, her eyes… They bore into mine so fiercely I flinch. Oblivious, Vadim comes to relieve her of her artistic burden and heads for the door. "Let's go."

She follows him, but when she glances back, I nearly lunge from the bed to grab her, barely able to suppress a fierce desire to hold her in my arms until she never sports such an expression again. Fear. Raw, naked terror so potent I'm rendered silent in the face of it.

CHAPTER TWELVE

I barely have the chance to mourn his absence before I sense Vadim return just as I'm dozing off. He slips into the room without a word, reclaiming his post beside me. I shiver, content, as warmth feathers my forehead—the shadow of a chaste kiss.

As I continue to feign sleep, his fingers capture mine, lifting them from my crumpled blankets. I make myself limp, my breathing steady. Maybe I'm curious as to what he'll do? And he doesn't disappoint.

With breathtaking care, he brings my fingers to his mouth, or so I assume from the warm bursts of air ghosting my knuckles. The feel of his lips a second later—grazing the back of my hand reverently—makes me shiver. Damn this man...

He gently strokes whatever parts of me he can reach. Runs through my hair with aching gentleness. He lavishes me in silent praise, all in secret without an audience to preen for.

And even though my eyes remain closed, I know that this is *him*—a man Irina was never, ever privy to.

The real, unfiltered Vadim.

I WAKE up to find a watchful gaze directed my way, its owner wearing another stripped-down suit—this time with a navy dress shirt and no jacket. The moment I start to lift my head from the pillows, he races to get me a pitcher of water and small pieces of fruit, fussing to make sure I'm hydrated and fed.

Once my nurse comes in and performs her assessment, then the doctor—who deems me stable enough to leave—I find myself discharged and promptly carried into a waiting car a little after noon.

"Where's Magda?" I ask once I find the backseat empty.

Vadim's chosen to drive us himself, and he chuckles as he settles into the driver's seat, his lip twitching. "Forcing Ena to teach her gardening techniques. Well, perhaps not necessarily against his will." His expression turns wistful as he navigates the steering wheel with one hand, the other placed firmly on my knee. "I don't think I've ever seen the bastard smile," he admits. "At anyone."

Satisfied, I sit back in my seat, oddly amused by the prospect. But then my thoughts turn to more dangerous topics as my injuries throb, even after a dose of—much less potent than my initial dosage—pain medication.

"How did she get past him?" I ask, eyeing Vadim warily. "Irina?"

He frowns, all traces of joy vanishing from his face. "I suspect she timed it. Watched him long enough to know his schedule—when he'd be the easiest to circumvent. She was always like that. Cunning."

An assessment that brings up another chilling suspicion circling my brain. "Magda… Do you think she remembers Irina?"

He cocks his head, his brow furrowing. If he's considered such a possibility himself, I can't tell. "What makes you ask that?"

Several reasons come to mind. Her aversion to roses, for one. Not to mention her almost obsessive need for her teddy bear—a bear, that I'm starting to realize, may symbolize more to her than just a sentimental gift. A fact bolstered by a certain picture she'd chosen to hide within it.

He can protect you, she told me after giving me her drawing —which I've kept tucked within my discharge paperwork.

For all of her intellect, she's still seven at heart. A child prone to magical beliefs of monsters and mystery—and one who trusts in Vadim's presence so strongly that, in her mind, he could protect her from anything. Even her worst nightmares…

"It's nothing," I finally say, rather than bother him with a bunch of random observations that may not mean anything. "But have you talked to her yet? About what she might remember of her life before you found her?"

It's a topic that feels far too intimate for me to broach again. Only her father should have reign over that arena.

…Shouldn't he?

"No," he confesses. "I haven't. Not yet. According to her records, she had decent nutrition and healthcare prior to being discovered. But…" He frowns and lifts his hand from me, stroking it through his hair.

"But?" I prod when he falls silent.

"Her diabetes was newly onset, so her blood sugars had been wildly uncontrolled—but that is typical with this illness. Otherwise, there wasn't a mark on her."

But I know firsthand that abuse can extend far beyond the physical. Some of the worst wounds are the ones inflicted upon your soul. As strange as it feels to admit, even to myself, Irina's attack—while hurting like a bitch—doesn't sting anywhere near as badly as some of the verbal blows Jim dished out. Injuries to my self-esteem that I'm still recovering from years later.

The thought of Magda suffering even a fraction of the same…

"She doesn't *need* Irina," Vadim says, injecting himself into my scattered thoughts. "Irina's heart has only ever had room for herself. But you? Bleeding and injured, your sole concern was that Magda didn't see you in such a state."

Awe colors his voice, making my cheeks catch fire. He makes it sound so momentous—so unfathomable to him. That the welfare of another could supersede even someone's personal pain.

Not that I'm the only one capable of that kind of selflessness.

"You're such a good dad to her," I tell him once the internal rage has worn off, and I can objectively review his actions over the past few days. "To Magda. She adores you—"

"And you," he says almost hesitantly as if he's not sure how I'll handle that knowledge. His gaze finds me warily though he keeps most of his attention on the road. "I can't get her to stop asking when we'll go to California again."

I laugh, wincing as my left side twinges. "If my parents have their way, then probably for every major holiday at least. A few of the minor ones too. You do realize they'll be expecting us for Christmas, don't you?"

A smile softens the line of his mouth, and it is breathtaking. I sense him sneak another peek at me and his eyes brim with a hint of something that may or may not be…hope?

"Another chance to practice my gift-giving skills," he says earnestly.

"Wine for my mother. Beer for my father. And as long as you don't buy the entire toy store for Magda, I think you'll do just fine."

It's only when I see the pained edge to his expression that I realize something I don't have the heart to ask out loud. Has he ever spent a Christmas with family? With anyone other than Ena?

I make a mental note to myself to spoil him lavishly when the time comes—shower blow jobs galore. When I'm through, he'll look forward to the holiday season with a childlike sense of joy.

I'll fix all of the broken memories his childhood denied him.

Even if it kills me.

CHAPTER THIRTEEN

I t isn't until Vadim parks in an unfamiliar driveway—one barricaded behind a high stone wall and wrought iron gate—that I recognize the stout, clinical gray mansion as our new home.

In so many ways, it's not as impressive as the last.

Dour and relatively plain, it lacks the charm of the beautiful house overlooking the cove—instead, commanding a ruthlessly manicured plot of land cast in shadow by that massive wall spanning the entire perimeter. Once inside, I find the décor seriously lacking. Or, as my mother would say, "Where is the sunlight, darling?"

Without the aid of bay windows to provide said natural light, or a view of a body of water, Vadim's dour color scheme creates an almost prison-like atmosphere. One bolstered by the strange men I spot patrolling various sections of the property.

Gone are the days of Ena's out of sight, out of mind approach to security, it seems.

We find the old bodyguard himself sitting at a square table in a spacious dining room at the center of the floor plan. In addition to his typical battered leather jacket, he sports a new, unusual accessory draped around his neck—a bright pink feathery boa. Across from him sits Magda, her gaze intent on what looks to be a pink tea set arranged in between them. Carefully, Magda lifts an empty cup and places it before Ena.

"You drink it," she says as if narrating a play.

He nods. "Okay."

"And now you're poisoned," Magda says, deadpanned. "So…you have to die."

Ena shrugs. "Okay."

"That's it?" Magda purses her lips, fighting to maintain her serious frown. Despite her best attempts, a smile breaks through within seconds. "You're supposed to be *dead*," she exclaims, throwing her hands into the air. "Try making death noises or something! Play pretend. Let's go again—"

"It looks like the queen needs to work on her poisoning skills," I call from the doorway as Vadim comes up behind me.

Magda looks up, her smile unfurling in full. "Tiffy!"

"Easy, *chérie*," Vadim scolds gently as she races over and snatches my hand, tugging me to her makeshift royal tea party. "She's still very sore."

"Never too sore for palace intrigue," I say, forcing a grin as Magda ushers me into the chair beside Ena.

Once she reclaims her throne, she glances at the bodyguard, her frown apologetic. "You're not the princess anymore," she tells him, though judging from his stoic expression, I doubt the man is too heartbroken by his demotion in status.

Something far more serious seems to be on his mind. Guilt? His dark eyes shift toward me and quickly dart away. "Okay," he grunts, starting to rise to his feet.

"*But*," Magda says, making him pause mid-motion. "You can be my royal henchman. Tiffy will play the princess. Now, henchman—" Her eyes take on a gleeful, calculated gleam. "Pour the tea!"

What unfolds next is an enthralling, heart-stopping game of royal politicking during which I die five times, and Ena has to robotically endorse the maniacal musings of his mad queen. All the while, Vadim hovers in the background, his expression guarded and yet completely decipherable.

He watches his daughter, his gaze soft with a love no one would deny. He smiles when she squeals in delight during the twists and turns of her "game," and I think he's spellbound by every machination of her imagination. But pretty soon, I'm equally as enthralled by him.

As much as I try to deny it, Irina's petty jabs *did* sting. They still do—and entirely not out of concern for Vadim and his potential motives either. He may want another child one day, but so do I. *Badly,* I'm starting to realize. More than I thought I ever would.

"Pay attention, Tiffany," Magda scolds as the daylight wanes beyond the windows. Already, Vadim had to switch on an overhead lamp just to provide enough illumination for us to see by. "I've just declared you an illegitimate heir to the throne. You are banished from the kingdom, and my evil henchman has come to take you away forever! What do you do?"

I frown, thinking it over. Then I tap my chin. "I think I'll ask, why I've been banished," I decide.

But Magda's expression falls flat. "Because you're sick," she says tonelessly. "And no one wants you anymore."

I stiffen, my gaze darting around the room. Vadim's vanished—presumably to make dinner—and Ena already managed to escape his role nearly an hour ago. There's no one else left to witness the pain transforming her features, and I have a suspicion that our "game" isn't so hypothetical anymore.

If it ever were, to begin with.

"The *queen* is saying this?" I say cautiously, twisting my pink teacup between my fingers.

She nods.

"Hmm. And what about the king?"

She looks away, her expression distant. "He doesn't want you either. So the mean men come to take you away…"

My throat is dry, my heart pounding at the sheer horror I suspect I'm only getting the faintest glimpse of. Is *that* why Irina abandoned her? Because of her illness? A condition that she clearly inherited from Vadim?

Not to mention Magda's obvious fear of men built like Maxim. How had she described him? *"Is the big scary man here?"*

Did that fear also stem from Irina? Had the woman arranged for some brutal henchman to yank Magda from whatever home she'd known, dumping her at an orphanage? It would certainly explain her reaction to Maxim, and Milton to an extent.

And, that obvious atrocity aside, my worst fear is that Magda knows well enough of her mother's intentions. All along, she's known. Even more tragic, she's carried that pain believing the worst—Vadim didn't want her. Irina *told* her he didn't want her.

When I find my voice again, I clear my throat to banish any traces of anger. "You know what I'd do?" I set my teacup aside, fold my hands and lean forward, forcing her to meet my gaze head-on. "I'd tell the queen to shove it. I am a princess, and I have more powers than she could ever dream of."

She raises an eyebrow, her lips quirked downward. "Like what?"

"Like…" *Make this good, Tiffy.* "I'm charming, and pretty, and I'm damn good at shopping. I'll scour the whole damn world and hunt down a cure. Then I'll use my wits to secure a lifetime supply of it. Cursed or not, I'm stronger for it either way."

She wrinkles her nose, unconvinced.

"*And,*" I add, thinking fast. My eyes settle on a tuft of white centered on her lap, barely visible above the table. "I know that I'm never alone in my adventures. Because the king *does* want me—more than anything else in the world. In fact, he sent me a protector to always look out for me when I'm afraid, or lonely. And since the evil queen is a liar, I'll know that he must have been cursed too. That's why he isn't there," I add as she shifts, her fingers creeping toward It, burying in his plush fur. "And that when he wakes up, he'll find me. He will always find me, no matter what."

"Why?" she asks, her voice so hollow that I nearly lunge across the table to grab one of her hands, gripping it tightly.

"Because he loves *you,*" I tell her so fiercely, my voice cracks. "He will always love you. Always."

Silently, she wrangles her fingers from mine. Then, she slips from her chair and scurries around the table. Before I have the sense to steel myself, she's climbing onto my lap, burying her face in the crook of my shoulder.

"Oh, honey..." Without a thought given for my stitches, I wrap my arms around her, squeezing as tight as I'm able to. "And when the king does find you, he'll have a crazy bitch girlfriend who will stab the queen's eyes out if she ever comes near you again. You hear me?"

She says nothing, but I rock her in silence, inhaling the scent of her hair and the fruity shampoo Vadim must have bought for her. I stroke my fingers through her braided curls and reassure her in every way I can that my words are more than just a boastful fairytale.

I will personally fight to make them true.

AFTER PUTTING MAGDA TO BED, I'm limping when I finally creep into a master suite—admittedly nowhere near as spacious or appealing as the old one. There I find Vadim hovering near the bed. The second he spots me, he's by my side, lifting me into his arms.

"You've overexerted yourself," he scolds, carrying me over to the bed. "Lie still. I need to check if you've broken any sutures."

I pout and submit to his inspection. With utmost care, he strips my clothes, leaving them on the floor and manipulates me until I'm lying face down, his fingers gingerly peeling back my bandages.

"No damage," he declares after a moment. "But, I'm inclined to put you on mandatory bed rest."

I lift my head hopefully. "Sexy bedrest?"

He shakes his head, stroking down my lower back in a way that inspires thoughts of *anything* but resting. "I'm afraid not," he says, contradicting the desire conveyed by every swipe of his fingers. "You will have to go without until your wounds heal. That is final."

"Is that so?" I play dirty and reach out, inching toward the front of his slacks.

"Very final," he insists, groaning as I cup him, finding him straining the tailored fabric.

I'm not the only one who will go without, it seems. Still teasing him, I flex my fingers, watching his expression shift as he turns onto his side, facing me.

"Where did you go after dinner?" I ask cautiously. Once mine and Magda's tea party ended, he'd served us another one of his delicious homemade meals and then vanished, leaving us to play a round of monopoly—during which I got my ass thoroughly kicked.

He frowns and captures my rebellious hand, moving it to settle on his chest. "Something you said piqued my curiosity," he admits. "I made another round of calls to my contacts in the hopes of finding out more about Magda's origins. Anything I can use to—" He breaks off, his jaw clenched, but I can guess the words he's holding back.

He's tracking down anything he can use against Irina. At least in her legal battle if she persists in her quest to block his custody.

"Any luck?" I ask hopefully, but he shakes his head.

"No. It's like she appeared from thin air. And I'll be honest…" He rakes one of his hands through his hair, sighing in exasperation. "Hiram was the one behind most of the arrangements in those early days when I was alerted to her existence. I still don't know many of the details. I doubt Magda remembers much, either—though how can I ask her to? She was so young."

Meeting his gaze, I flex my fingers over his chest. "I think Magda remembers her," I tell him. "I think… I think she's *afraid* of her. Terrified. I can't really explain it in much detail, but I think Irina abandoned her the second she became diagnosed with diabetes."

Or, in her twisted, sick opinion—*flawed.*

"It's possible," he grates, his eyes flashing. "But what makes you say that?"

"Call it a hunch," I say wistfully. "Or, to be more accurate, fairytale logic. You know how Magda likes to play games of the queen and the princess? What if they aren't games to her at all?"

And one overarching theme becomes painfully apparent the more I think on it. *You've been poisoned,* she declared to preface almost every one of her "tea parties." *Poisoned by the queen…*

Could Irina have drugged her? Or, given her a drink of some kind that her childish brain interpreted as much. I'm so lost in the thought that I barely notice I'm in

Vadim's arms until his voice drips into my ear, sensually low.

"I say that Magdalene's past is the past," he growls, his tone both stern and husky. "I will strive to make her future so bright she looks back on any prior memories as a faint shadow. A beautiful future. One in which she has everything she could ever ask for or need—while her parents are forced to sneak away every now and again to indulge in their filthiest desires."

I swallow hard. Parents? Not to mention the way the man can utter the word "filthy." An answering ache resonates down my spine, and I pout. No fair.

"Where will we sneak to?" I ask him, reaching up to run my fingers through his abused, wild curls.

His lips twitch thoughtfully. "I may have to declare my renewed interest in the club," he suggests, nuzzling at the nape of my neck. "I'm envisioning a private suite filled with those apparatuses I ordered for you."

My toes curl. I could squeal in excitement, and the potential of healing has never seemed better. "Well then, you better get building," I tell him, slapping his chest playfully. "Though I insist on watching. But, that means you may have to make up with your brother, if only to prevent the off chance of you killing each other should you enter the same vicinity."

His eyes darken at the prospect, though I figure I'm more amused than alarmed at the display. He reminds me almost of a stubborn child, refusing to end a grudge too soon, if only to salvage his pride.

"I once promised I'd smooth things over between you two, didn't I?" I point out. Poor, naïve past Tiffy. She had no fucking clue. "What happened between you and him? Maxim?"

That muscle in his jaw twitches, his gaze drifting away from me—at the last second, however, something draws him back. "We grew up in hell," he states, encasing me in his arms. "But for whatever reason, Maxim showed me kindness more than once." His voice is gruff, as if the confession physically hurts him to voice. "But unlike you, he didn't boldly acknowledge his actions. It's more like…he strived to punish me for them. For wanting to reciprocate them. As a result, we've spent almost thirty fucking years spitting on each other. I don't think even he understands why."

It's such a raw admission from him. One I don't take lightly. Bracing my hand over his chest, I risk planting a kiss over his heart, letting my breath warm that precious space.

"I will *always* acknowledge you," I tell him. "Always. As long as you keep me well supplied with sex—but it won't be transactional. What you give, I will gladly reciprocate."

He laughs in that beautiful, haunting way. "And what you wish, you shall receive."

I nestle against him, lulled into a daze by the thrum of his heartbeat. I know that—despite all of our pillow talk—

there's so much more between us awaiting to be addressed. Nuances, we need to put into words. Boundaries that need adjusting.

But, as I allow him to redress me and then drift off, I have to admit that I'm more than looking forward to it.

Each grueling, sweaty, sensual bit of "negotiation."

CHAPTER FOURTEEN

The door to our room flies open with a bang, rousing me from a light sleep and making Vadim lurch upright, wrenching the covers back. His rigid posture conveys power—a desire to protect so vicious I'm awed in the face of it.

But just as quickly he transforms as our intruder makes herself known in frantic little steps, her braids askew, her bear dangling from one hand.

"*Chérie?*" He reaches for her hesitantly, his brows drawn. "What's wrong—"

"I don't like it here," she declares, lunging onto the bed. As I watch in shock, she squirms in between us, curling into a ball, her face buried in the body of her bear. "I hate this place. I want to go home."

"Home?" Vadim asks, as if horribly confused by the prospect. He reaches out, stroking her back. When she doesn't recoil, he tentatively braces his arm around her, and almost instantly, she's burrowing into his chest, her tiny limbs shaking.

"*Home*," she insists plaintively, in a tone I've never heard her use. "I want to go home! With my pony. I want my old room. I don't like it here!"

"Alright. Alright…" He relents with little resistance, petting through her hair. His expression is puzzled—confused even. As if he isn't quite sure of the allure that would drive a child to his arms in the middle of the night. Or why she might instinctively love the home he labored to prepare for her. But I think he's catching on quickly.

His eyes meet mine, alight with the beginnings of a life-altering revelation. With Magda in between us, I risk reaching over her to stroke his chest and nod in encouragement.

"Super dad," I mouth to him, much to his surprise.

Slowly, he settles her tiny figure against him, cradling her carefully, his gaze awestruck. I realize now that—not even in his most optimistic of potential futures—did he envision a moment like this. One so sweet, *I* almost feel like the intruder…

Until Magda hooks her tiny hand around my wrist as if sensing the possibility that I might pull away. I surrender to her grasp, thanking my lucky stars that Vadim and I are at least clothed during this midnight intrusion.

It seems our forced abstinence worked out for the best, in the end.

And, I suspect judging from Vadim's wistful gaze, better than he could have ever dared to hope.

DESPITE VADIM's prior intention to sell the house, "home" turns out to be pretty much as we'd left it. As I peer into the foyer, I have a mental image of him studiously overseeing a team of movers, ensuring they replaced everything in the same exact position—minus any bloodstains in the kitchen or signs of a psychotic blond.

Even so, I'm surprised by just how strongly a sense of dread paralyzes me as I linger on the threshold. Especially considering that I had no problem entering the home I shared with Jim after he *figuratively* stabbed me in the back.

But now?

My hands shake, and breathing becomes a struggle. If I'm honest with myself, I know exactly why I'm on edge. It's not fear of Irina that makes me linger in the fresh air, unable to enter those four walls. It's the crushing reality of who might never come to exist to fill this home at all. The rooms beside Magda's that might never gain an occupant. The wonderful, albeit lonely life she'll have as an only child—spoken from experience.

Unless, of course, her father remarried someone else capable of expanding his family tenfold.

"Are you alright?" Vadim wonders, his gaze intense with concern, his hand on my lower back.

Forcing a smile, I nod. "Yeah… Besides, it looks like someone's happy."

Oblivious to my discomfort, Magda tears through the lower level, a whirlwind of energy. Her joy gives me the courage necessary to cross the threshold, and I find myself caught in her wake, laughing as she eagerly unpacks her clothes in her room.

"Can I go play with Ainsley?" she asks Vadim once our things are put away, and we've had lunch at the dining room table. "Please?" She bats her eyelashes, playing his heartstrings like a fiddle. I almost feel bad for the man.

Helpless, he looks to me, but I shrug innocently, leaving him to drown.

"I…"

"Ena will take," a firm voice pitches in before the bodyguard himself marches into the kitchen. "And there is cake. In fridge." He looks at me, his gaze conveying something unspoken that catches me off guard. I vaguely remember Vadim mentioning something about a special chocolate cake Ena sometimes bakes. Dare I hope for a truce?

The old bodyguard turns away before I can be sure, shuffling to the sliding glass door leading to the terrace.

"Come," he grunts, his tone unusually soft, directed at the tiny figure leaping to her feet.

"Really?" Magda skips toward him, clutching It to her chest. No one would ever know that a horrific attack took place in this very room just a few days ago. At least, if it weren't for the way she's starting to carry her bear almost every waking moment. She's already worn at It's newly sewn head, and I'm sure he'll wind up decapitated again before long.

And yet, she beams as she glances at Vadim. "Can we? Please?"

Sighing, he gives a nod of approval. "Alright."

She races off, her loyal henchman in tow. The second they slip beyond view, I rise from my chair and slink toward Vadim. Given the fact that I'm still very much in pain—my muscles stiff with disuse—I wind up lurching toward him more than anything sensual. Still, he reaches for me, settling me gingerly onto his lap.

"We should have some alone time," I declare, pressing my lips to the side of his throat. Against his flesh, I murmur, "I declare our brief abstinence officially over."

He chuckles, his hands on my hips, his expression pained once I slip my hand between us and cup the front of his slacks. "You've barely healed," he points out as I flinch the second I strain my side too much.

Shrugging him off, I persist, rocking my palm against him until he groans in capitulation. "Be naughty with me for just a moment," I beg, shamelessly licking a path down to his collar bone. "I'll even let you have a slice of my cake after. I promise it'll be worth it..."

"Not if I cause you any pain, it won't," he warns, always the stoic. Still, when I start to work my fingers into the clasp of his pants, he stands, lifting me in his arms. Before I regain my bearings, he carries me to the center island. Dazed, I grip the edge of the marble surface as he sinks to his knees, cursing under his breath.

I'm not the only one impatient, it seems.

"Don't move," he commands as his fingers creep beneath the waistband of my "healing attire"—a pair of his sweats. I shiver in anticipation, my eyelids threatening to shut as his heat bastes my belly and below.

A true torturer, he takes his time, unwrapping me as meticulously as one would a cherished present. I can't prevent a moan from escaping my throat as I'm fully bared to him, deliciously exposed.

With his gaze fixated on my flesh, he grunts in appreciation. "And to think," he murmurs, more to himself than to me. "I was almost foolish enough to risk losing this…"

This. A prize that he claims with a single, devastating stroke of his thumb, making me lurch into his touch, a gasp breaking loose.

"Beautiful." He sounds like a repentant sinner, more than ready to prostrate himself before an altar in a quest for redemption. And damn, does he endeavor to earn every ounce of mercy…

I gasp as his lips nudge my inner thigh, swiftly inching downward, forcing me to cling to the counter. As a result, I wind up opening myself to him further—a vulnerability that he eagerly takes advantage of. Soft, his tongue feathers over my piercing first in teasing, slight swipes. Followed by his lips. His teeth.

Everything.

I whine, gripping the counter to the point of pain, too far gone to feel the discomfort in my back as I arch into his embrace. Holy crap, he's gotten too damn good at this since the last time. Far too soon, I'm nearing the brink, drowning in the quick, searing glances he throws my way in between every tasting lick and nibble.

Like I'm his alone…

To consume.

Own.

Destroy.

When my orgasm finally arrives with the strength of a freight train slamming into me, I moan shamelessly, my voice echoing throughout the room. The only way to save face is to fist my hand in his hair and tug, drawing him to his feet. Still holding him captive, I spin, switching positions.

Taking care not to rip my sutures, I sink down carefully, relying on his touch to steady me. Then I impatiently tug his pants down and eagerly return the favor.

"*Merde!*" He hisses as I flick the end of his piercing with my tongue and suckle, swallowing him whole, holding his gaze as I do so.

His eyes flicker, unfocused, and heavy-lidded. One flick of my tongue, and he's experiencing another revelation, after revelation, after *revelation*. Before me, the man is born anew, empowered with a lifetime's worth of pleasure he's spent so long denying himself.

Soon, he's rocking into me, grating out various broken bits of French. I make a mental note to do everything I can to learn the language as I suck, sending him spiraling into his own release. Spent, I lean against his thigh, stroking patterns into his perfect flesh. It's so easy to just coexist with him, even in the aftermath of such a filthy, intimate act.

There is no shame between us. No more boundaries. Just silence, and understanding, and a peace so heavy it hurts.

And to think, I've spent so damn long denying myself of this. Will I let a bitch like Irina barge in and take this fragile calm away?

Hell no.

But a part of me warns that I may not have a choice…

"Shit!" Vadim jolts to attention, gently helping me to my feet, before scrambling to adjust his pants and wash his hands in the sink. Confused, I copy him, even as my brain struggles to process what set him off.

"What's wrong?" I follow the line of his gaze and quickly discover the source of his alarm.

A tiny figure races across the terrace—but gone is her exuberant energy from earlier. Tears spill down her cheeks, her cries audible even before Vadim lurches to the door and wrenches it open. He has her in his arms in an instant, and as I follow him out, I spot two figures hurrying from the woods in her wake.

One is a huffing Ena, his gaze alert despite the obvious exertion of having run after a seven-year-old.

By his side is a tiny blond, her expression constricted with concern. Spotting me, she sighs in exasperation. "He didn't mean to! I tried to tell her that he only *looks* scary—"

"What's wrong, *ma chérie?*" Vadim murmurs to Magda, stroking her hair. "What happened?"

She shakes her head, hiding her face in the crook of his shoulder. Frowning, he glances at Ena, who shrugs.

"I know." With a maturity well beyond her young years, the smaller girl steps forward, her gaze focused on her friend. "Max came home," she explains. "I tried to tell her that he only looks scary. Come back, and you'll see, Mags. Promise! I bet he'll even play tea party with us if we ask him to—"

"No! I don't want to go away!" I barely recognize the childish whimper as belonging to Magda. She's trembling, her chest heaving with choking, gasping sobs. "I don't. Don't let me," she wails, clinging to Vadim, who looks stricken in the face of her fear. "Don't let him take me—"

"No one is taking you anywhere," Vadim insists. He cuts his gaze to Ena, radiating authority. "Secure the perimeter."

The man nods and marches off. "Yes, Sir."

Left behind is Ainsley, her bottom lip trembling, her eyes welling. Before another disaster can ensue, I step forward and gingerly link my hand in hers.

"I'll take her home," I say, starting off in the direction of Maxim's property before Vadim can argue.

I glance over my shoulder to find him carrying Magda into the house, speaking to her calmly all the while.

"I'm sorry," Ainsley whines, her nostrils flaring. "He's not mean, honest!"

"I believe you, honey." Though internally, I'm questioning a little girl's interpretation of "mean" where a man as imposing as Maxim is concerned. Halfway to the house, we're met by a panting figure who races from the underbrush.

"Thank God!" Francesca exclaims, clutching at her chest. She races to her sister's side, bundling the girl in her arms. Despite my best efforts, Ainsley is crying soon enough, and my heart breaks for both girls for very different reasons.

"Mind if I join you?" I ask Francesca as she starts back toward her house. She looks alarmed and glances warily over her shoulder—but eventually, she nods. "Sure."

She comforts her sister the entire trip back, and the girl sports the beginnings of a smile by the time the house looms above. A towering figure stands waiting to greet her near the edge of the terrace.

She squirms from her sister's arms and races over, tugging insistently on the pantleg of a man most would eagerly avoid. Dressed in black from head to toe, he stands with his arms crossed, his blond hair streaming loosely behind him, his gaze on me.

"I'm sorry," Ainsley tells him, her voice hitching. "I don't know why she got so scared."

But I do. Stepping forward, I force myself to meet the man's steely gaze. "Can we talk?"

From the corner of my eye, I see Francesca stiffen, but Maxim? He eyes me for so long I nearly sway with relief when he finally nods and turns into the house. Inside, I'm once again reminded of the glaring similarities—and differences—between the two brothers.

This house has a softness to it Vadim's lacks. Perhaps it lies in the pops of color sprinkled throughout the relatively muted color scheme—hints of red, yellow, and blue in the form of pillows or throw blankets or potted plants. Or the scattered toys that hint toward a bustling family life. Or it could just be that Maxim, as foreboding as he seems, dominating this spacious room, has settled into a relationship that may or may not have softened some of his harsher edges. At least where Ainsley is concerned. Maybe even Magdalene?

Clearing my throat, I face him. *Here goes nothing.* "Vadim needs you," I blurt in a rush. "Now, more than ever. I don't know what's between you two." Something tells me that Maxim's tale of their feud may differ slightly from the one Vadim told. The details don't matter. "He needs you. Your niece, needs you."

He flinches as something unreadable crosses over his dark, unsettling eyes. "Niece?" He grunts as his rumbling voice echoes through the room. "You believe that?"

"I know it," I counter swiftly. Crossing my arms, I level him with an eyebrow cocked, ignoring the fire searing through my shoulder. "Do you really want to deny that? You can look at her and see for yourself. And you can see that they both need you."

"Is that so?" He lumbers to a far corner of the room, turning his back to me. Without the distracting intensity of facing him head-on, I'm left to inspect the rest of his bulk, adding up more clues to cement the brothers' strange idiosyncrasies. Their panache for tailored, Italian-style suits for one. Maxim's is black, and yet despite wearing it, there's a primal intensity to his form that doesn't portray quite the level of icy businessman Vadim can. This man looks less business and more...not legal. I recall a hint of a conversation I heard between Vadim and his friend Milton. I'm more convinced than ever—Maxim—much in the way Irina hinted about Vadim—doesn't play by anyone's rules.

Hopefully, not Irina's.

"Someone is trying to hurt him," I say in response to his obvious skepticism. Vadim once joked that Maxim probably thought he was Magdalene in a child-sized suit, and I'm starting to realize that statement might not have been entirely an exaggeration. "Someone is trying to hurt his *daughter.* Does that mean anything to you? Or do you enjoy having little girls run from you in terror?"

He grimaces, and I have my answer. *No.*

"Vadim may need you when the time comes," I add, taking a step toward him. "If you give a damn at all, you'll answer the door when he does."

"Oh?" Maxim scoffs, whirling to face me. I assume some form of an insult is poised on his tongue when he stiffens, his eyes homing in on my left hip. "You're bleeding," he says.

Shit. Sure enough, without the overriding concern for Ainsley or Magda clouding my senses, I can feel the fiery pain ripping down my left side in full force now. A glance downward reveals a splotch of scarlet seeping through the gray fabric of my borrowed sweatshirt.

After trudging over a mile through the woods, it's not surprising to assume I may have ripped some of my stitches.

"Well..." Wincing, I start for the back door, praying to God that I don't track blood all over the floor. "I'll be leaving—"

"No." The big man rocks on his heels as if wrestling with indecision. Finally, he sighs and cocks his head. "Lucius!"

As if conjured from thin air, the kind, older gentleman, who I'm beginning to suspect may be a saint, appears near the doorway leading to the foyer. "Sir?"

Maxim nods curtly in my direction and then marches for the terrace. "Take her home."

"Yes, Sir." Lucius beckons me forward only to pale when he sees the blood staining my ensemble.

"It's just a scratch," I insist with a faint grin.

Minutes later, I'm racing up the front path and barreling into Vadim's house. I find him in the process of leaving Magda's room, closing the door softly behind him. From beyond his shoulder, I see her asleep on her bed, clutching It to her chest with one hand, while her other stuffed toys form a protective perimeter around her. Courtesy of her father, I suspect.

His eyes meet mine, brimming with a tenderness that makes my chest tighten. At least until he notices the blood and yanks me into his arms. Dazed, I find myself being lowered onto the bed seconds later, wrenched to lie face down as he draws my sweatshirt up.

"Damn it," he hisses in disgust. "You've ripped them."

I sigh dejectedly, pouting. "Are you going to play sexy doctor and stitch me back up?"

"No," he says without an ounce of humor. Rising to his full height, he draws a cell phone from his pocket. "This is well beyond my skill set."

A hint of unease seeps in at the thought of being poked and prodded by a real doctor. "What if I promise never to get up again?" I say mournfully.

"Nice try." He shoots me a stern look before dialing a number into his phone and bringing the device to his ear. "I need your help," he says to someone I suspect most definitely isn't Maxim. "Preferably now."

CHAPTER FIFTEEN

As it turns out, he called Milton. The man must be a doctor of some kind because he stitches me back up in no time, but with a stern warning as he packs up his supplies. "Rip these, and you'll have a nasty set of scars to look forward to."

Adequately cowed, I lie flat as the two men exit the bedroom, heading downstairs.

And the second they're out of earshot, I slither onto the floor and practically crawl to the mouth of the stairs, straining my ears to listen.

"So, I'm beginning to suspect that you *didn't* cause Maxim's headaches in Moscow," Milton declares, his voice drifting from the direction of the kitchen. "The attack was too vicious. Even you aren't *that* bloody ruthless. He managed to salvage what he could of the supply, but the setback will take months to fully recover from. I suspect that was the aim all along—he'll be distracted for a while, at least."

"Good," Vadim says with chilling vitriol. "Maybe the bastard will finally realize that I'm not the only Boogeyman lurking in the shadows."

"Trust me," Milton insists with a harsh laugh, "he is well aware of that. Anatoli is still 'lurking' as you put it. Even now, I bet the old fucker is itching to get back into the game. Especially after losing Sevastyn."

"Dear old grandfather?" Vadim says with a hostility that makes me suspect he doesn't cherish this particular family member the way I do my old "Pop-Pop." "I will admit I've left the old bastard alive solely because he torments little Maxi so damn well. And, perhaps I'd been arrogant enough to assume that, with Sevastyn dead, he couldn't get up to much trouble on his own."

The viciousness in his tone is chilling—a reminder of the cold aspects of his personality the fatherly tendencies in him obscure so well.

"Enough," Milton scolds. "Let me tell you why I'm here. You remember when you told me about your problem?"

"Irina," Vadim hisses. "You've tracked her?"

"Someone who goes by that name anyway, yes. You won't like what I've learned, though," he adds gruffly. "Especially where your daughter is concerned."

Vadim sucks in a breath, and I imagine his eyes taking on that cold, ruthless gleam I've wisely grown wary of. "Tell me."

"She's a prominent player in the Circle. What's left of it, anyway. You mentioned Sevastyn? Well, without him at its head, the trade's been all but splintered," Milton says, his voice wracked with utter loathing.

And my stomach turns. *Circle. Trade.* Do they mean the horrific crimes Vadim suffered as a child? A slave trade.

"Your Irina's found herself scrambling for territory," Milton continues. "Though, her come-up was relatively quick, to begin with. The bitch got her hands on a large sum of money in a fairly short timeframe a few years back. Now, she runs her own ring—not with children, but women. All unwilling, exploited, or sold, nonetheless. She trades them to the highest bidder and has made quite the name for herself, mainly using aliases, mind you, but my contacts are clever. I'm sure it's her. She prefers to operate primarily under the name 'The Madam.'"

"*Fils de pute!* Son of a bitch," Vadim snarls. A faint thud resonates throughout the house as if he slammed his fist against a firm surface like a table. Or the wall. "And she has the nerve to seek me out? To toy with *me*. I'll kill her—"

"You may not have to," Milton suggests. "She's made plenty of enemies for herself. Give me time, and I'm sure I can spin the right kind of trap. Hell, you might be able to sell *her* for a profit."

My heart stops. Given the man's grim tone, something tells me that wasn't a figurative statement.

"Don't joke," Vadim counters, and I manage to breathe again. He sounds disgusted by the suggestion, at least. Or is that pure rage coloring his voice? "My only concern is Magdalene. I won't let that bitch harm her—"

"Neither will I," Milton swears, his voice hard. "If you're antsy, I was able to track down a lead on the orphanage she came from. Ask around, and you may find more information. The identity of who alerted you to her, at least… Because here is the part you really won't like—two years ago, rumor is 'The Madam' was looking to traffic a little girl. Caused quite the stir if you can imagine. Her aim wasn't the trade, mind you. Just the black-market adoption circuit—"

"Like that makes it any fucking better!" Vadim's voice breaks. He sounds horrified. Gutted. It takes everything I have—and the fact that I'm terrified to stand up—not to run down to him, eavesdropping be damned. "I was hoping the bitch had given her up out of…I don't know, *love*? For Magdalene's sake. How can a child face the fact that their own mother wanted to sell her like chattel?"

"*We* did," Milton says in a tone that makes me suspect he too has a traumatic past behind him. One comparable to Vadim's. Or worse. "And we fucking survived, didn't we? So will she. She has you. And if you want this information, maybe you can find out who did rescue her. And why."

He leaves the offer in the air, and by the time the two men return to the foyer, I'm not sure whether Vadim has accepted the information or not.

As Milton leaves, I slither back toward the bedroom as quickly as I dare. I nearly make it to the bed when a set of heavy footsteps breaches the threshold, and a disapproving voice rings out, "Caught you."

"Damn it." I risk glancing at him, my eyes bug-wide, my lower lip protruding. Somehow, it's easy to suppress the horror of what I've heard. Too easy. Denial. "*Please* don't punish me. Too hard. We can start with a spanking."

"Insolent witch." He cracks a smile despite the concern twisting his features into a haggard, grim expression that tugs at my heart like nothing else. Crossing to me, he takes me into his arms but doesn't set me down right away. His eyes stare into mine, demanding an answer to a question he doesn't ask out loud just yet.

Did I overhear?

And if so…

Am I bothered by what I've learned?

I match his silence with my own nonverbal answer. Arching toward him, I let our lips meet. He stiffens in response, his lips parting. The second they do, I loop my hand around his neck, extending the kiss as much as I dare. When he finally pulls back, I'm panting, both thrilled and wary.

"I heard everything," I confess, my stomach heavy as those dark revelations loom overhead.

He sighs, averting his gaze from me. "And?"

"I want you to explain it to me," I say, surprised by how calm I sound, all things considered.

That muscle in his jaw twitches as he sets me down onto the edge of the bed. Then he starts to pace, his hands sinking into his hair. "Explain. The supposed mother of my child trades in women the same way *we* were traded. She wanted to sell her own daughter. And I didn't know a damn thing until someone literally dropped the news of her existence into my lap. At every turn, I seem to keep failing her—"

"You haven't," I insist, my voice breaking. He's distant again, glowering into his past, swaying with the weight of it all. "You're angry," I add, stating the obvious. In some ways, it helps to say as much out loud. To acknowledge his obvious disgust at these dark, twisted things. Even though, from his scattered conversations with Milton, I sense that he's more familiar with these horrific aspects of the world than I can even imagine.

Irina all but taunted as much.

"You should follow-up on the information Milton offered you," I say softly, skirting the larger question of his real identity. For now. "For your sake."

Because he needs this, I realize. Answers—even if they're offered on a fragile bit of thread. If anything, he needs them for Magda. Her peace of mind. Her sanity.

But as stubborn as he is, I don't think he can admit it out loud just yet. So he sinks onto the bed, reaching for me. Again, our lips collide, his tongue stealing deep. I grasp at him, surrendering myself to every searching kiss. Every groan he utters into my open mouth. Soon enough, we wind up tangled together, though he makes sure that I'm on top of him, lying on my stomach so as to not risk my stitches.

Groaning, he nuzzles the nape of my neck, smoothing his hands down my hips. "I will think about your suggestion," he finally says. "It would require traveling upstate. Arrangements would have to be made, appointments organized." He frowns at the prospect, and I can't tell what he's decided upon when he sighs in defeat. "Give me a few days to decide."

"Okay." I seal the promise with a kiss and rest my face against his chest, listening to his heartbeat. "I'm sorry for spying. But," I add in my own defense, "I was just being a good fake wife, after all."

"Don't be," he says, deceptively soft. "Because when you heal, I fully intend to punish you."

I flinch, utterly thrilled by the threat. "Then add another crime to the tally, good Sir, because…" I suck in a breath and sneak a peek at his face. He looks so beautiful, so calm. I savor the expression selfishly before I confess, "I spoke to Maxim."

He hisses out a breath, his nostrils flaring. Anger, yes—but nowhere near the extent I might have expected.

"Did he scare her purposefully?" he asks in a tone so murderous my toes curl.

"No," I say quickly. "He didn't. But… I think I know why she might have reacted to seeing him the way she did."

The same way she's reacted to him since their very first—albeit traumatic for Magda—meeting.

"Because of Irina?" Vadim questions coldly, his eyes fixated on something in the distance. Years away, I suspect, far in the past. "I'm sure she kept goons around who frightened her. She kept begging me not to let her be taken from me —" He breaks off, scowling, and I almost regret breaching the topic at all.

"But you won't," I say confidently. "You won't let anyone frighten her ever again."

"You're right," he agrees, pressing his lips against my forehead. "Because I aim to cut off the source of her fears. Right at the fucking head."

I cringe at the ferocity in his voice—not that I can blame him for the violent imagery.

Such a fate would be a fitting end for Irina's figurative role as Magda's mad queen.

CHAPTER SIXTEEN

We must fall asleep with our limbs entwined, still fully dressed, because I'm startled to awareness when Vadim's arms stiffen around me as the door to the room swings open. Once again, we've been interrupted by a small figure who doesn't wait for an invitation.

Instead, she lurches onto the bed and burrows her way in between us, seeking out the safety of Vadim's arms, which I'd been enjoying until now. As a result, I'm forced to make room as she slithers in to take my place.

Her father, however, has already switched into dad mode. "What's wrong?" he murmurs to her, so gently that even I'm soothed by his tone. "I thought you liked the house?"

"I do," Magda insists against his chest. "But it's too dark in my room."

I raise an eyebrow. "Too dark?"

"We can turn on the lights, *chérie*," Vadim offers. His confusion matches mine.

"No," Magda whines the second he starts to pull away. "I don't want to."

The independent girl who first came here a few weeks ago had no problem sleeping on her own. Though, back then, she wasn't reminded of the aspects of her past that still obviously scare her. This new aversion, I suspect, has everything to do with what happened with Maxim. Whatever memories seeing him triggered, haunt her badly enough that she'll risk her pride just to find safety in her father's arms.

It would be heart-warming if it weren't so tragic. I can't stop myself from stroking my hand down her back, sensing her trembling beneath her nightgown.

"It's dark," she repeats, still clinging to Vadim, her body curled into a stubborn ball. "I want to sleep *here*."

She doesn't bother asking, not that the man holding her would ever have the heart to refuse her if she did. Sighing, I crack a smile and shift over to make room.

"I guess it's okay for tonight," I say.

Always prepared, Vadim repositions himself to somehow embrace us both on either side of him. Like leeches, we nestle into his warmth, draining him of all the comfort he has to offer.

And, he seems to possess more than enough for us both. When morning finally comes, he disentangles from our mass of limbs long enough to return minutes later with breakfast food piled on a tray and a jug of orange juice.

Sensing a shift in the mood, we eat in silence and wind up lounging in the master bed, sandwiched together—Vadim in the middle—with Magda and me on opposite ends. And, of course, It somewhere in between. For the first time, I realize that the bedroom even has a flat-screen television affixed to the far wall, defaulted to the news station. After flipping through the channels, we settle on watching cartoons and promptly vegetate the rest of the day.

The time spent in this way reveals a strange new aspect of our dynamic. The doting father. The clingy daughter. The pseudo-mother popping pain pills every few hours just to stay coherent. When evening comes, Vadim retreats again to bring back pizza, and we only leave at various intervals to get ready for bed—him assisting Magda—before we all wind up back in the master suite.

This time, she doesn't even bother to give an excuse before burrowing beneath the blankets, not that Vadim or I ask for one. With her nestled in between us, we fall asleep in the middle of a show about rambunctious undersea critters and wake up to very much the same routine. Again, the cycle repeats the next day.

And the next.

By the end of the week, I'm forced to confront a horrible realization as I wake up with Magda's foot in my stomach and Vadim's breath fanning over my forehead. We've barely left the room, let alone the house in days. Our only outside interaction at all came in the form of Milton stopping by to remove my stitches.

Otherwise, we've been on an island unto ourselves—and I think Magda's fingers are starting to leave permanent marks on Vadim's forearms.

There is no dancing around it—we haven't just been indulging in the lazy inclinations of a seven-year-old. We've been *coddling* her. In essence, we've become *those* people. One of those weird families so fearful of the outside world and the danger it may bring that they collapse in on themselves. Eventually, we'll have Magda encased in bubble wrap and only leave the house to fetch the mail. Though, with Ena around, we may not even get to do that.

Somewhere during Vadim rousing himself like a zombie to trudge down to the kitchen, I come to a conclusion.

"Rise and shine, princess!" I ruffle Magda's hair until she blinks up at me, deliriously innocent and half asleep. "You too, Sir." I slap Vadim on the ass as he rises to his feet.

Then I shimmy to the edge of the mattress and tentatively stand. After days of being damn near bedridden, I have to sway just to regain my balance. Once I do, I'm surprised to find my left side feels marginally better. Enough that I can march into the bathroom, leaving my bedmates staring after me. When I emerge—having brushed my teeth and run my wet fingers through my hair—I snap to command their attention.

"Hop to it! We're going riding."

Vadim raises an eyebrow. "Do you want to injure yourself again?" he asks, ever the spoilsport.

Undeterred, I wiggle my arms and only wince a little. "I'm nearly healed," I say. "As long as we go slow, I'll be fine. And the fresh air will do us all some good."

He doesn't look fully convinced. Nonetheless, he copies my lead, heading toward the closet.

But he's not the only one needing persuading, it seems.

"Why?" Magda wonders, her voice bordering on a whine. With It against her chest, she burrows beneath the blankets and promptly disappears beneath them, she's so tiny in such a large bed. "I don't want to," she declares, her voice muffled.

"Sure, you do." I shuffle forward and yank the blankets from over her, revealing her pouting at me with an intensity that makes my heart soften and melt.

"Can't we watch more cartoons?" she asks plaintively. "I don't *want* to go outside."

Her eyes flicker in the direction of a certain neighbor's property, and I sigh in exasperation. The entire display is almost enough to make me give in. Almost…

But then I envision myself as a helicopter mom with badly permed hair leading Magda around by a child leash and promptly change my mind.

"No. Come on, you love riding," I say, doing my best to cajole her. Judging from her stubborn frown, it's going to be an uphill battle. "You can show me how to ride Magnus," I add, naming the horse Vadim procured for me. "I haven't even gotten to test him out yet."

"And," Vadim pitches in, returning from the closet fully dressed in a pair of jodhpurs and a black T-shirt, "we can race her on my Zzazza. With you as my copilot, I'm sure we'll win, even at a slower pace."

I look at him in mock indignation. "You're on! What do you say, Mags?"

She eyes us warily, mulling it over. Finally, she crawls off the bed and marches toward her room, her head down, her shoulders slumped in defeat. I follow and make a show out of rifling through her riding outfits—mysteriously, it seems at least ten more sets have joined the first one Vadim bought her since the last time she's ridden—settling on a bold, scarlet jacket, white blouse, and black pants.

The clothing tempts her when even my best jokes don't. She's still brooding during our quick breakfast and the entire walk out to the stable. I almost fear I've made a mistake, but the second she spots the face of her pony peeking eagerly from over the door of her stall, her entire face brightens.

By the time the three of us are out on the trail—me riding my black stallion Magnus, with Vadim and Magda astride his beautiful Zzazza—I have no more doubts. We needed this, all of us. Fresh air. Peace. The tranquility we find in exploring the furthest reaches of the property by horseback.

Vadim picked his property well. It spans way more ground than one would think when observing the space solely from the house. Alone, he commands a good bit of the waterfront and the surrounding woods. A series of old paths lend themselves well to becoming decent trails with a bit of work to flesh them out.

Something even Magda picks up on. "Could I ride my pony here one day with Ainsley?" she asks midway in. It's the first complete sentence she's said since leaving the house, but her expression has brightened at least. Gone is the surly frown, and her eyes gleam as she looks back to find Vadim nodding.

"Of course, *chérie*. I'm sure you could."

Content with that answer, she settles against his chest. By the time we return to the house, she's almost fully shaken the foul mood entirely. After dinner, I help her up to bed and promptly discover that Vadim has made some minor changes to our previous routine.

"You have to brush it *this* way," Magda commands, showing me how to coax the brush through her hair, supposedly the same way her father does. Once I've finally arranged the braids to her liking and tucked her beneath the blankets, I retreat for the door.

"Oh!"

I turn around to find her lurching upright, riffling through her end table until she withdraws her cell phone from a drawer. As I watch her dial a number in confusion, she looks up and says, "I promised Harry and Gigi I'd call them once a week."

"Harry and Gigi?" She mentions the prospect of calling these mystery people with such earnest seriousness that I'm at a complete loss. Until I realize. "You mean my parents?"

She nods and settles against her pillow with the phone pressed to her ear. "Vadim said I could. Harry is going to tell me about his strawberry plants, and Gigi said she was going to send me dress-up clothes—" She breaks off, cocking her head to listen, and I'm promptly forgotten. "Hi," she says in her charming way, so similar to Vadim's disarming cadence. It's like she's studied his tactics for manipulation as an art form. "Yes, I've been in the muck…"

I leave her to it, escaping down to the kitchen to find Vadim washing the dishes, looking deliciously domestic.

"You gave her permission to call my parents once a week?" I ask, slipping my arms around him from behind. "How very kind of you. They're smitten. I think they might have kidnapped her if we didn't leave when we did." My voice turns wistful as I reflect on just how quickly my parents have taken to her. To him.

Jim was lucky to get a Christmas card and a coupon in the mail for his birthday.

"She insisted," Vadim says, frowning. He turns to face me, cupping my chin against his palm. "But… I've decided. She deserves her answers, and I intend to find them."

"I think you should," I say softly.

His furrowed brows betray that he doesn't fully like the prospect, but his fingers part my hair, tilting me back for a searching, slow kiss. "And, though I'm not sure how long it will take, I believe you may be safer with me," he adds.

I feel my nose wrinkle. "What about Magda?"

His gaze darkens as he contemplates the possibility of leaving her behind, even for a little while. "Ena will watch over her."

"Or," I say, tentatively licking my lips. "She can still have Ena's protection, *and* the benefit of being around someone who can actually participate in a game of tea party."

He raises an eyebrow. "Oh?"

I nod. "And an uncle who, admittedly, is big and scary enough to protect her from anyone who might harm her, let alone Irina—"

"You want me to leave my daughter with Maxim?" He breaks away from me, scowling at the mere idea.

But I don't relent, following him into his study. "What scenario do you think will benefit her more in the long run? Having a friend her own age to play with, and getting to know her uncle—learning not to fear him to the point that she can't even sleep in her own bed for a week—or huddling here with Ena watching cartoons all day and trying to make him pretend to be a princess? By the time we come back, I'm sure she'll be starting to put down roots into the flooring."

He scoffs, unconvinced. "What makes you think he would even agree to it?" He whirls to face me, but rather than angry, he just looks…helpless. Like a drowning man who knows a lifeline is within reach—but he's afraid it will vanish the second he grasps it.

"I think he will," I say, stepping into him, letting our bodies connect and collide. "If you *ask* him to."

He's still frowning, embodying Magda's surly, brooding mood from this morning. But eventually, he sighs, wrapping his arms around me—though taking care with my injuries. "Maybe. But…"

I rest my head on his chest, wiggling into his touch. "But?"

"But if Maxim refuses to watch Magdalene, then *you* have to tell Ena he'll be on tea party duty."

I giggle, picturing the image in my head. "Deal."

Sending Magda to Maxim's for a harmless playdate, during which she can bond with both her uncle and pseudo-cousin, sounded promising in theory. A win-win, actually. The reality, however, turns out to be a lesson in child wrangling as Magda refuses to get out of the car once she recognizes the house we're parked in front of.

With her arms crossed, her persistent utterances of "No," quickly devolve to high-pitched shouting. Soon, her stoic façade gives way entirely to wracking sobs and real, enormous tears spilling down her cheeks as Vadim finally coaxes her from the backseat.

"Oh, *ma chérie*..." He rocks her in his arms, murmuring soothingly to her in French while, from the house, a curious press of faces watches us from the windows.

"Look at me," Vadim finally urges in a tone stern enough to make her risk lifting her head from his shoulder. Her bloodshot eyes scan his imploringly as her white-knuckled hands grip his forearms to what I'm sure is the point of pain. "I will never put you in danger," Vadim tells her. "Do you believe that? That I will always do what is best for you?"

Slowly, Magda nods even as her eyes continue to spill over. Her bottom lip trembles, her expression so stricken...

I relent first. "Maybe we should go back—"

"No." Vadim crouches down, settling his daughter on his knee. Gingerly he wipes away her tears and smooths the wild curls back from her face. She has no choice but to quiet down and listen to him. "My brave girl is going to wait here while I go inside, *oui?*"

He sounds so confident and assured for her. When I can tell from how the muscle in his jaw twitches that inside, he's thinking—*I'll go inside, and hopefully, Maxim refuses to take you, and this is all rendered moot, and we can watch cartoons for the rest of the week.* And yet, he does his best not to reveal his doubts. He smothers his own unease, entirely for her.

"Why don't you stay with Mr. Ena?"

Following his cue, Ena steps forward to take her hand, and she promptly clings to his hip, the princess, and her trusty henchman.

Together Vadim and I approach the house only to have the door opened from within the moment we reach it. Lucius isn't the one standing guard on the other end, this time. A wary Francesca greets us instead, her eyes guarded as they flick over Vadim.

And looming behind her, the picture of brute strength, is Maxim, his posture tense, dark eyes flashing. I sense myself instinctively step back, letting the brothers square each other up in their unique, calculating ways. Maxim glowers while Vadim eyes him coldly, his unease painfully apparent.

"Hello," Francesca says softly, and yet her voice alone seems to crack the tension enough that Maxim uncurls his hands out of fists. "What brought you over?" she prompts, her eyes on me.

Sighing, I take my cue and forge a path inside, leaving Vadim to follow in my wake. "We wanted to see if Magda could spend the day while we—"

"She can sense your hostility, you do realize," Vadim says in a deadly quiet tone. My alarm bells go off, and I instantly regret suggesting this option. Nothing, it seems, can ease thirty years of animosity overnight. Not even the welfare of a little girl.

"Your hatred toward me," Vadim continues in a hiss, still positioned in the doorway, his head cocked, gaze ice-cold. "You scared the hell out of her. We couldn't get her out of bed for a week. She would rather hide inside than feel safe venturing out of her own home. Because of *you*."

For all of his coldness…

Something in Maxim's expression gives for a split second, and I know the accusation hit home. His jaw twitches, his lips parting before slamming shut into a fearsome scowl.

"So what?" he tosses back, his accent thick. "You demand I leave? Try to buy this property out from under me, again?"

Vadim grits his teeth, and I sense something in him falter. Spite? Guilt? He's wavering on a precipice, and one wrong act will send him hurtling over it—both of them.

The only way to salvage this, I suspect, is to throw caution to the wind and lay the cards on the table.

"Magda wants to spend the day with Ainsley," I blurt out. "Vadim and I will be out of town for a few hours, if you wouldn't mind her playing here."

"It will be good for them," Francesca pitches in. Following my lead, she steps forward, bracing her hand on Maxim's forearm and bit by bit some of the crackling tension eases. A minuscule bit. "They can play outside—"

"But can *he* refrain from taking out his hatred toward me on a child?" Vadim wonders, though I suspect that question is directed more at himself than anyone else. And I can tell from the set of his jaw alone that he wants to believe it. He does. But he's spent so much of his life expecting the worst from those around him.

His first instinct is always to suspect.

"Can you?" he demands of Maxim.

The other man grits his teeth. "Can I trust you not to steal a child?" he counters. "Related to you by blood or not."

They eye each other fiercely, but as the seconds pass, they don't come to blows at least.

Finally, I can't take the silence anymore.

"I'll go get Magda."

I race for the door as both men swivel in my direction with equally fierce expressions. Vadim flinches toward me. To stop me?

"Yes," Francesca encourages from beyond the fray before he can voice any refusal out loud. "I'll go get Ains."

Taking my cue, I hasten outside and find Magda still clinging to Ena's pantleg so tightly the bodyguard has to adjust his posture just to withstand her weight thrown against his one leg. Her eyes dart to the house—searching for Vadim?

When I reach for her, though, she takes my hand and reluctantly follows me inside. My heart pounds, my throat tightening as I realize that bringing a traumatized seven-year-old into the thick of a brooding feud between two powerful men may not be the best course of action.

But right when I hesitate, Vadim appears in the doorway to the house. Gone is his hateful mask. He looks neutral again, his composed, poised self.

Meeting his daughter's gaze, he inclines his head for her to follow. Her trust in him is apparent solely in the fact that she does, even as her grip on me tightens to the point I feel myself wince.

Maxim is no longer in view, I realize, as we cross the spacious living room for a door leading out to their terrace. It seems the other man has migrated outside, his posture tense, his back to us as we step out to join him.

When he turns to face Magda, I exhale sharply. A blind man could sense the sheer amount of discipline he's utilizing to keep his expression neutral. Some of the ice leaves those cold, dark eyes, rendering him slightly less "big and scary." But apparently not enough.

Releasing me, Magda contorts herself to cling to Vadim's leg, forcing him to stop short. It's such a striking contrast to the brave little girl who had spurned him just a few short weeks ago. Though I think this new display of emotion is merely a testament to how much she's opened herself up to him. How much she's learning to trust him.

And Vadim's pained frown tells me that he is well aware of that fragile bond. Sighing, he sinks down to her level and cradles her chin against his palm, urging her to meet his gaze.

"I know you're afraid." He brushes some of her tears away and smooths back her curls. "But you don't need to be. Here, you can play with your friend and focus on your tea parties."

She shakes her head. "Why are you leaving me? Again!"

"I'm not," he says firmly. "I will never leave you. Besides, Mr. Ena whom I trust more than anyone else in the world will stay with you, yours to command. I'll return as soon as I can, and you have your cell phone, yes?" He brushes his hand along the fanny pack that's become a near-permanent fixture around her waist. "If you ever feel unsafe, I will return within an instant."

He sounds so damn reassuring, his expression persistently calm. Even she can't resist. Her bottom lip trembles, her eyes still watering, but she loosens her grip on him enough for him to point to Maxim.

"And I'm not leaving you with just anyone," he says, his voice a deep, soothing hum. "This is your uncle, *chérie*. He will protect you while I'm gone. And if he doesn't…" His eyes flash. "Then he will answer to me."

If Maxim takes offense to the threat, he surprisingly doesn't say as much. With his face still arranged in that careful, neutral mask, he stalks forward and crouches, extending his hand in Magda's direction, even as she flinches back.

"I hear you like ponies," he says, his accent sounding more charming than threatening. "Would you like to see mine?"

Magda glances warily at her father, who nods in encouragement. "It's okay."

Slowly, she places her tiny hand on Maxim's enormous one and allows him to lead her toward the edge of the terrace. Even so, she looks back at Vadim, her bloodshot eyes frantic.

"It will be alright," he says so fiercely even her fear can't withstand his assurance. "I promise you."

She nods and turns back to Maxim. To the man's credit, he meets her gaze with gentle acknowledgment, and something in my heart twists a little. These brothers...

It's like they were designed to repel all assumptions of care, empathy, or compassion, only to reveal an uncanny knack for emoting all three when pushed to do so. At least by those they deemed worthy of such emotions.

Case and point, a tiny figure races from the house and snatches up Maxim's other hand without an ounce of fear.

"Wait for me!" Surging ahead, Ainsley winds up pulling her two companions behind her, forging the way to the stable. "I can't wait for you to see my pony," she prattles to Magda. "You'll love him!"

"Score one for super dad," I murmur as Vadim rises to his feet, his expression constricted. I know that nothing in the world was probably harder for him to endure than this moment—save leaving Magda in the first place, of course. Regardless, his jaw is clenched with resignation as we exit the house and return to the car.

"She'll be fine," I insist as he glances back at the house at least ten times before finally climbing into the driver's seat.

Without looking my way, he mutters under his breath, "She better be."

CHAPTER SEVENTEEN

For some reason—despite the fact that he's rarely relied on a massive show of security in the time I've known him—I'm surprised to discover our road trip seems to consist of just me and him. No driver. No Ena.

His trusted friend hasn't been sidelined, of course, but merely reassigned to cover a target Vadim values above all else. And yet, his seemingly second most important target, he's decided to guard personally.

It betrays such a confidence in his own skillset, and a level of concern for me—one declared without him having to strut down a boardwalk to show me off. With his actions alone, he proves the lengths he's willing to go.

But have I been willing to do the same?

"Don't tell me you're so far unimpressed by our solo excursion," Vadim remarks dryly, drawing my attention to him. He's smiling, I find, his lips in a rare, lazy grin that makes my heart sputter further. At the same time, he looks so tired.

His eyes are bloodshot, his expression haggard. A sudden thought hits me—he probably hasn't slept much at all these past few days. With Magda in his arms, maybe he'd been too afraid to—too worried about failing her trust in him to ever drop his guard.

So, he put her first over his own discomfort.

"I'm more than impressed," I confess, though our impending destination is far from my mind.

He frowns, stroking the back of my hand. "And here I was, assuming you were disappointed we've forsaken the private jet."

I puff up with mock indignation. "I'm with you for the designer clothing, remember? Not the limitless travel."

He laughs, but something darkens his expression. Doubt?

"And, I'm with you for the sex," I add, nestling against him before his paranoia can fester. "And your patience. Your kindness. And your ass. And…" I bring my mouth near his ear, my voice husky. "Your filthy brain."

His posture relaxes, a sly grin playing over his lips. But even dirty talk can't seem to placate him for long. Within seconds, he's scowling again—but before I can even prompt him for a reason, he sighs. "There is always one possibility," he says softly. "One I've considered since the day I learned of Magda's existence."

"Oh?" His expression warns me that whatever his suspicion, it doesn't inspire warm and fuzzy feelings.

He cocks his head, meeting my gaze, still stroking my hand. "There is always the chance that she isn't mine. That Irina crafted an elaborate deception just to convince me she was. I had test results commissioned from a private laboratory, but…" He shrugs. "I am not so foolish to believe that even my most rigorous testing is infallible."

I don't know what to say, so I bite my lip and try to see the dilemma from his angle. It *is* possible—in the mind of a paranoid man so mistrustful of the world around him. But even so, there are aspects of Magda too authentically him to have been faked. Her mannerisms. Her facial features. Her illness.

"I think she's yours through and through," I tell him. "Biologically or not." But another realization makes me observe him from the corner of my eye. "Is that why you were afraid to adopt her before now?"

He flinches. "No! I mean…" He rakes a hand through his hair, disrupting the mussed curls. "It isn't easy for me to let people into my life," he confesses. "I know Irina. I know her games. And I knew that I couldn't survive letting a child in —mine or not—and losing her. Or worse, having her utilized as a pawn. If I kept her at a distance, it would be better for us both…"

Until he couldn't. Until the desire for a family got the best of him, and he took on that risk. Whatever Irina's plan may be, he won't give up Magda without a fight.

"She *is* mine now," he says as if reading my mind. His eyes brim with a raw emotion I can't name. Devotion? Love? Desperation? "No one will take her from me. No one."

I can't resist slipping my hand within his as a silent gesture of reassurance. But I know, as a sleepy, small town appears on the horizon, that my vulnerable Vadim will have to take a backseat to his more ruthless personality.

And that I better hold on for the ride.

THE BUILDING where Magda was abandoned turns out to be a small, modest brick-and-mortar front for what seems to be a nonprofit child advocacy program.

"The United States no longer relies on the traditional concept of an orphanage," a woman explains as she leads us on a tour of a spacious series of wide, open rooms decorated with framed photos of children, seemingly from all over the world.

"That's why I remember it so clearly, the day Magdalene showed up," she says. "I couldn't fathom it—someone just dropping a little girl here, all alone, without even checking to make sure staff were even on the property. Thank God a janitor saw her when he did. Naturally, we called the police, but we do have the capacity to take in children in emergency situations, so she stayed here in the facility for a few days as they attempted to establish her identity. You know, I was sure that she had been kidnapped. A little girl so well-groomed and impeccably dressed. I think her clothing was worth more than my salary." She breaks off with a nervous laugh and shakes her head, her smile fading. "But… She didn't cry like you'd think a normal child might. She didn't ask for her mother or father, or anything of the sort. It was almost as if she knew."

"Knew what?" Vadim prompts. I've never seen his expression so rigid, his eyes dark and distant.

"That she had been abandoned," the woman says with an apologetic nod. "Honestly, I haven't stopped thinking about her since. I'm so glad that she's found an adoptive family—"

"How did you learn her name?" Vadim demands, so lost in his own thoughts that I doubt he realizes that he interrupted the woman at all. "Her birthday?" I can tell from the set to his jaw that it's physically paining him to ask more. Questions I suspect he already knows the answer to.

Did you learn anything about her mother? Her father? Her origins?

"She told us her name," the woman says, wrinkling her mouth. "Though, she had a slip of paper in her clothing. It had her name written on it, along with her birthday and immunization records—all validated, of course."

"A slip of paper?" Vadim raises an eyebrow, and I recognize the intense set to his jaw. He wasn't aware of that detail.

"Yes. The police took it in their initial investigation," the woman admits. "But… I made a copy. I'm not sure why, it all felt so strange. I think I felt compelled to remember it somehow. If you wait right here, I'll be back."

She disappears down a winding hallway while Vadim starts to pace, stroking his jaw, the gears in his brain whirring. I watch him, even as I find myself imagining this place two years ago, with a five-year-old Magda walking haughtily through its halls. She would have been even smaller, twice as frail, and under the assumption that neither parent wanted her. My heart breaks for that girl, and I'm more resolved now than ever to live up to the commitment Vadim admittedly goaded me into. Adopting her—no matter who may stand in the way.

"Here it is!" The woman returns brandishing a slip of neatly folded photocopy paper. Vadim scans the surface, his eyes widening.

"That logo…"

"You recognize it?" The woman tilts her head thoughtfully. "Eingel Industries is one of our main contributors. In fact, for well over a decade, their donation has far exceeded all others. It was an odd coincidence, but there's a factory not too far from here, and the workers tend to scatter their promotional materials all over. I'd thought her parents may have worked there, but honestly, it could have been taken from the local library just as plausibly."

Something I sense Vadim doubts. His hands shake as he scans the page over and over again. From over his shoulder, I make out a few lines written in crisp, neat handwriting. A series of unique flourishes make the style stand out—far more elegant than one might suspect of a desperate guardian dropping off an abandoned child.

Does he recognize it as Irina's?

"May I have this?" he asks of the woman.

"Of course. I'm so glad to hear that Magdalene is safe and thriving. I think about her often. I wonder… Does she still have that quirk when it comes to roses?"

Vadim frowns, still reading the note. "Roses?" From his tone, I doubt he understands the significance of that one statement.

But I do.

"Quirk?" I ask, turning my full attention toward the woman.

She purses her lips, wringing her hands. "It was around Valentine's day when she arrived—which was why I couldn't imagine someone bringing her *here*. It was freezing. Anyway, we host a few children's groups throughout the year, and we prepare crafts for them to complete during the holidays. That month, we had them design rose vases that we displayed throughout the facility. They truly were beautiful." She smiles faintly, only for the expression to drain from her face, replaced by utter confusion. "When poor little Magdalene stepped foot inside, she vomited. It was one of the first things she said—not to ask for her parents, but simply *'I hate that smell.'* We had to clear away any trace of the flowers from the area we kept her in. I was wondering if she had grown out of the aversion."

In some ways, she has. While playing with my parents in their garden, she can frolic amongst a sea of roses unbothered. But when sensed while caught off guard, she panics. So much so that she crawls into her father's bed at night and breaks down at the mere thought of someone taking her from him.

"Thank you for your help," Vadim says, leading the way to the door. I follow him out, and as we enter the car, I notice that he still has that note clenched in his fist, his gaze unfocused.

"What's wrong?" I ask, bracing my hand over his forearm as he settles beside me. "Is that handwriting... Is it Irina's?"

"No," he says hoarsely, looking hopelessly confused. "It's not."

I frown. "Do you think she had someone else—"

"Irina didn't write this," he says, as if he has to repeat it just to drill the fact into his own understanding. "But I know who did."

"Who?" I ask.

Carefully, he folds the paper and slips it into his breast pocket. With his gaze on the window nearest him, he says, so softly, I almost don't hear him, "Hiram Gorgoshev."

CHAPTER EIGHTEEN

The weight of his statement casts a pall over the entire mood of our impromptu trip. I'm at a loss for words, truly unsure of what to say.

Not that anything I could voice would be able to penetrate the cloud of unease hanging over Vadim. It's so heavy I feel as though if I reach out to touch him, I'll feel an invisible barrier barring my path—his wall, rebuilt higher than ever.

Hiram, his mentor, and father figure who entrusted his business to him… *That* man had somehow written a note that wound up on Magdalene the day she arrived at the crisis center. A crisis center primarily funded by said company.

It's almost too convoluted a web to unravel all at once.

And Vadim especially seems perplexed by this new twist in the puzzle that is Magdalene's past. By the time we're nearly an hour into our drive, he finally speaks.

"I knew there were things he never told me," he says gruffly. "I'm not a fool. But this… Did he plan this with that bitch? Goad me to take in Magdalene for his own gain?" His voice trembles, coarse with anger, and my heart aches for him. Cracks.

In his mind, such a betrayal makes sense—it's the only way he's learned to see the world. Always on the defense. But something tells me that the explanation may not be so simple. Maybe reinforced simply by the fact that a man who would do so much for a young, tormented boy to cross his path—even going so far as to give him his name—wouldn't be so cruel as to gamble that trust on a reckless whim. Would he?

"He's probably laughing at me from the grave," Vadim adds with a harsh, callous scoff. "I've still carried his name all this time. I was going to give my daughter *his* name."

He glowers, his hands clenched over the steering wheel, his eyes flashing a vitriol he doesn't even display toward his brother. All I can do is place my hand on his shoulder and let him rage.

"Is there anything he left you that might give you a clue as to his motives?" I ask, gingerly giving Hiram the benefit of the doubt.

Vadim blinks as if he didn't think to consider the possibility for himself. "I had most of his estate liquidated," he explains, raking a hand through his hair repeatedly. "But some personal effects I had shipped to the city and placed in storage. I never had the heart to go through them."

"So let's do it now," I suggest, hoping I sound braver than I feel. "Together."

He eyes me warily, and I see the faintest hint of his wall starting to splinter. I feel so attuned to him in this moment, I swear I'm reading his mind. Once again, he's grappling with his decision to trust me. Hiram supposedly betrayed him, am I next?

I meet his gaze unflinchingly, hoping that whatever he finds gives him enough reassurance to trust me. At least for now.

After a few tense seconds, he sighs and steers the car onto an off-ramp heading toward Fair Haven. Sensing the need to remain silent, I let him stew for nearly the entire drive.

It's only when we arrive before a prestigious bank in the heart of the city that I manage to blurt, "So this is where billionaires get all those fancy limitless cards from."

My awe is quickly tempered, however, when Vadim exits the car, stone-faced, and reaches back for me. Together, we enter a minimally designed lobby where a teller guides us to a private room supposedly designed to store personal effects.

As we wait on leather loungers, the woman returns with a few small items balanced on a silver tray.

"Take all the time you need," she explains as she sets the tray onto a wooden table before us.

The second she's gone, I sit forward and eagerly peruse each object. There isn't much—perhaps Vadim's ruthless minimalism isn't a trait he picked up on his own, but one he learned from Hiram? A leather-bound journal, a gold-set watch on a leather band, and finally, a black metal lockbox make up the bulk of his few personal effects.

The last item draws my interest the most, but I sit back as Vadim takes his time inspecting the arrangement. Finally, he reaches out, fingering the watch first.

"He told me once, he'd leave this to me," he says, more to himself than to anyone else. Sighing, he turns his attention to the notebook, warily flipping through the first few pages. With a pained expression, he sets it aside and then finally opens the lockbox.

I find myself leaning forward, eagerly peering within—only to frown in confusion. Hiram Gorgoshev cherished few things in life, it seems. A small stack of documents, and a selection of glossy snapshots tied together with a delicate strip of ribbon. But not just any photos.

I recognize the little girl staring plaintively from the topmost one—so does Vadim. He snatches the entire stack and spreads them out over the table, his expression increasingly constricted. Magda stars in every last one, spanning at least most, if not her entire short lifespan. A wide-eyed, stoic baby. A blankly staring toddler. A presumably five-year-old girl photographed without flashing so much as a smile.

Vadim lifts that one, his hand shaking so badly. It slips through his grasp and lands face-down, revealing a slash of cruelly elegant script written on the back: *Proud of your creation?* Every picture sports some variation of a message, each one seemingly more mocking than the last.

So innocent. So perfect. How many such well-bred creatures did you deny the world when you grew a soul, Hiram?

Do you see his face? I do. What would he say?

And finally…

Do you deny she's a result of your 'research?' Flawed, like everything you touch.

The author of these cruel messages needs no explanation. Irina wrote them, using the pointed language to taunt Hiram. Blackmail him? And the last one, adorning the oldest photo of Magda, mentioned that damn, hateful word. Flawed.

In disgust, Vadim swipes his hand over the photos, scattering them further. Then he snatches the remaining stack of documents from the lockbox and scours them with a deepening frown.

"What is it?" I ask as he lurches to his feet, his gaze on one page in particular.

He shakes his head rather than tell me. Then he retreats to a corner of the room while withdrawing a cell phone from his pocket. In hushed tones, he relays something fervently to whoever is listening on the other end, but I only manage to catch snippets. "…Verify. The one Hiram used. Yes. See if you can track him down."

As I strain my ears to listen, I reach for one of the documents he'd left behind. All it contains is an itemized list. An invoice? I struggle to decipher the final details. A series of names… Countries? Each one is followed by a date and a scribbled response in different handwriting that makes me suspect they had been written in after the fact.

Gone.

Left in June.

No sign.

Witnesses saw a child but no sign.

Was Hiram tracking someone? Someone with a child who apparently bounced from city to city—even country to country. And judging from the number of invoices, his surveillance of that mysterious figure spanned months if not years.

"He knew," Vadim rasps. I look up to find him stowing his cell phone in his pocket, apparently speaking to me now. "Irina kept in contact with him. The bastard even had her traced. Put a bounty on her head—"

"I'm sorry." I rise to my feet and approach him. Everything we've learned takes a backseat to the betrayal I know he's feeling. And I'm already steeling myself to withstand his instinctive way of reacting when hurt.

His eyes cut down to mine, blazing with mistrust. "How do I know you aren't working with her as well?" he demands. "Am I supposed to believe it was a coincidence that you appeared in my life when you did? How good you are with her. It could be an act. It could…" He deflates, raking his hands through his hair, his gaze unreadable. "No," he decides, shaking his head. "No."

What exactly about me makes him change his mind, he doesn't say. Instead, he sinks onto the edge of the leather chaise and sighs.

"Hiram's man was the one who brought Magda to the crisis center." He tosses the crumbled invoice onto the table, eyeing it in disgust. "He tracked Irina to Fair Haven of all places. His mercenary took Magda—terrified her in the process—and then…he abandoned her."

"And then that man sent you that note?" I ask cautiously.

He shrugs. "It makes sense. Or at least it would if Hiram were the kind of man who thrived in deceit."

"But he wasn't," I say, going off his obvious distress. "So there must be another explanation." Desperate to help him find one, I grab the journal and flip through the pages. Hiram was a man of few words, most of them spent reflecting on his take on the current stocks, or his viewpoint on the current events that day. I'm starting to feel my search is in vain when I stumble across a page near the very end that isn't like the others.

It's longer for one, with Vadim's name sprinkled throughout. It's a summary of his accomplishments at the time, more like an exhaustive list. His ascent in the biotechnical industry. His many accolades regarding his education and various business acquisitions. And at the very end, he'd written simply—*he is ready for anything.*

My throat constricts at the realization of just how true those words are, but for whatever reason, I can't bring myself to voice them.

"Let's go." Vadim stands, leaving everything on the table but the stack of invoices. "If we leave now, we can make it back before dark. I'll call Magdalene."

He's already in the hallway by the time I manage to stand. Before I leave the room, however, I can't stop myself from gathering everything into the lockbox and tucking it under my arm. When I rejoin Vadim out in the car, he spots my bounty, but he already has his cell phone against his ear, and the person on the other end takes precedence over all else.

"Having fun?" he asks in a jovial tone that's such a startling contrast to his glowering expression. The man sure can turn on the charm when he needs to. Even I would be convinced if I didn't happen to be staring directly at him. Whatever Magda says makes some warmth creep back into his gaze even as his frown deepens. "You want to stay the night," he says, sounding surprised by that fact. His eyes meet mine, wavering with indecision. "I…"

"Yes." I gently ease the phone from his grasp. Magda's excited chirping is audible even before I fully press the device against my ear.

"…and we went hiking. And they said we could camp in the backyard! Can I stay? Please?"

I barely recognize this little girl, brimming with the full extent of a seven-year-old's excitement. Even Vadim seems to realize that, despite his feelings toward Maxim, raining on her parade now would be cruel.

"That sounds great, honey," I say, deciding for him. "Of course, you can stay. We'll pick you up first thing in the morning."

Vadim eyes me both grudgingly and with a hint of something that might be relief as I return the phone to him. After talking to Magda for a few more minutes, he finally hangs up.

"This is a good thing," I insist in response to his distant gaze. "She gets to spend time with her family, and you get to digest what you've learned. You deserve to feel betrayed. But, you also deserve to think things through and have doubts about what the information may seem to present. It's okay to not want to believe the worst in anyone."

"Is it?" he wonders, flicking his gaze toward me.

"Yes." I nod. "And, it's especially easy to when you have a diversion. Let's take advantage of the absence of little ears and paint the town red."

I feel so smug with my offer, but Vadim's lips don't even twitch in the hint of a smile.

"Red with Irina's blood?" he wonders in a tone that makes me suck in a breath.

"N-Not quite. More like…dinner and wine?"

He sighs but starts driving, presumably toward a restaurant here in the city. After settling Hiram's estate on the floor of the car—and conveniently out of sight—I lean against him, slipping my hand in his.

He doesn't pull away at least, but by no means is he content with any of the events today has brought his way. Were I not here, I think he'd go off on his own and brood. Maybe spiral into one of the dark moods I've briefly witnessed, and that Ena has warned me about.

And I make a promise to myself to do everything within my power to prevent that from happening.

No matter the cost.

adim's version of wining and dining centers around a gorgeous French restaurant in the heart of the city. The food is amazing, the wine even better, and as we sit at a private table amongst beautiful ambiance, one could easily assume it'd make for the most romantic tension ever.

Or not.

My date scowls during the entire meal and barely touches his food, too distracted by the thoughts in his head. It's like I can see them, dancing across his expression one by one. Fear of losing Magda. Anger at Irina. Pain at the thought of Hiram's betrayal.

By the time our waiter clears away our plates, I'm resigned to what I feel is my only course of action left, other than to let him brood.

"Talk to me," I demand, reaching across the table to clasp one of his hands. He stiffens, refocusing on me. It's like he forgot I was even here, so lost in his own torment. "Tell me what you're feeling. Or..." I lick my lips, recalling the one method of communication between us that never seems to fail. "You can show me."

He raises an eyebrow and lifts his hand from beneath mine only to capture my wrist. Curiosity alights those dangerous eyes, and I feel a thrill shoot through me.

"Show?" he wonders gruffly.

I nod and casually finger the low neckline of my dress with my free hand, deliberately drawing his attention downward. "If you don't want to talk to me, then show me. Let me feel what you're feeling."

His lips press together in a thoughtful gesture. "Sexual torment?" he muses in a tone so dark... I almost—*almost* have second thoughts. If only the logical part of my brain isn't instantly drowned out by the lustful part, who relishes the avenues ventured by his twisted whims.

"I'm here for you," I tell him, sounding more earnest than I think I have about anything in my life—other than when I said the same to Magda. "Let me be here."

He stands, pulling me to my feet. In a whirlwind blur, we leave the restaurant and return to the car. It isn't long into the drive that I become eerily familiar with the direction we're headed in.

But before anything of note appears on the horizon, Vadim makes time for something far more important than sex.

"Goodnight, *ma chérie*," he says into his cell phone, once again speaking to Magda. My heart swells as some softness seeps into the hardened lines of his expression as he lets her regale him with more of her day. But I think real tears prick my eyes as, instead of hanging up, he offers the phone to me.

"Goodnight, honey," I tell her, sensing from her slurred reply that she's already half asleep.

The brief, domestic moment makes for a startling contrast to our eventual destination—an infamous club that happens to be partially owned by the man beside me.

An ominous shiver runs down my spine as he takes my hand, and we exit the car. Once inside the familiar ebony walls, Vadim leads me boldly through an archway in the direction opposite the club floor. It doesn't appear to lead to the upstairs level either, but some new taboo section, and I have to admit my interest is piqued.

"I mentioned to Milton that I wished to expand my private use of the club," he explains as my eyes excitedly scan the corners, hunting for any hint of where we might be headed. So far, all that greets me is a long, winding hallway draped in shadow. "He and Maxim both have rooms here," he adds, steering me forward as the corridor begins to curve. "He granted my request."

That being his own "private space," presumably lurking beyond a massive ebony door waiting up ahead. That ominous tingle strengthens, turning into a shudder I can't suppress. Excitement becomes a palpable thing—I can almost taste it.

Dark, dangerous kink.

Still, I try my best to cut the tension. "Milton granted your request," I parrot, leaning against him playfully. "Is he in charge?"

"No," Vadim says, his tone suddenly serious. He brings me to a stop as we reach the door. With one hand, he pushes it open, while the other captures the side of my face, forcing me to meet his gaze directly. "*You* are in charge," he tells me huskily. Before I've even processed those words, he gently shoves me back, forcing me to stagger over the threshold of the room. "Always… Of how much of yourself you are willing to submit. Of how far you'll allow me to go. Of your trust. Of *me*."

Sensory overload. Especially as I find myself turning to take in the room we're in—a beautiful, haunting space decorated almost entirely in hues of black and navy. The man has certainly researched kink down to an art form. I blink as my brain races to take in every last detail.

There are windows, large and rectangular with a view overlooking what appears to be an enclosed courtyard complete with a bubbling, black marble fountain. Plush, ebony carpeting lends to a mysterious aura only enhanced by matching curtains. A lone leather chaise positioned near the windows serves as the sole piece of traditional furniture.

Because everything else is so very NSFW.

"Holy crap," I whisper as my eyes fall over one promising structure directly ahead. Extending from the ceiling in a display of expert craftsmanship is a round, circular base hung upright with two strips of material dangling from the bottom. Longer, larger sections dangle directly from the ceiling, framing it at all four corners.

It's a fancy version of a sex swing.

Beyond it, I recognize the pillory from the house, along with a few hanging cabinets, no doubt containing more goodies.

"A fitting enough playground?" Vadim wonders, coming up behind me. I'm too busy staring to answer him right away. Awed, I continue to take in the meticulously compiled décor—and all the while, his hands slide down my shoulders, removing my dress as they go.

I'm only vaguely aware of the material falling to my hips— and promptly tugged down the rest of the way. All I can do is surrender to his touch as my attention fixates back on the swing. My thoughts whirl, quickly envisioning how many naughty, twisted things he could do to me on it.

But, as he runs his fingers through my hair, smoothing the strands back from my neck, I suspect that I haven't even come close to what he's planned. Not by a longshot.

"Do you trust me?" he asks near my ear, his voice a low rasp.

My heart stutters. Breaths quicken. Excitement builds, nearly impossible to contain.

"Yes," I croak, sensing him lower something from above my head. His hands brush my cheeks as I blink to recognize a black strip of silk being positioned before my eyes. His tie?

Make that a makeshift blindfold, in this instance.

I don't resist as he loops the silk around my head, tying it in the back. Warm and dangerously soft, I sense the shape of his fingers dance down my forearms, finding my wrists next. With gentle pressure, he urges me forward, forcing me to follow his prompting blind.

And it is an experience unto itself. Trust had a different meaning before this moment—being naked, at his mercy, completely under his control.

At the same time, he tied the blindfold loosely enough that I have to keep my head still to prevent it from slipping. An oversight? Or by intention…

The latter, I suspect, predicated on one twisted bit of reasoning. If I want to see where this new game goes, I have to commit fully. There is no room for doubt or hesitation. The second I falter, his illusion will quite literally fall as well.

Sneaky devil.

The implicit insinuation is that every step, every bit of obedience to his touch, is entirely of my own free will and completely at his discretion.

"Kneel," he whispers against the column of my throat, his voice sensually warm.

I start to obey before he even finishes getting the word out, sinking to my knees on the plush carpeting.

"So beautiful," he praises thickly, sounding somewhere above me, still behind. "Now lie flat, onto your stomach."

My unease only grows in the most delicious of ways. Taking care with my back, I ease myself down onto my belly. From this position, I'm painfully aware of just how vulnerable I am. Open and naked to any assault he deigns to dish out.

For now, he seems content to make me wait. I breathe in and out, my face pressed against the flooring, him presumably watching down on me. Surprisingly, I feel anything but degraded. I know without even having to see his face, his expression is only one of lust.

And desire.

But just as I start to relax, I sense movement near my right. His footsteps? They're muffled, harder to track. I can only interpret him moving maybe a few feet away before he returns. A hiss of air betrays him sinking to his knees, I think, his fingers trailing down to my wrist. Something softer than flesh replaces his touch a heartbeat later. Silk? He loops it around, securing it tightly, but the sensation is nowhere near painful.

With a deliberate series of movements, he does the same to my other wrist. A subtle bit of tensing makes me suspect that my binds aren't manacles this time. They don't feel secured together, or even to the floor or any nearby surface. From up above instead?

I'm distracted from my suspicions as my ankle is next to receive the mysterious silk treatment. Then the other. Finally, his hands rove up to my waist, smoothing over the bones in my hips.

"Beautiful," he breathes before silken fabric brushes over my lower back in a teasing swipe. The gesture urges me to arch inward, allowing him to loop the fabric underneath. When I lie back down, I sense a swath of the silken material wide enough to stretch from my upper thighs to my navel.

"Do you trust me?" he asks again, but this time his tone makes me shiver in anticipation. It's low. Hoarse. Alluring.

And too damn smug beneath it all.

"Y-Yes," I whisper. The word barely escapes my lips before…

Ascent. Glorious, heart-stopping, mind-bending ascent. I don't know how he does it. The fabric carefully looped around my limbs goes taut, but not constricting, Regardless, the sudden tension lifts me from the floor completely—my belly first, then my wrists and ankles, suspending me seemingly by a thread.

A startled gasp escapes my throat. I can't even tell how high up I am—or if there is anything beneath me should I fall. But before I can voice my doubts fully, a stern voice reminds me, "You trust me."

That's all he has to say for it to click. So, *this* is the swing he envisioned for us—a completely different concept to the sturdy, more traditional base I helped him build what feels like a lifetime ago. Even now, I'm swaying, my body lying limp in this virtual harness.

But the logistics of my predicament aside, his care for me is readily apparent. He made sure there is no pressure on my back, for one. The position of the strap beneath my hips is expertly placed, ensuring that the tension is spread out evenly, preventing any one limb from taking too much stress.

It betrays an impeccable attention to detail, and I have a feeling that—as he has with most of his toys—he ensured this was designed with my specific measurements in mind.

"Are you afraid?" Vadim wonders, sounding somewhere in front of me. I almost reach out for him, feeling disarmingly unmoored. Lost. But his voice is like an anchor, imparting a calmness that heats me down to my core. "Don't be," he urges in a tone like sin. So deep, rumbling in earnest. "You never need to fear me. That isn't what I crave from you. But do you know what I *do* crave?"

My belly flips, sensing him even closer. A prickle of heat along my cheek alludes to his nearness. Then…

Whoosh!

I fall.

Stop short.

Raise again even higher.

Descend twice as fast.

It's *almost* too much. Almost. But the tension of the fabric is just a hairsbreadth on the side of more restraining than restricting. My body feels unnaturally loose—less like I'm a fly stuck in a spider's web, but more as though I am the spider. One whose web is being meticulously manipulated by a beast with devious intentions in mind.

But in the end, I still have some level of control.

Or not.

A featherlight touch along my jaw has me inclining my head toward the source, desperate for any clue of what lies in store.

"So beautiful," I hear Vadim say, his voice throaty and gruff. That gentle touch steadily inches downward, brushing the trembling column of my throat. "You wanted me to show you how I feel?" What I think is his thumb caresses my windpipe. "This."

Again, my binds are manipulated. The world shifts, and in a dizzying display of motion, I sense that I'm now suspended at an angle, slanted with my head downward judging from the blood rushing toward it. The strip beneath my belly still provides enough support that I don't feel in danger of falling. Just disoriented like hell.

"Always on edge," Vadim explains, his voice even closer. A prickling heat over my shoulder blades makes me envision him standing before me, stroking his fingers through my hair. "Like everything I knew no longer provides the same structure. The same support. You've taken that away from me."

Have I? I suck in a breath, mulling over the description.

"No one else would ever dare," he adds in a dangerous murmur. The air shifts again as the binds around my wrist tighten while the ones around my ankles loosen. My stomach flips as I wind up upright, leaning slightly against the strip across my belly, my hands stretched above me, while my legs are slightly bent behind me.

I definitely hear him now, moving to stand nearby. Then I feel him. A slow, hungry kiss against my eager mouth. Groping fingers cupping my breasts.

But, even as my body melts beneath his ministrations, I'm painfully aware of the fact that I'm unable to touch him in return. A shudder runs through me as I recall his deliberate phrasing. *You've taken that away from me.* So, he's retaliated by robbing me of any chance to turn the tables. Taking away my own sense of support.

But damn is it a glorious exchange. In return, he gives me a teasing, sparse bit of contact I never knew I needed. My body contorted like this, every nerve and sensation are enhanced tenfold. I can feel every ridge of his fingers. The softness of his tongue. Being helpless is surprisingly…

Kinky.

But I never forget his grated statement, or the way he said it. *You've taken…*

And in return, he devours. I'm never sure of where he's standing or how exactly he's touching me. Just that he is—near, there, everywhere somehow all at once. I'm a puppet on his strings, capable of moving only as much as he'll allow.

It's so disorienting. I lose track of up and down. Left and right. Gravity. My sense of direction comes solely from him. His mouth, grazing my jaw, inching down to my breast, encasing the nipple. Sucking…pain. Warmth of his tongue to soothe the sting. Then again.

Again.

Again.

I don't realize how turned-on I am until he adjusts my legs, making them chafe and bringing painful awareness to the moisture gathering there—that's how distracted he has me. I'm feeding off every bit of physical contact he's willing to give. I'm thriving on it. Growing mad on it…

But it's as if he's avoiding true stimulation on purpose, making me wait. Ache. Throb in a way I never have. My thoughts start to dissipate, scattered by his searching, grasping fingers. Down to my hips. Up across my ribcage and around to my healing scars. One by one, he gives every wound his own unique brand of attention, caressing the flesh around each with worshiping reverence before turning to my breasts again. Lower.

But never too low.

I'm biting my lip so hard I taste blood just to keep from voicing a plea. Sweat slicks my skin, making the fabric chafe with every swaying motion, but the slight friction only enhances my sensitivity more. A moan breaks loose before I can help it, but the low sound seems to trigger something in him.

Finally, his touch slips between my splayed legs, his voice dripping into my ear. "I have you," he tells me throatily as one of his fingers invades, working past my contracting muscles. "Don't I? I have you."

Mindless, I nod, lost to the feeling of his touch.

"You will never leave me."

Never, a part of me whispers as he thrusts that invading digit, making my eyes roll back into my head. It's like he's drugging me with every deliberate motion, making me susceptible to any command he dishes out.

"And you will finally tell me what you've danced around confessing all this time, won't you?"

Tell? Then it clicks. My eyelids flutter against the fabric of his makeshift blindfold. "Let me see you," I whisper, my voice hoarse. "Please. I need to see you."

I sense him hesitate, presumably unsure of my motives— always battling that closed-off, paranoid part of himself. Finally…

His fingers brush the planes of my cheeks before the blindfold is lifted away, and I can take in his face. Those beautiful dark eyes watch me warily, still too proud to beg. So he demands instead, stroking me from the inside out, wringing a strangled gasp from me in lieu of words.

He wanted me to feel what he does? I show him, arching shamelessly into his touch, forcing my body to sway, at the mercy of his contraption. I let his fingers work their magic, turning my insides to putty, my brain to mush. I allow any lingering doubts to drain away, my blood drugged on lust as our gazes meet.

"I love you," I tell him, meaning every word. The conviction in my own voice terrifies me, but I can't deny it any longer.

And this is true surrender.

And corruption.

"I love you—"

Growling, he steps into me, at the same time reaching up to snatch one of the strips holding my wrists aloft. The sharp shift in angle draws me against him, and his free hand grips my hip, snatching me the rest of the way. His lips pry mine apart, his tongue plunging in between as his finger strokes a brutal friction that makes me moan openly, senseless.

He's still fully dressed, I realize somewhere at the back of my mind. A fact he quickly rectifies, snatching open his slacks with a sharp tug of his free hand while his opposite fingers withdraw from me.

Bucking his hips, he enters me hard, lowering his mouth to my throat, his teeth catching the tender flesh there. "Again," he rasps in between harsh thrusts that leave me reeling. "Again—"

"I love you." I marvel at how easily the words come now. No hesitation. No shame. I'm as locked into the confession as I am to the apparatus he's created for me, surrendering of my own free will.

CHAPTER TWENTY

I'm only vaguely aware of the moment he releases me from the straps, cradling me into his arms. His jacket encases me, a prison of tailored cotton, as he carries me from the room and then the club entirely. I can sense the change in the atmosphere—the sensual tension traded for welcome calm—right up until the moment he finally brings me over the threshold of our home and utter contentment sets in. Now I know why Magda missed it so much during our brief absence—the smell. The familiar feeling in the air that makes me relax into his arms as he takes me into our room.

We're on the bed, my limbs still slick with sweat when he drags me closer, his lips pressed to my forehead. "I love you," he tells me in a low, fierce hum more beautiful than any other sound in the world. "I love you."

MAGDA GETS the benefit of having her playdate extended to midafternoon as I spend the morning recovering in bed, and Vadim pampers me with mind-blowing attention to detail. He bathes me first, then feeds me a hot breakfast of eggs and toast—I'm starting to appreciate how his research has broadened into culinary skills. When we finally get dressed and drive the short distance to Maxim's home, Vadim's still so relaxed there's barely any clue as to his unease.

It's only when he finally parks in the driveway and steps from the car that a frown tugs on his mouth as his gaze fixates on the front door. His right hand sinks into his pocket, and I envision him grasping his cell phone, ready to call Magda the second he doesn't catch sight of her.

But as the seconds pass, he doesn't take a step toward the house.

"Come on, Mr. Brooding," I tease, stepping forward to slip my hand in his. But inside, I'm just as uneasy.

Can the brothers extend their terse truce for longer than a few seconds at a time?

God only knows.

I aim for optimism, however, as we approach the front door. I think it's the first time that it isn't automatically opened from the inside. Instead, we're forced to knock, and Vadim's wary expression deepens into flat out dread.

Seconds pass in silence before audible footsteps approach from inside the home. Finally, the door cracks, revealing an unfamiliar face so unexpected that I blink.

"They're in the back," a teenager declares, his dark hair shaggy and untamed. He must be sixteen or seventeen, at least, nearly as tall as Vadim. Is he one of Francesca's siblings? I think I vaguely recognize him from the "party" I attended all those weeks ago.

Without a more thorough introduction, he inclines his head for us to follow him inside and leads the way out onto the terrace.

One look at what awaits us on the lawn, and I feel my eyes threaten to fall from my head. Beside me, Vadim's jaw tightens, his gaze unreadable.

"Off with his head!" Magda shrieks. Somehow she got a hold of one of my old pageant dresses—a bright pink chiffon that hangs on her tiny frame, clashing with her fanny pack. Wearing an equally extravagant dress is Ainsley, crouched beside her, cackling maniacally.

Both girls look poised to lunge at the poor, unfortunate figure caught in their midst.

"Get him!" Ainsley calls, leading the charge.

Both girls proceed to throw themselves at their victim—the only fact impeding their attack is that their opponent dwarfs them in both size and stature. Nonetheless, he's a good sport and playfully keels over to accept his fate.

All circumstances aside, it's an oddly heartwarming thing to witness. Maybe I'm not the only one who feels as much—Vadim's watching as well, his expression blank. Mistrustful, still? Even if he is, he doesn't march forward to draw Magda's attention.

He merely watches the scene unfold, and I imagine him envisioning all the many ways he was denied one similar to it. A peaceful, happy childhood spent playing games with his brother on their lawn, safe and protected.

The longer he observes them, the more pained his expression becomes until, finally, I feel compelled to brace my hand over his shoulder.

"Let's give her a little bit more time, huh?"

His only sign of acknowledgment is a terse nod before he turns on his heel, retreating inside the house. I spare the trio one last glance—they're so caught up in their game, Maxim it seems has turned the tables on his two charges, lifting them into the air one by one. Neither one seems to notice our arrival or our absence.

We retreat back to the house, and by the time Magda finally returns, courtesy of Ena, she's a rumpled, exhausted shadow of the earlier, energetic princess. She can barely keep her eyes open during dinner, and Vadim has to carry her up to bed.

Once she's down, I follow him into the master suite, but even as I run my hands down his back, inching toward his front, I sense he's not fully here. Especially when I tug at the fastenings of his pants, and he doesn't react.

"Earth to Vadim," I murmur against the back of his neck, but I'm worried. I'd almost forgotten just how far away he can seem when his thoughts are focused inward. Like we're miles apart, separated by infinity. "Tell me what's wrong," I urge him, moving my hands to cup his hips.

"Maxim," he says coldly, but his voice lacks the vitriol I'm used to hearing where his brother is concerned. "Given how much you've been eavesdropping, you're probably aware, but someone has been causing his business interests trouble in Russia. I'll spare you the nitty details—let's just say that everything my brother has a hand in isn't necessarily legal, so his position is a bit more precarious than you'd think."

"Legal," I say, tasting the word carefully. It tastes dangerous. Like a trigger to a potential avalanche of unwelcome information—like the aspects of him that Irina alluded to. Mocked me over. "And what about you?" I ask him softly, my eyes on the line of his jaw—it tightens. "Is everything you do *completely* legal?"

He sighs and grasps my hands, spinning around to face me in the same motion. I wind up caught in his embrace, forced to crane my neck to meet his gaze. Gone is any ounce of a barrier—he lets me see all of him clearly. The shadows bathe his beautiful features in a mixture of darkness and light. Much like who he is at his core, I suspect. A man capable of the tenderest love imaginable...

And yet equally ruthless, shaped by the hell he grew up in. Is it fair to even expect such a creature to play by the rules of the very world that chewed him up and spit him out?

I can't decide as his eyes scan mine, hunting for a reaction. I'm not sure what he finds. Dread? Concern? Desperation just to learn more about him?

"I would lie to you," he tells me as his thumb ghosts my cheek in a reverent caress. "I would. If I knew that it would shape your opinion of me... I would lie merely to keep you. But in the end, it wouldn't. Trust?" He makes the word sound more foreign to him than any other concept, flicking his tongue along his lower lip just to sample the aftermath. Lowering his mouth to my ear, his arms shift around me, crushing me against him. "That's what you want, isn't it? My trust. I could entrust the truth to you. But warn me now if it could change this. Us."

I inhale sharply, startled by the raw heat in his voice. What the hell could he reveal? And would anything truly change my opinion of him? It could. That's the scary fucking part —never mind my trust in him, do I trust my heart to have picked the right man to claim it?

It didn't do so good of a job the last time.

"It could," I confess, flinching as he stiffens. "But you need to trust me to handle the truth."

"So ask me," he commands, his voice concealing the hint of a dare. "I will tell you anything you want to know."

I swallow hard; the gravity of the offer isn't lost on me. Tentatively, I decide to start with the obvious, horrible suspicion tossing around my brain ever since Irina first implied it. "Do… Do you hurt people?" I don't even know how else to phrase it. "Like how you were—"

"No!" He wrenches back from me, his expression pained. "I do not trade in people. Never."

"Okay," I murmur, smoothing my fingers along his jaw until he stills, his nostrils flaring at the mere suggestion. "So, what is it you do, then?"

Illegal or not, anything has to be better than human trafficking.

Right?

"You need to understand something about my family…" He moves to the bed, sitting on the edge with his back to me. His shoulders are rigid, his posture taking on the tense, stone-like stiffness that's become a hallmark of when he reflects on his past. I can't imagine how painful this is for him to face—and the true magnitude of darkness those memories may hold. "My father belonged to a family well-known in Russia and beyond for their ruthless grip on power. The *Koslovs*."

He says that name the same way he referred to Irina and her exploits while speaking to Milton. With utter disgust and loathing.

"Various branches dabble in their own aspects of crime— some so evil you couldn't fathom them. As far as Maxim and I are concerned, our father dealt primarily in weapons. Stealing them from various military strongholds or manufacturers and then selling them to the highest bidder on the black market. Whether it be to mercenaries, or crime lords terrorizing parts of Africa, money dictates the sale rather than morality."

"So, is that what Maxim does?" I ask, advancing toward him. "He sells weapons?"

"And more." He inclines his head as if gauging for himself just how much more I'm willing to hear. In the end, he says, "His club? He uses it primarily as a front to swindle blackmail and favors from powerful clients or rivals. He doesn't employ the same tactics my old master did, mind you, but the aim is the same."

"I might have been able to guess that much eventually," I admit, thinking of Geoff, the man I met there. He made scoring entry to the club sound comparable to winning the lottery, though he had also implied the shadowy nature of Maxim and his operations. "So what is it you do?"

"Me?" He sighs, and from this angle, I catch how his eyes flicker toward the windows, cold and distant. "I have a stranglehold on one of the premier pharmaceutical manufacturers in the world. When I took control, Eingel was little more than a blip on the map—a small, though pioneering, biotechnical firm. Now, they corner the lion's share of the market. Insulin. Lab equipment. Research studies regarding various vaccines to illnesses, some of them newly discovered. But one drug that makes up most of our portfolio is one used by paramedics to treat heroin overdoses. It's a fairly new delivery system, allowing it to be given with the same ease one might use to administer an epinephrine pen."

"But?" I croak, sensing a horrible caveat looming on the horizon.

He shifts to face me, his expression open and wary. It's his unease that makes me steel myself against the truth. His seeming resignation to the fact that whatever he's about to reveal, I won't accept. And yet he's taking the risk to trust me with it, all the same.

"The drug is a form of Naloxone, engineered to be effective within seconds of administration. But I ensure its demand more than matches the supply."

He pauses deliberately, as if forcing me to ask the magic words.

"How?"

"By taking steps to ensure the flow of heroin continues unabated," he says. "Using my influence to ensure incoming shipments into the city aren't entirely seized by law enforcement, for one. Supplying dealers through untraceable methods. No matter how fierce a campaign some praise-hungry politician mounts against 'the war on drugs,' my interests are never threatened."

He sounds ice-cold. No bluster. No bravado. One hundred percent honest.

And I feel *punched*. Swaying, I grapple for the edge of the mattress and sink onto it. "We can't mention that to my parents at Christmas dinner," I croak. I'm surprised when I blink to find moisture building behind my eyes. Out of shock? Fear? Or perhaps just pure sadness for the fact that someone as beautiful, and intelligent can never rise fully above the darkness that bore him.

"Tell me why," I whisper before the horror can build to an unbearable level. "I want to hear you explain it to me."

The bed shifts as he stands, his steps heavy. "Maxim was given control of our family's assets from the time he was ten years old," he confesses. "I was given *nothing*. Always, I had to fight and scrape to gain a fraction of what the chosen heir had handed to him on a silver platter. Always. You don't understand… In our world, power is money. Money is *life*. If I couldn't outwit them, garner my own resources to stay ahead, I would have drowned before I realized the water was even above my head. It is a cruel world, and cruel measures are required to survive in it. I refuse to lie down like a good dog. Never again will I be used as a toy in another's game."

His voice… That isn't Vadim talking. I imagine it's his father, or worse—some other phantom who threatened or harmed him in the past. Even now, seemingly successful with more money than any man could ask for, he's still running. Still fighting.

Can he ever truly be at peace?

"I can't pretend like I agree with any of this," I admit, my eyes welling, throat constricting. "I can't. I can't understand it—but I can admit that I have never been faced with what you have. You want my trust, then you have it. That doesn't mean acceptance."

He stops, his back to me. "So what does it mean?"

I suck in a breath at the ice in his tone. It's not the chilling, detached way he's spoken to me when cutting me off from Magda or accusing me of wanting to use him. This anger, I suspect, is fully focused inward, solely at the boy he used to be, desperate to outwit his brother at every turn. Craving to prove his worth in any way he could. A part of me wants to…

But in the end, I can't blame that little boy for who he is now.

I don't have that right.

"Should I prepare the plane to fly you to California?" he wonders. But he sounds so hollow, I doubt he's joking. Resigned. He's *that* convinced I'll leave him merely for hearing the truth.

"I'm not running, am I?" I ask hoarsely. "I'm listening. I'm processing…" Sighing, I rise to my feet, advancing toward him on trembling limbs. "I love you."

The space where his arm meets his shoulder is a refuge I seek out, burying my face in that hollow as my arms go around him to settle over his stomach. "That means facing the good and the bad. You're more than the person I met in a bar on a whim. I can't expect everything about you to be tailor-made for my life and expectations. But… Neither can you when it comes to me. So I'm asking for the same mercy. Be honest with me."

His fingers flutter over mine, hesitant as if he's not fully convinced I won't pull away. "Anything."

"What do you really expect from us? I need to know. Is it children? B-Biological children—" God, how selfish is it that this topic stings more than the reality of him supplying an entire illegal drug trade to spur the sales of his company's assets. Damn Irina. Her smug grin is in my head, her snide accusations ever looming. I can't escape them no matter how hard I fucking try. Walking away from a glorified drug dealer due to my own moral compass is one thing. Having him cast me aside because of the failings of my own body is another.

It's so selfish…

But there it is.

"I want to hear it from you," I tell him, my words muffled by the fabric of his suit jacket. "Please. Just tell me—"

"I don't deserve one child." His voice resonates throughout his entire body, guttural with pure conviction. "Let alone more. I'm not so arrogant as to *demand* more."

He shifts, prying me from him only to spin me into the embrace of his chest. With utter gentleness, his fingers brush my chin, coaxing me into facing him. Those eyes swallow me whole, absolving my guilt, my fear.

He looks at me like someone seeing sunlight after years spent in the dark. With too much awe, he looks at me—more than any one woman could ever deserve. Ever live up to.

But he doesn't make it feel unwarranted—and that's the terrifying part.

"Love," he murmurs, trailing his lips across my forehead. Then down. Over my cheek and against my mouth. "I won't demand more from you than what you can offer. Again."

I sway, seeking out the contours of his body for stability.

"Push me away like that again, and I'll kill you," I tell him seriously. "Your reputation or not."

"My reputation…" He chuckles, and some of that persistent pain leaves his gaze. Just enough to make him seem more exhausted than calculating for once. A man so used to going to war with the world, he's still mistrustful of peace. "But that is why Irina's recent actions don't make sense," he admits, his lips contorting into a frown as the pressing reality at the forefront asserts itself again. "I never told her about Maxim. To go after him, she has an aim in mind far beyond aggravating me."

In a funny way, it's striking that he can only realize as much now, with a tiny fraction of his animosity toward Maxim cooled for Magda's sake.

"Like?" I press.

His brow furrows, revealing a mere glimpse of a man ruthless enough to rebuild the world around him as he saw fit. "Like… She dug too deep into my past and decided to make a deal with the devil."

I feel my eyebrow raising. "Don't tell me Lucifer himself is another relative."

"My grandfather," he says, without missing a beat. The scary part? He doesn't sound like he's joking. "Anatoli Koslov. A bastard cruel enough to sow an empire of thieving, scheming degenerates. Maxim defied him. I'd thought he'd slunk off to Moscow by now."

"You think Irina…made a deal with him somehow?"

"No," he says quickly, but he frowns, raking a hand through his hair. "Unless… Fuck!" He turns, pacing with renewed focus. "How the fuck didn't I see it before? Why would a woman like Irina have a child? *My* child. I can tell you she never expressed a maternal interest before. But to the Koslovs? A child is a commodity," he says darkly, his hands curling into fists. "One easily bought and sold. My past? I still have yet to tell you the full extent."

He inhales raggedly, his body swaying, his eyes unfocused.

"I'm here," I say, bracing my hand against his chest. "I'm here."

"My mother sold me to my father. To the Koslovs," he says. "And when I failed to challenge Maxim, I was given to our uncle, Sevastyn. *His* realm was far different than trading in guns," he admits, his voice rasping. "Through him… I was sold to The Collector."

"Oh my god…" It's too horrifying to fathom. I refuse to, pressing my face against his chest, sensing his heart pound frantically underneath.

"Maxim has not always played by our grandfather's rules," he adds. "Securing an heir should have been his primary focus the moment he came of age—but he hasn't. Deliberately, I suspect, though the bastard would never admit as much to me. As far as Anatoli is concerned, having a child of Koslov blood—no matter their origins—would be a preferable backup. Even the child of a worthless bastard long since sold."

My heart breaks for him. As cold as he sounds, and as ruthless as he can be, admitting as much guts him. I know it does.

"You think that's why Irina had Magda? To sell her to your family?"

"If she is prominent in the trade, then she knew Sevastyn," he grates, his expression horrified. "No one could enter that realm without kissing that bastard's ring. But if that was her aim, to curry favor with a child, they would have no interest in a girl."

And, in a cruel twist of fate, once Magda became diagnosed with diabetes, Irina had no interest in her either.

"But why keep her?" I ask, more to myself than him. "If the Koslovs didn't want her, and obviously her bond to her wasn't that strong considering she abandoned her, why keep her at all for the first five years of her life?"

Something in Vadim's expression shifts. He's having one of his many revelations, but this one is different. It crushes him. "Money," he rasps. "Money she could extort via blackmail."

"From you?"

He shakes his head. "Of the man whose research may have led to her creation being possible in the first place. Irina somehow stole the remnants of our employer's sick experiments—but those experiments were only possible due to Hiram Gorgoshev and his expertise."

And once selling Magda to the Koslovs was no longer an option, Irina decided to use her as a cash cow instead, extorting money from Hiram to keep her child's origins secret. My heart throbs for her, Magda. I can't imagine anyone ever treating their own child so callously.

But at least in her case, she wound up in the arms of someone who will go to the ends of the earth to protect her.

"I know what the bitch wants," Vadim growls. "Why she's chosen now to come back. Sevastyn's dead. Without him, I'm sure her sick fucking realm is in shambles. She wants to ally with the Koslovs to ensure her revenue isn't affected."

And she'll use her own daughter as a bargaining chip to do so. It's such a sad, selfish motive, but something warns me that it's only a fraction of what may be really driving Irina. I can't ignore how she looked when speaking about him. That possessiveness.

And pain at the thought of being forgotten by him.

"What are you going to do?" I ask, running my fingers over the planes of his chest.

He catches my wrist, his expression softening as he forces his attention outward.

"Irina would only feel bold enough to go after Maxim if she assumed I wouldn't put the pieces together in time."

"I guess your relationship must not be a secret then."

"But if I go to him directly... If we combine our resources..." He frowns, not liking the idea even as the words leave his mouth. "He'd never agree to it."

"But if he did?" I prod.

He grimaces at the mere thought and strokes his chin. "We could head her off. Formulate countermeasures to wipe out her and the fucking ring while we're at it. Milton would help."

"So then ask him." I plant my lips against his jaw and feather a path of them down to the center of his chest. "If you need a better reason, I promise to reward you handsomely after."

"That is a tempting offer..." He captures my waist, anchoring me against him. In this position, I've never felt smaller in his shadow, nestled against him like something cherished and delicate. Protected.

"Whatever you do, I'll support you."

Even if it means accepting the unforgivable.

CHAPTER TWENTY-ONE

He wakes up early, rolling away from me without a word. I can tell from the set of his jaw alone not to question. Not to speak. Instead, I watch from the safety of the blankets as he stands and enters the bathroom. Minutes later, he emerges dripping wet, his gaze set in a grim mask of determination.

Lost in his thoughts, he takes his time picking out his suit, and when I finally rise and join him, I find him scouring his selection of hanging ties.

"This one," I say, stepping forward to gently remove a navy blue one from the rack. I loop it around his neck as he watches me, his gaze so open my toes curl the few times I sneak a glimpse at it directly.

Once he's fully dressed, I stand on tiptoe and plant a kiss against his pursed lips.

"I'll be waiting for you when you come back," I tell him huskily.

Though for what exactly? Those plans seem up in the air as tiny footsteps approach from down the hall, and the door is opened from the outside.

"Can we go swimming today?" Magda asks, still half asleep, her braids crooked, It tucked under one arm.

Vadim chuckles, his expression softening as he takes her in. "As long as it's not too cold out," he says, smoothing his hand over one of her braids. His touch lingers, eventually finding her chin—gently, as if giving her every opportunity to pull away. When she doesn't, he tilts her head back to face him. "You need all the practice you can get if we're to summer at the beach, *oui*?"

Her smile is so damn ripe even her stoic nature isn't enough to suppress it. "Really?"

He nods, drawing his hand away to adjust his collar. "I'm looking into a boat as well. Would you like to fish?"

She eyes him warily and nods, padding after him into the hall. "Can we get a yacht? And have a party on it…"

"A yacht?" Vadim sounds utterly perplexed by the request, and I feel my cheeks flush. Note to self—watch my terminology around the child next time.

I slip into a robe and follow, my lips stretched into a grin as I watch them interact. Once we've had breakfast, Vadim leaves, no doubt heading to face a challenge far more intimidating than lounging by the pool.

And I try not to stress over the possibilities of what could happen between him and his brother. Luckily, the sun is shining, and it's warm enough out that I feel brave enough to risk another shot at swimming lessons.

"What do you say?" I ask my co-pilot, posted beside me, as I wash the dishes. "How about a swim?"

She darts off while I take my time entering the master suite, trying to pick which one of my outfits I'll sacrifice to the waters of the pool. I've barely begun perusing my options when I spot a luxurious black shopping bag I definitely do not remember purchasing myself. Inside, I find not one, but several beautiful, stylish swim sets to choose from.

The bastard even got me a particularly risqué bikini in emerald green.

I'm smiling as I pick a modest navy-blue one-piece for now, and I've just managed to get it on when a tiny voice calls from the mouth of the closet. "Are you ready yet?"

I peek out to find that I'm not the only one who found a few presents in her wardrobe. Magda's fully decked out in a charming yellow one-piece decorated with white polka-dots, complete with a matching set of sunglasses and her fanny pack.

"Hold your horses, sailor-girl," I tell her playfully. "And you don't want your phone to get wet. Leave the bag in your room, and go wait for me downstairs. I'll be there in a second."

"Five minutes?" she prods, every bit as manipulative as her father.

I relent with a sigh. "Five minutes."

Within two, I already hear frantic shouting coming from down below.

"I'm coming," I call out. "Just give me one second." With a pile of towels slung over my arm, I pad down the stairs. As I round the corner of the kitchen, I call out, "I hope you're ready to learn how to doggie paddle—"

A piercing scream cuts me off mid-sentence, followed by a monstrous splash. My heart stops. Before I know it, I'm racing onto the terrace. My eyes fixate on the pool—and the tiny figure flailing in the center.

I stop thinking. The next second I'm in the water, diving down just as she slips beneath the surface. Adrenaline and instinct control my limbs, giving me a strength I didn't know I possessed to grab her in my arms and spring toward the surface.

I gulp at the air, kicking toward the edge of the pool on autopilot as my attention turns to the girl in my arms. She's quiet. Too quiet.

"Magda!" I spin her around, my thoughts racing as I struggle to recall the first steps of CPR. Two large blue eyes blink up at me, stunned but alert.

I manage to haul her onto the edge of the pool and climb out after her before relief barrels through me like a sucker punch. My hands shake as I stroke the hair from her face, my eyes on her chest. Only when my voice reaches back to me—high pitched and frantic—do I realize that I've been speaking to her this whole time.

"What were you thinking, coming out here without me? Are you okay? Magda! Say something."

But she's silent, even though—physically at least—she seems to be okay. I draw her into my arms anyway, squeezing so tightly I think she'd protest if she weren't in shock. Soon any anger I may have felt turns to a crippling, overwhelming sense of guilt. I stroke my hands down her back, my voice soothing. "It's okay, honey. You're okay…"

But she isn't.

"What the hell?" Red splotches mar her left arm, noticeable only when I start to pull back. Alarm shoots through me like a lance. They don't look like a rash or a harmless reaction to the water. They're scratches. As if someone grabbed her there. Brutally.

"Honey…" I force her to face me. "Tell me what happened."

I've never seen her like this. Dazed. Distant. Much like Vadim in his very worst of mind states. When it seems like nothing short of screaming can reach him. When his past has all but consumed him.

I snatch Magda into my arms and carry her back into the house, my heart pounding. I wrench the sliding glass door shut and lock it. Then I race to the cutlery drawer and grab the biggest knife I can. Brandishing it in one hand, I curl my free arm around Magda—though she's clinging to me so tightly on her own.

At first glance, nothing looks out of place. The kitchen is as pristine as always, the dining table cleared of dishes or dust for that matter. The heightened sense of unease that has me scanning the corners could be attributed to paranoia.

But then I hear it. Laughter. Faint and distant, it comes from the direction of the terrace. I whip around to find a beautiful blond lazily skirting around the pool. In her hand is a pistol, aimed squarely at the glass door.

There isn't time to panic. I just run, barreling upstairs before I even process why. In Magda's room, I rip her from me, crouching down to her level.

"Get your cell phone, honey," I tell her, making my voice as stern as I can. "Call your dad and hide. No matter what, stay hidden, okay?"

She nods, and some twisted semblance of relief eases my fear. I stroke her hair and then close the door, returning downstairs. It's stupid. I should be hiding too. Running in search of a guard or wait for Vadim.

But deep down, I know in the pit of my gut that nothing I do will deter Irina for long. She doesn't want a chase.

She wants a fight.

The kitchen is her battlefield. She sits at the dining table amid a sea of shattered glass—remnants of the sliding glass door. She eyes me from above her neatly folded hands, the gun out of sight.

"You've called him already, I'm sure," she says, her lips parted into a beautiful smile. Her outfit this time is a ruby red dress that enhances her curves, playing off the gold in her hair. "Good. It's best we keep this quick—"

"Keep what quick?" I counter, adjusting my grip on the knife. I stride toward the counter, putting it in between us, my eyes on her hands. If she goes for her gun, I might be able to duck quickly enough to avoid the first bullet.

But the longer I keep her talking, the more time Magda has to hide.

"You don't want your daughter," I point out, cocking my head with a confidence I don't feel. "You already had the chance to kill me, and you didn't take it. What now?"

"Now?" She giggles, her eyes sparkling. "*You* were never a factor," she tells me. "Just a toy. A diversion. And Magdalene, while I may have no use for her, she does serve one purpose..."

"Vadim," I croak. "You know he'd do anything for her. So why try to drown her?" Anger makes my voice tremble in a way I've never heard it before. I barely recognize this woman.

But embodying her gives me an insight I'd never have before my brief introduction into Vadim's world.

"You didn't," I say, changing my opinion as Irina's eyes darken with disgust. Annoyance.

And then it hits me. The red marks. Magda's fear. It all paints a horrifying picture—rather than let her mother drag her away, she jumped into a pool, knowing she couldn't swim. Or, even more chilling, she made the most noise she could, trusting me to hear her. Save her.

"Do you think Vadim will really allow you to hold her life over him?" I ask incredulously. "He'll kill you."

"Perhaps." She shrugs, but in a fluid, graceful motion, she snatches the gun from its hiding place on her lap and aims it squarely in my direction. "Or, he may be too distracted by grief at your death. I'm curious to see it. Something tells me that he'll get over you quickly." She smiles wickedly, her eyes gleaming. "Magdalene or no, he could have a flawless child to dote over soon enough."

It takes everything I have in me to let the barb go unchallenged. Distracting me is what she wants. Instead, I try to read between the lines, finding the meaning in what she *isn't* saying.

"You must be desperate for money," I decide, honing in on her clenching jaw. *Bingo.* "To come crawling to him after a decade. What? Did the amount you blackmailed from Hiram run dry?"

Her eyes narrow; I've caught her off guard again. "Hiram. You say the man's name as if you know him. But you don't, do you? No. And neither did Vadim." She stands, still aiming the gun, though she twirls it by the handle, around and around—a twisted game of roulette.

"Hiram was too smart for his own good. So smart, he accepted the challenge set down by a monster—help him preserve his toys so that he could make more whenever the mood struck him. Children that he wouldn't have to go through the trouble of buying on the black market, stealing or smuggling. Homegrown stock. I don't think the old man knew the full extent of what he'd signed up for," she acknowledges with a shrug. "I'm sure he couldn't face his shame before his perfect little Dima. That he was the one behind the program that saw him strapped down, his essence ripped away. And for what? A broken little girl child so genetically flawed, she carried on his curse."

"You mean you couldn't sell her," I snap, my voice shaking with anger. "To his family. That's the real reason why you gave birth to her, isn't it?"

She raises an eyebrow, and I know I've hit a bullseye. "His family... Do you even know a hint of their reputation? I think not, or you wouldn't mention them so cavalierly." Smug once more, she cocks her chin, a smirk playing over her red lips. "So what if I aimed to give them a child? They would have welcomed Dima back into the fold then. He might have thanked me."

"But Magda was a girl," I point out. "So, you blackmailed Hiram for money instead."

"Hiram, Hiram." She sadly shakes her head. "A poor man, so wracked with guilt and fear of what his poor Vadim would do if he knew his savior contributed to the hell we lived through. He was pathetic."

Or he was human. A human who loved a man like his son, enough that he'd do anything to protect him the only way he knew how.

"Why now?" I demand. "Why come back now?" But then I remember something Vadim voiced, his own suspicion. "Your sick little sex ring is in jeopardy? You need more money. How disgusting."

"You are *very* mouthy," she spits, her eyes flashing. "It seems even Dima fed you tidbits to keep you quiet. Though you still have no idea, do you? His world. The crimes he's ingrained himself within. The darkness that lurks inside of him. One day, he'll give you a real taste—but I don't think you'll enjoy it much."

She pivots to face me, her expression cold. "You will never know him. No matter what lies he spins to placate you, you will never know the full extent. Money? That man commands more than money—"

"Power," I finish for her. "Is that it? You want protection." She flinches, and I know I've hit a sore spot. Like a shark sensing blood, I latch on, caution be damned. "The little boy you used and threw away now runs the world. But he doesn't even want you. He's had plenty of time to seek you out. Plenty of resources. He's used them to claim his daughter, but never you. Why?"

She flicks her wrist, pointing the gun at me once more. "Should I kill you quickly?" she muses, tilting the barrel toward my head. "Or slowly?" She turns her attention to my chest and licks her lips. "*Slow*, I think—"

"Mommy!"

God, no... In slow motion, I turn to the foyer, helpless to stop a tiny figure from racing into the room. Shouting, I lunge from behind the counter, but she's too fast. As I watch in horror, she runs up to her mother...

And throws her arms around her waist.

"Mommy," she wails plaintively, her face in Irina's hip, her tiny hands fisting in her skirt. "Mommy..."

It's a display that shouldn't sting nearly half as much as it does. Doubt creeps in, stealing away my resolve. Could I truly fight this battle with Magda as a bystander? Especially if—instead of fearing—she actually loves her mother?

The answer is simple—no.

And well aware of that fact, Irina faces me, her gaze alight with triumph. She lowers her free hand toward her daughter's head, her fingers unnaturally stiff. Then she flinches and shoves her off so violently her tiny body goes flying into the row of counters with a sickening thud.

"No!" I run to her, wrapping her in my arms, using my body as a barrier between her and our assailant.

"Little bitch," Irina hisses, swatting at her side. "Enough of this game—"

She aims her gun, heedless of the child in view—and I push all concern for myself out of my brain. Pushing Magda out of range, I pivot on my heel and lunge, swinging with the knife recklessly. Sheer surprise works to my advantage. I catch her off guard, knocking her against the table. The gun flies from her hand, but she lashes out, swiping her nails through the flesh of my cheek.

Growling, she kicks me back and scrambles for her gun. But before she can grab it, she staggers. Falls. Convulses, her eyes rolling.

A monstrous shout resonates from the foyer before I can even process what's happening. A heartbeat later, Vadim races into the room, Maxim hot on his heels. He takes one look at Irina and then me, his posture tense.

"Get the gun," he snaps to his brother—an act of trust so startling that I don't think he even realizes what he's done. His sole focus is on his daughter, overriding even a decades' long feud. He lunges for her over the sea of broken glass, stopping short only when he notices me. "Are you alright?"

I nod. "I'm fine."

With that, we both turn to Magda, and my heart sinks. She's hunched on the floor, staring blankly.

Vadim tentatively takes a step toward her. "Magdalene?"

She inclines her head toward him, but her blue eyes are fixated on her mother's body, watching as the woman's limbs contort uncontrollably. A brief stint of binge-watching medical dramas gives me a vague clue as to what's happening—she's seizing.

"She's not shot," Maxim declares, his tone cold. He's standing over Irina, scanning her body with a predatory intensity that makes me shiver. Meeting Vadim's gaze, he extends her discarded gun.

Vadim steps forward and takes it, hissing in disgust. "What the hell happened—"

I have no idea why or how—but in response to Vadim's concerned frown, Magda lifts her hand. In it is a tiny syringe, and a horrible explanation for Irina's state becomes clear.

"You gave her insulin?" Vadim's expression shifts as he crosses to her, crouching before her. Gingerly, he strokes her cheeks, forcing her to face him. "How much did you give her? How much?" he asks gently.

Magda shrugs and drops the syringe at his feet.

"The whole thing?" Vadim looks at Irina, his gaze unreadable.

"What does that mean?" Maxim demands, seemingly as confused as I am. But then something Vadim told Magda echoes in my mind—*no one else should ever take your medicine but you...*

"It means... We need to call Milton. Now." Standing, Vadim forces himself to leave his daughter, turning to the unconscious blond. "Tiffany. Can you take her upstairs to dry off?"

I force myself to move, gathering Magda into my arms. I carry her past Maxim, slipping upstairs. Once we're in her room, however, I can't seem to let her go.

"What were you thinking, huh?" I demand against her scalp. "You could have been hurt, honey. I told you to hide. I told you…"

She doesn't say anything, but her arms go around me in return, holding me just as tightly.

And *neither* of us can seem to let go.

CHAPTER TWENTY-TWO

Hours later, Vadim and Ena have temporarily boarded up the terrace door. Irina is gone to only God knows where and Magda—somehow—is sleeping in her bed. I linger near her more than I should, planting kisses over her forehead and smoothing my hands along her back until I'm sure she's asleep.

When I creep downstairs to check the progress of the cleanup, I find Vadim, leaning against a counter, his face in his hands. "She killed two guards," he explains, fixing me with a haggard, exhausted expression.

"Is she dead?"

He sighs. "No. Though she easily could be, with the amount of insulin in her system. But... I couldn't let Magdalene grow up believing she killed her own mother. Irina doesn't deserve to impact her life any more than she already has."

"So where is she?" I gather up the nerve to ask, fearful of the answer.

And he knows it. "Do you want me to say I let her go?" he wonders tiredly, shooting me a searching glance. "That she repented and is in prison forever and will never harm another soul? I will not lie to you—"

"And I don't want you to. So, tell me the truth," I prod.

"Why? Do you want to be disgusted? Do you want to hear that I sold her to the highest bidder? That the bitch will suffer for ever daring to touch my daughter? My family? Would that bother you?"

"It might," I admit. "But I think I'll get over it."

He cocks his head, not expecting that answer. Maybe he can hear it in my voice—I'm not lying. Compelled to explain, I let the true depth of my conflicted emotions wash over me. Disgust. Fear. Hate.

All of those things old Tiffy—even in the midst of her divorce—could never imagine feeling to this extent.

"Magda jumped in the pool just to keep Irina from taking her away." I can't disguise my horror. "How can a seven-year-old be forced to choose between drowning or her own mother? She can't swim. She was *that* afraid of her. If I didn't hear her… If I didn't get to her in time…"

"She's intelligent," Vadim states. I'm in his arms before I know it, crushed to his chest, and I relent to the embrace. "She *knew* you'd get to her in time."

And she must have known that Irina wouldn't even bother. The thought is so grim that any lingering unease I may have felt at her fate is instantly washed away.

As the Sunday school teacher deep within me might say—an eye for an eye.

But I appear to be the only one in a grudge-holding mood —one glaring event of the day stands out, and I rear back, poised to watch his expression.

"You and Maxim…"

He winces, his lips curling.

But I'm ruthless. "You brought *Maxim* with you. He *helped* you." I sound so childish, like I'm taunting him—but I can't help the silly glee that has me grinning. "You two were quite the dynamic duo—"

"I met him at the club," Vadim says, his tone far more somber than mine. "I intended to discuss our mutual headache. As it seems, our interests converged far more quickly than I initially thought."

Some of my excitement deflates at his frown. His eyes take on that distant gleam that they do when only one person is on his mind. "Magda called you," I say, my voice rasping. "God, she must have been terrified."

His brow furrows in surprise. "Commanding actually," he says, a rare smile sneaking onto his mouth. "She demanded I come to rescue you. I tried to convince her to hide somewhere safe and wait for me, but she hung up." He looks torn between fear and grudging admiration.

"It seems she didn't just inherit your good looks," I tease, stepping into him again, letting my head rest against his chest. "She got your stubbornness too."

Chuckling, he brings his hand to my scalp, cradling me against him. "It seems she picked up some traits from you as well," he murmurs, sounding amused once more. "Your remarkable ability to enthrall those around you, for one. I only had to say her name for Maxim to come."

His voice deepens, revealing just how much that confuses him. His brother came when he needed him the most.

Could the rift between those two ever be mended?

I picture two beautiful little girls, and I'm hopeful that they might be up to the task.

It should be impossible to expect things to return to normal after the events of the past few days. In some ways, they still aren't. Vadim and I wake up to find Magda squirming in between us, her bear firmly wedged under her arm, her fanny pack still on.

But she's the first one to spring from the mattress, padding downstairs, chattering excitedly.

"Can Ainsley sleep over here today?" she asks over a bowl of cereal. She seems oblivious to the fact that Vadim and I are perched on opposite ends of her, waiting for the second we might have to swoop in and comfort her.

The pink sundress she's wearing exposes her arms—and the mottled bruises down the length of one. Vadim was concerned enough by them to have Milton come over in the middle of the night and examine her. Supposedly, there is no lasting damage.

She'll be fine.

But she doesn't even seem to notice. "Huh?" she prods after shoveling a spoonful of cereal into her mouth. She eyes Vadim questioningly until he snaps to awareness.

"Yes, *ma chérie?*"

"Can we go back to California soon? I want to be on a boat."

"Of course. We can leave by the end of the week," he ruffles her braids, but the line of his jaw betrays concern. He didn't miss the same note in her voice that I did—the same way she'd "asked" to sleep in our bed for a week after being spooked by Maxim.

But once she finishes her food and skips off to the garden—watched over by Ena, there's no sign of trauma at all. Which is a testament to childish fortitude because I can't even look at the terrace door—newly replaced overnight—without flinching.

"I asked Milton for recommendations for a child psychologist," Vadim tells me as we clear the dishes. "Once we settle on one, I'll have her start regular sessions." He moves toward the stairs next, and I find myself following him, too distracted by my own worries for Magda.

"What if Irina comes after us again?" It's a fear that won't stop nibbling, and it leads my thoughts down a dark path. Like the musing that next time, Magda won't be the one to inject the bitch with a lethal dose of insulin.

"She won't," Vadim says. He sounds so damn sure of that. I start to question, but something in his gaze warns me not to. Some aspects of his world, I'm better off not knowing about.

So I turn my attention to what I'd much rather study—him. He grunts in surprise when I slink toward him and press my body against the hardness of his. We're in the bedroom, and the row of windows makes for a fitting surface for him to push me against while ensuring we can both still see Magda frolicking about her budding garden, Ena in tow.

I stand on tiptoe and nibble along his jaw, tugging at the front of his slacks.

"Wait." He looks pained as he grasps my wrists, halting my assault. His eyes take on that dark, wary gleam as if he's hesitating on the verge of a decision. Sighing, he relents and releases me to reach into his pocket. "I haven't asked you to marry me," he states while presenting a small black box balanced on the center of his palm. "I still won't. Not until you're ready. But…"

He lifts the lid of the box, and I sway at the sheer opulence of what lurks beneath it. A ring—but one so delicately, beautifully crafted that I know it received the same careful attention to detail that his kinky endeavors did. It's beyond anything I could have imagined, and my throat tightens.

"Vadim…"

"I want you to know what awaits you if you do accept," he explains, his gaze alight with such raw emotion my heart swells, unable to contain it all.

Gently, I place my hand over his, forcing him to lower the ring. "I can't accept this," I tell him, hating the tension that tightens his jaw—the disappointment he can't even try to hide.

Disappointment that turns to confusion as I sink to my knees and return my attention to the front of his slacks.

"I do believe that it is *my* turn to propose." I free his cock and promptly tease the tip of his piercing with my tongue. "Mr. Vadim Gorgoshev," I declare in between devious tastes of him. "Will you marry me?"

I think he says yes, nearly drowned out by his groans as I take him as far into my mouth as I can.

When I draw back, he looks dazed. Like a man trapped in a dream, one he definitely doesn't want to wake up from.

"There is one condition," I tell him, though I'm not even sure how serious a thought it is. "I've always wanted a double wedding."

He raises an eyebrow, but when I curl my fist around him and press my lips against the crown, he promptly loses his ability to argue.

And if this proposal is anything to go off of, this marriage won't be anything like my last. My heart swells with that knowledge, and I watch him through my lashes, prepared to earn the ring I know lurks in the box still clenched in his fist. His face is the picture of awe. Rapture…

Horror.

"Damn," he whispers a split second before my ears pick up the noise triggering his alarm—tiny footsteps skipping down the hall in our direction. I barely manage to lurch to my feet—while he wrestles himself back into his pants—before the door opens and Magda marches in.

"Mr. Ena wants you," she says to Vadim, her button nose wrinkled in confusion as Vadim staggers to her side, still smoothing his clothing into place.

"H-He told you to tell me?"

Magda nods while I suppress a grin. Sending a child to do his dirty work could be a hallmark of the old bodyguard slacking—or his knowledge of what he might have interrupted as well as the inkling that his employer would spare poor Magda his wrath. Which he does with a wry grin that warms me down to my core. Taking her hand, he leads the way downstairs, where Ena lurks in the kitchen, scowling at the scene visible through the newly replaced terrace door.

"Ainsley!" Shirking her father's grasp, Magda surges forward, and Ena has just enough time to wrench open the sliding glass door before she can career right through it.

Sure enough, her target is already racing to meet her, her blond hair flying out behind her. Smiling, I scan her wake for a familiar figure and promptly feel my mouth drop open.

"Jesus Christ," I whisper. I have to resist the urge to rub my eyes just to make sure the stoic figure striding across the lawn is real.

"What the hell does he want?" Vadim murmurs, though he sounds genuinely curious rather than hostile—another fact contributing to my dropped jaw.

But his question winds up presenting its own answer—it's obvious to anyone watching just what Maxim wants.

"Uncle Max!" Magda's voice is audible from here, chirpy in the familiar way that took her own father weeks of trust-building to achieve. She skips to him, looping her hand within his, chatting animatedly the entire while.

And as his dark eyes take her in, they ignite with a warmth I figure might be visible from space. His posture relaxes as his lips quirk in the semblance of an expression that on any other man could be called a smile.

As Ainsley claims his other hand, I'm convinced that, foreboding figure or not, his heart has been stolen more than once.

As has the love of the man standing beside me. His hand flattens against my waist as if anchoring me to him is the only way he can stop himself from marching forward. Mistrust is always his first instinct—especially where Maxim is concerned—but in this case, I can sense the effort he exerts to stay still.

To watch.

To let his brother enjoy the simple gift they've both been denied for so long—family.

Did you enjoy the final installment of Vadim and Tiffany's Trilogy? Sign up to be alerted about all things Club XXX!

A WORD FROM THE AUTHOR

Hey there!

Thank you so much for reading! If you enjoyed the story, please leave a review and recommend the book to any friend you think would love this twisted world. You'd have my eternal gratitude. Even a short sentence goes a long way!

Then, come join the rest of us dark romance lovers in my Facebook Group where you can get snippets, sneak peeks of upcoming books and even help vote on aspects of future novels.

Come to the dark side:
https://www.facebook.com/groups/lanasbeautifulmonsters/

WANT MORE STUFF TO READ?
Join my newsletter and get a **free book**! Plus, you get to stay updated with any new releases, random giveaways and exclusive sneak peeks!
https://www.lanaskybooks.com/newsletter

Other Novels: https://lanaskybooks.com/

FREE BOOK - JOIN MY NEWSLETTER

Dark, Twisted Romance

Join my newsletter and get a **free book**! Plus, you get to stay updated with any new releases, random giveaways and exclusive sneak peeks!

https://www.lanaskybooks.com/newsletter

Lana Sky is a reclusive writer in the United States who spends most of her time daydreaming about complex male characters and parenting her Cockapoo Joey. She writes dark, twisted romance across several genres. Her titles include everything from mafia romance to vampires.

facebook.com/AuthorLanaSky

twitter.com/lanasky101

amazon.com/author/lanasky

pinterest.com/lanasky101

goodreads.com/lanasky

instagram.com/lanasky101

bookbub.com/authors/lana-sky

ALSO BY LANA SKY

For more titles by Lana Sky, please visit:

https://www.lanaskybooks.com

www.ingramcontent.com/pod-product-compliance
Lightning Source LLC
Chambersburg PA
CBHW071727190726

48292CB00003B/642